THE DEVIL BEHIND ME

THE DEVIL BEHIND ME

by

Frederick E. Smith

Dales Large Print Books
Long Preston, North Yorkshire,
BD23 4ND, England.

British Library Cataloguing in Publication Data.

Smith, Frederick E.
    The devil behind me.

    A catalogue record of this book is
    available from the British Library

    ISBN   978-1-84262-855-3 pbk

First published in Great Britain 1962 by
Hodder & Stoughton Ltd.

Copyright © Frederick E. Smith, 1962

Cover illustration © Alexandre Cappellari by arrangement with
Arcangel Images Ltd.

The moral right of the author has been asserted

Published in Large Print 2012 by arrangement with
Frederick E. Smith

Dales Large Print is an imprint of Library Magna Books Ltd.

Printed and bound in Great Britain by
T.J. (International) Ltd., Cornwall, PL28 8RW

To
HARRY AND POLDI SHOOSMITH
with affection

I wish to acknowledge my debt to the Swedish Tourist Traffic Association, the Swedish State Railways, and in particular Mr G. Rosvall, for their help given me both in Lappland and in Sweden when preparing this book.

CHAPTER 1

I noticed her the moment I topped the grassy dune that separated the road from the sea. She was standing on one of the beach fortifications; her poised figure, silhouetted against the fading sky, making me think of a wild animal that had been suddenly alerted.

I paused, watching her. She was too far away for her features to be distinct, but I saw she was tall and slim, was wearing a windcheater and slacks, and that her dark hair was bound back in a pony-tail. Following her gaze down the seaweed-strewn, pebbly beach I saw the distant figures of two men approaching the fortification. One of them appeared to be a huge man, towering a full head over his companion, but the failing light made further identification impossible as yet.

Something about the tableau held me motionless. The girl's tensed figure, silhouetted against the crimson Baltic sunset. The steel-bright scimitar of moon poised above her. The angular hulk of the beach pillbox, half of it grass-covered, half bare rock, rising from the beach. The hushed whisper of the waves. The still air that trembled slightly.

11

I took another look at the approaching men. The big man, whom the girl seemed to be watching, stooped down and picked something up from the beach. He showed it to his companion, threw it away, and began walking forward again. I saw now that they were Swedish soldiers. The girl seemed to recognise them at the same time, for her attention relaxed and she turned away. It was then I noticed she was not alone. A man was sitting a few feet below her, half-hidden from me by a rock. From his posture he too appeared to have been watching the approaching soldiers; now he straightened and raised a face that looked pale in the failing light. She reached down and for a brief moment their hands met.

It looked like a gesture of reassurance, of relief from tension. As I watched, the girl seated herself alongside him. The fortification was forty yards to my left, below the dune, and curiosity made me move towards it. My movement instantly drew the attention of the girl, and I felt both of them watching me as I approached and reached a point above them.

I tried to keep my gaze as casual as possible as I looked down. In spite of the poor light and the fifteen yards or so still between us, I could see now that the girl had features as attractive as her long, supple body. Details eluded me, but I had an impression of a broad forehead, high cheekbones, and dark, watchful eyes. An interesting face, full of intelligence, strength, and something else that both intrigued and puzzled me.

I wanted to examine her companion, but she occupied my attention in the few seconds of passing, and when I looked back a shoulder on the dune hid them from sight.

As I paused I heard the crunch of the approaching soldiers' feet. One of them called out something in Swedish, no doubt a greeting to the couple above them. Their grey uniforms came into my view. They entered the pillbox, to emerge a moment later and continue in my direction. I guessed they were carrying out some kind of routine inspection of the fortifications. One waved a friendly hand as they passed below. They took a glance into the last pillbox at the side of the harbour, then climbed the dune and made their way to the main road.

I followed them slowly, pausing again at the end of the dune. The fishing harbour lay below me, its water tinted pink in the sunset. It was small and picturesque, and looked snugly content behind the two encircling stone jetties that held it protectively from the sea. I took a last backward glance, could see nothing of the man and girl, and slid down the dune to the cobbled path alongside the harbour. It led me by a pile of fish crates to a second, smaller harbour, in which was moored a number of small fishing boats and yachts. With time to spare, I took a look at one or two of the latter before following the path to the other side of the harbour. A pebbly bank sheltered it at this side: I climbed it, passed a fisherman's cottage and a small café, and three minutes later came out again on the main coast road.

My hotel was only three hundred yards ahead. Its lights were already switched on and were shining warmly from the cluster of trees that surrounded it. I wandered along, one half of my mind luxuriously making and discarding plans for my holiday, as yet only three days old, the other half speculating on the girl I had just seen.

I wondered if she were a local inhabitant. Her figure could be Swedish, but surely not her features or colouring. French, perhaps, or Belgian. Even German – there was a daily boat service from Travemünde to Trelleborg... Then I smiled at myself. As if one could classify races by appearance. She could even be English and have taken the Danish route to Sweden as I had myself.

A squirrel ran out from behind a bush, scurried a short distance along the road ahead of me, and stopped. It eyed me watchfully as I approached, waited until I was a few yards away, and then leapt for a nearby tree. It raced up the straight trunk, danced acrobatically along an outflung branch, and lay watching me again as I passed below.

I turned off the road into the drive of the Stranden Hotel. It was a small hotel, about seven miles east of Trelleborg. Chance alone had brought me to it. I'd stayed in Odense the previous night and had planned to drive along the southern Swedish coast as far as Simrishamn or even Kristianstad that day. But I'd omitted to make Knudshoved on the ferries, and a three-hour wait at Hassalvad and another two-hour delay at Copenhagen had thrown my time-table askew. Not that I minded: I don't like cut-and-dried holidays. But in the light of what was to follow it is worth mentioning, if only to show what fate can have in store for those who do not plan their lives too precisely.

I entered the Stranden and was making for the staircase when a sudden impulse made me turn left instead. There was a small lounge here with a verandah window that overlooked the drive and the sea. It was empty; I took a table and lit a cigarette.

The minutes passed: the sunset faded into a saffron afterglow and I was just deciding that my time would be far better spent in having a pre-dinner shower when a man and woman appeared at the end of the drive. As they approached I knew my hunch was right: they were also staying at the hotel.

There was no mistaking the girl: she was nearly as tall as the man, and I guessed his height at five foot ten or eleven. As they drew nearer I had the odd feeling – premonition is the only word that covers it – that because of them something quite unexpected and dangerous was going to happen to me. Premonition has a melodramatic sound, and I don't like the word, but anyone who has experienced danger will admit it has an aura of its own. Something of that aura must have brought me to the window to watch out for them.

I gave the man most of my attention this time. He had a large frame but was very thin, with slightly bowed shoulders, thinning dark hair, and a pale, drawn face. There was a tight, brittle look about him: he reminded me of the poor devils I'd seen released from the concentration camps at the end of the war – still looking and living as though in the shadow of the torture chamber. As I watched he stumbled over a stone on the drive. The girl caught his arm and helped him steady himself, murmuring something I could not hear.

To enter the Stranden they had to climb half a dozen steps which brought them level with the end window of the verandah. As the girl reached it she turned her face towards me and I realised that all the time she'd known I was watching them. We were no more than eight feet apart now, with only the window between us, and as her eyes met mine I saw they were level and wide-set. They looked bluish-grey in the twilight, and in tranquillity they would have been beautiful. But at this moment they made me think of rock pools into which sand had been thrown. Only in this case the sand was fear...

I sat very still, waiting for them to go up to their rooms. Then I went back into the hall. No one was in attendance at the desk and I went over to it. The Stranden had two registers, one for Swedish guests, one for foreigners, and I took a look at both. There were no new entries in the first. In the second was my own with the usual particulars required by the police: *Name:* John Drayton, *date of birth* 9/4/23, *Nationality:* British. *Last place of stay:* Odense. Etc. Etc. Directly below it, made that same day, were two other entries. Anna Frandl ... 8/10/28 ... Deutsch ... Travemünde... And under it: Carl Frandl ... 21/1/19 ... Deutsch ... Travemünde...

Anna and Carl Frandl. Either brother and sister or man and wife. I took another glance at the register and saw they had booked for one night only. Then I had the feeling someone was watching me and turned sharply round. On the lower step of the staircase was the girl, Anna Frandl.

She was still dressed in slacks but had discarded the windcheater. A black, fine wool sweater clung round her slim waist and showed the high, full curve of her breasts. She swung away as I turned, and entered the lounge, impressing me again by the grace and litheness of her movements. She paused by a table and flicked over the pages of a magazine. Everything about her indicated she was curious about me and wished to question me but was nervous of doing so.

I hesitated, watching her for a moment, then went slowly upstairs to my room, where I just managed a shower and change before the dinner gong sounded. Anna was five minutes late in entering the dining room and she came alone. She was wearing a black tailored costume and her hair was now swept up into a bun. She had no jewellery whatever except a hand-painted miniature on the lapel of her coat, and she looked as regal as a queen.

Carl Frandl made no appearance as the meal progressed and I couldn't help wondering if I had anything to do with his absence. There seemed little doubt they were afraid of something, and it could well be that my curiosity had alarmed them. More than once I caught the girl's eyes watching me, and the uncomfortable feeling grew on me that I had given myself some responsibility to ease her mind. At the same time I wasn't unaware of the irony of the situation. Premonition leading to curiosity, curiosity to responsibility, responsibility to contact, contact to...? A pretty chain that had a fatalistic shape about it.

I told myself I was thinking like a damned fool, and in that frame of mind took my coffee out on the open terrace. Afterwards, feeling restless, I wandered down the drive to the road. I turned off at the darkened café, passed the fisherman's cottage and a maze of poles used for drying nets, and a minute later was making my way out over the rough stones of the narrow eastern jetty. It terminated in a rough boss of stone: I climbed it, lit a cigarette, and sat down.

It was peaceful out there. The sky had that luminous quality found in Scandinavia in the summer, when it seems that any moment the aurora borealis will rise like a phosphorescent blue veil from the horizon. Twenty yards ahead of me across the harbour entrance was the other jetty. Beyond it was the beach where I had first seen Anna and Carl Frandl. A line of fishermen's poles ran out to sea here, their thin black silhouettes just reaching the shivering silver path laid down by the moon. Half a mile beyond them, on a dark promontory, a small lighthouse flashed its fussy, friendly warning. The waves, little more than ripples, washed the jetty alongside me with a neutral murmur that accentuated rather than diminished the silence.

It was the kind of night that, for no other reason than that it is beautiful, brings memories back. I sat thinking of mine, the bitter and the sweet, and time became a great nebulous cloud in which I drifted backwards and forwards at will.

It was the harsh squawk of a startled jackdaw in the trees near the cottage that brought me back to the present. I listened, caught a faint scrabble of pebbles, and a minute later heard the tap-tap of high-heeled shoes coming down the jetty.

There was a light springiness about the footsteps that made me feel pretty certain they belonged to Anna Frandl. I waited until they were almost upon me, then turned slowly round.

She was dressed in the same slim-fitting black costume she had worn at dinner, her only concession to the night air being a stole flung around her shoulders. She was bare-headed, and the moonlight added a sheen to her swept-up, glossy hair. In spite of the sophistication of her clothes she went with the stars and the sea as naturally as the tall pines alongside the road.

As I turned, she paused. Knowing her nervousness of me I thought I might have to break the silence first, but there I under-estimated the strength of her character. After that initial hesitation, barely more than a check of step, she walked to the foot of the boss and stared up at me.

'*Guten Abend, mein Herr. Kann ich Sie einen*

Augenblick sprechen?'

I rose to my feet. My German is quite fluent, but I had a feeling it might be better to keep to English at the moment. 'Good evening, Miss Frandl. What can I do for you?'

She spoke English with a husky accent that was fascinating. 'There is something I would like to ask you. May I join you for a moment?'

'It'll be a pleasure. Let me help you up.'

She accepted my hand, more out of courtesy than of need, and a second later was standing on the weatherworn stone beside me, bringing with her an elusive scent of perfume. I pointed to a shelf in the rocks. 'Won't you sit down?'

She seated herself and accepted the cigarette I offered her. Her face, although pale, was calm, and only the moonlight, shining into her eyes, betrayed her fear.

'There doesn't seem any need to introduce ourselves,' I said, giving her a lead. 'Hotel registers are useful things, aren't they?'

She inhaled deeply on her cigarette and then turned to me, her voice low but determined. 'That is what I wish to ask you, Mr Drayton. Why have you this interest in us? Who are you?'

'Interest?' I said, watching her face.

Her breath was coming a little more quickly now. 'Yes. You watched us from the

21

top of the dune. You looked out for us from the lounge window. And then I saw you looking up our names in the hotel register. What is your reason for all this?'

I was thinking of her companion. Why was he not doing this work instead of her? Before I could speak she went on:

'Tonight I too looked in the register. It says your name is John Drayton and that you are English. Is that true?'

'Quite true,' I said. 'Why shouldn't it be?'

There was a puzzled shadow between her dark eyebrows. 'Then why are you so curious about us?' One of her long, slender hands moved nervously, only a few inches but enough to betray the emotions hidden beneath her outward composure. 'Will you tell me?' She paused, then went on in a low, intense voice: 'It is very important to us that we know.'

I leaned forward, catching that elusive perfume again. 'It's none of my business and I'm not asking you for reasons, but it's pretty clear to me that you and your husband, or whoever he is, are afraid of something. And because you are afraid you're suspicious of everyone who gives you a second glance. Well, you can stop worrying about me. I'm an Englishman having a holiday touring around Sweden, and I'm not interested in anyone's affairs but my own. Does that make you any happier?'

A little of the tension was leaving her, although her eyes were still wary. 'But then why were you watching us so closely?'

Of all my reasons I chose the one I thought would cause her to relax the most. 'Miss Frandl, you're a very attractive girl. You make men look twice at you. But that doesn't make us bigger wolves than we are.'

There was nothing coquettish about the look she gave me. As I learned later, she was one of those rare women who accept their beauty as a gift instead of a talent.

'And it was nothing more than that with you?'

I hesitated. For one thing, I was curious to know more about her fear: for another, it was difficult to lie with those eyes of hers right on my face. 'Not altogether,' I admitted. 'It was your attitude that first drew my attention. You were looking at those two soldiers as though they were someone you were terrified of. It wasn't until I drew closer that I saw how attractive you were. Put the two things together, add a dash of presentiment, and you've got the whole story.'

Her voice was sharp, a little unsteady. 'Presentiment! What do you mean?'

'Nothing,' I said, impatient with myself. 'I just mean that because of those things I became interested in you and your companion. May I ask who he is?'

'He is my brother,' she said slowly.

I was strangely glad. 'And he has been worrying about my curiosity too, has he?'

'Yes. He has been…' She broke off, giving her head a slight shake. 'It is nothing. Please do not ask me more.'

Once again I wondered why she had to do the dirty work for him. In the silence that followed I sat studying her. She was a lovely picture out there in the moonlight. Watching her, I had the feeling that in spite of the calm of her face and her refusal to elaborate her fears, she was under great strain, and badly in need of a confidant. But hers was the kind of strength that makes no concession to personal comfort if the slightest risks are involved. Sensing this, I made no effort to force the pace until I remembered she and Carl were leaving the following day.

'I saw from the register that you and your brother are staying here only one night.'

Any question concerning Carl seemed to make her cautious, and it was a few seconds before she answered this one. 'We intended leaving, yes, but now we may have to stay. My brother is not well, and I think he must have a day's rest before he can continue.' Then, as though feeling she had said too much, she rose and held out her hand. 'I must go now. Thank you for reassuring me like this. I am sorry I disturbed you.'

I rose with her, smiling. 'I'm not sorry. I've enjoyed your company. But one thing before you go. If I'd been the person you suspected, wouldn't it have been dangerous for you, a woman, to have come alone like this?'

She was picking up her handbag as I was speaking. My words seemed to halt her: she turned, and for the first time her eyes seemed to lose all their suspicion and to smile at me. 'Thank you for the thought. But you must not have any fears for me.'

I wondered why my voice suddenly sounded awkward. 'Just the same, you shouldn't make a habit of it.' A pause, and then: 'Let me see you back to the hotel. I'm going back myself now.'

She made no protest, and we walked in silence along the narrow jetty and up the path to the road. There I noticed with some satisfaction that in spite of her high heels I was two or three inches taller than she. As we walked along that dark road with the moonlit sea on our right, I became more and more conscious of her nearness as a woman. It was my first experience of the magnetism she was to have for me later, and it was the more startling that night because I am quite certain she made no effort to exert it.

On the terrace of the Stranden I asked her if she would take a glass of wine with me, but she shook her head.

'It is kind of you, but now I must go upstairs to see how Carl is feeling. I do not think I shall come down again tonight.'

'Then what about tomorrow?' I asked. 'I have my car with me, and I understand the scenery is beautiful around Ystad.'

If for no other reason than Carl, I had expected her to refuse. Instead, she paused as though my words had brought her a new thought.

She turned to me. 'Thank you. If Carl is well enough I would like that very much. But we can discuss it further in the morning. *Auf Wiedersehen*, Mr Drayton.'

And there it was, I thought wryly. Fate had arranged the contact – what followed now? I had half a dozen emotions as I watched her graceful figure ascend the staircase and vanish, and not the least of them was that nagging presentiment of danger. Yet in spite of it I felt oddly happy, in the way a man is happy before an unknown adventure.

CHAPTER 2

I awoke to sunshine the following morning. The smell of the country spiced with the tang of salt entered the bedroom as I opened the window wide. The sky was cloudless, and the sun, warm on my pyjama jacket, gave promise of the heat to follow.

Neither Anna nor her brother was visible when I went downstairs, nor did they appear later, even though I spent as long as possible over breakfast in the hope of seeing them. I smoked a couple of cigarettes in the lounge, took a stroll around the hotel, and on my return took another glance in the breakfast room. Apart from a jolly-faced Swedish woman and her two blond, sunburned children, it was now empty. It was past nine o'clock, and an uneasy thought made me go over to the reception desk. The plump, bespectacled receptionist spoke reasonable good English and I asked if the Frandls had booked to stay another day. He nodded.

'Ja, min herre. The lady made the reservation last night. The gentleman is not well – she phoned down this morning and asked for their breakfasts to be sent upstairs.'

I thanked him and moved away, wondering

what Carl suffered from. I entered the lounge, paged restlessly through a magazine, and finally, impatient with myself, decided to take a walk into the nearby village of Boste to do some shopping.

It was a pleasant two-mile walk, with the sea in view most of the way. I found what I wanted in Boste, had coffee in a small, open-air café on the outskirts, and then started back. The sun was hot now, making me take off my jacket.

It was nearly eleven when I got back to the Stranden. Before going upstairs I took a glance into the lounge and saw Anna and Carl at a table in the corner farthermost from the window. She noticed me immediately and I saw her touch his arm. I can't say the smile she gave me was the hundred-percent welcoming one I would have liked, but in a sense I had not expected it otherwise. She's had a whole night to remind herself of the danger of making friends with strangers, and no doubt Carl had given her a warning too.

Nevertheless, she made it clear I was welcome to join them. As I approached their table Carl rose to his feet.

I saw now that he had once been a handsome man, for his features were good and his body had once been athletic. But ill-health had undermined him as blight undermines a tree, sallowing his skin, stealing the life from his eyes, shrinking and bowing his body. He rose with difficulty and I noticed Anna's hand half-extended over his chair as though to support him. A nervous tic made him keep screwing up his gaunt face as if the light were too bright for him. Again I wondered at the nature of the complaint that had made such a wreck of a comparatively young man.

He was typically German at our introduction, touching his heels and bowing stiffly. His thin hand was clammy but as firm as his strength allowed. I felt a tremor running into it as I grasped it – the uneven shudder one gets in a car when the engine is misfiring. An odd sensation to feel in a human hand.

His English was halting but adequate. 'I am glad to meet you, Mr Drayton. Please join us.'

I sat down and turned my attention to Anna. She was wearing a square-necked, sleeveless frock of some blue material and looked cool, composed, and very attractive. Her eyes, however, without avoiding mine, were heedful and wary again. There was no doubt she had been having second thoughts about me.

I listened to her brother making conversation. 'Anna tells me you are touring in Sweden, Mr Drayton. Are you enjoying yourself?'

'Very much, thank you.'

'Have you been over here long?'

'No, I only left England three days ago.' I offered them both a cigarette, saying as casually as I could: 'What about you two? Are you also on vacation?'

His eyes turned to Anna as though he were having language difficulties. 'Vacation,' he muttered. *'Was hast Du ihm er zählt?'*

Anna did not answer him, addressing me instead. 'No; we are not on holiday. My brother has a small business in Germany and we are travelling in connection with it.' Smoothly she changed the trend of the conversation by pointing to my small hand-grip. 'I see you have been shopping. Have you been into Trelleborg this morning?'

I had to pull myself together to answer her question. Carl's muttered *Was hast Du ihm er zählt* had nothing to do with vacation. It meant: What have you told him?

'I've been into Boste, not Trelleborg,' I told her. 'I had a couple of postcards to send and a few things to buy. Have you been out yet? It's a perfect day.'

'Not yet. Carl has not been feeling well and has only just come down...'

A peculiar thing happened then. Carl, who was sitting facing the open door of the lounge, gave a sharp exclamation and stiffened in his chair. I turned quickly to see a man standing in the doorway. His back was turned to us, but two things were conspicuous about him: he was completely

30

bald, and he was massive in build. Carl, skin parchment-tight about his eyes and mouth, was staring at him as though he were the devil himself. Then, abruptly, he relaxed and closed his eyes in thanksgiving. I looked back and saw the bald man had now turned towards us and was entering the lounge. A small, pig-tailed girl followed him: it was obvious he was nothing more than a fond father with his child.

Carl's eyes were still closed and his forehead damp with sweat. Anna, her face as white as his own, was holding his hand and whispering things in German I could not hear.

I was on my feet. 'Is there anything I can do? A glass of water? Or brandy, perhaps?'

Her voice was unsteady, as though she too had received a shock. 'I don't think so, thank you. But it might help if we were left alone for a little while…'

I picked up my grip. 'Of course. But if there is anything I can do, please don't hesitate to call me. I'm in room 25.'

As I turned away she checked me, her voice low. 'About this afternoon, Mr Drayton. You will realise that in the circumstances I cannot go far away. But an hour or two while my brother is resting – I might be able to manage that.'

I was surprised at this, for everything had led me to believe our arrangements were

31

cancelled. 'See how things are this afternoon,' I told her. 'I'll be here after lunch and you can decide then. It won't inconvenience me; I've nothing planned for today.'

She thanked me with her eyes. Carl, although still very drawn, had recovered now and somehow pulled himself to his feet. There was both distress and humiliation in his voice. 'I'm sorry, Mr Drayton. These attacks of mine – they come at such inconvenient times...'

I was feeling sorry for the poor devil. It was a long time since I'd seen a man so frightened. 'I hope you'll feel better soon. Don't forget– if I can help at all, let me know.'

They thanked me and shook hands. I went out, leaving Anna comforting him in that low, husky voice of hers.

She came into the lounge just after 1.30. She was wearing a two-piece sun frock, sandals on her feet, and was carrying a canvas handbag. She came over to me as I rose.

'Carl is resting now, so I think I can go out for a little while. But I must be back no later than 5.30. Are you certain that is all right for you?'

I assured her it was. Noticing her canvas bag I asked if she intended having a swim. She shook her head. 'Unfortunately I didn't bring a costume to Sweden. But you mustn't let that stop you going in.'

We went out on the terrace. The sun was scorching down from a cloudless sky, although a certain stickiness in the air suggested rain might follow later. I led her to my car, an A70 Countryman which she seemed to examine with interest. I thought she was looking at the camping gear inside, and explained that I sometimes slept in the car when accommodation was difficult to find.

She asked me where I intended going. I turned to her. 'I thought of Ystad. As I said last night the coast there is supposed to be very beautiful.'

'How far away is it?'

'About 45 kilometres – three-quarters of an hour by car. Is that all right with you?'

She seemed doubtful, but finally nodded. 'Very well. But please do not let us be late back.'

I drove the Countryman hard and we were in Ystad in forty minutes. There was a charming strand beyond the town with the sea on one side of the road and pine woods on the other. The beach was crowded with holidaymakers and I drove a mile or two out before parking the car. We sat a moment in silence and then I turned to her.

'Would you care for a walk in the woods? It'll be cooler in there.'

Her slight delay in replying told me her

earlier wariness was still with her. But she agreed, and a minute later we were following a path through the tall pines. I made little attempt at conversation, feeling it were better she made the first moves.

The first indication she was beginning to relax came after we had been walking for fifteen minutes. The path brought us into a glade that was carpeted with ferns and wood violets. Trees stood on three sides of us, on the fourth we had a framed glimpse of the sea.

Her exclamation of pleasure was spontaneous. 'You were right. It is beautiful here. So quiet and peaceful...' At that she stopped short and turned away, as if regretting her outburst of emotion.

We walked out on to the beach. By this time we had left the holidaymakers far behind, and again I could feel her uneasiness as she gazed at the deserted sand dunes. I wondered what I could do to help her relax.

'Are you certain you don't mind if I have a swim?' I asked. 'I won't be more than ten minutes.'

There was relief in her eyes as she turned towards me. 'Of course I do not mind. I will wait for you down there,' and she pointed to a hollow fringed with sand grass.

I went round the other side of the dune, took my costume from the grip I'd brought with me, and changed into it. The sand was warm and yielding under my feet as I walked down to the water's edge. The waves were small, hardly more than ripples on a lake. I ran forward and dived in. There was no shock, the water was almost warm. I swam up and down for a few minutes and then stood up. Twenty yards from me half a dozen gulls were wrangling over a tit-bit on the water. It was very clear; looking down I could see the sand under my feet. A jellyfish floated by me, its body billowing like a translucent parachute. I watched a tiny crab, no larger than a half-crown scrabbling frantically for safety and throwing up a swirling cloud of sand behind him.

Looking up I saw Anna. She was sitting in the hollow with her arms around her knees, watching me. Behind her were the cool green woods, around her the bright, golden beach. Suddenly I had a feeling of elation, as inexplicable as it was real. It felt as if the hot sun were pouring its energy directly into my body, and the sensation of being alive was suddenly exquisite.

I stayed in the water another five minutes, then collected my towel and joined her. There was less reticence in her smile this time.

'You seemed to be enjoying yourself. Was the water warm?'

'Wonderful. So wonderful I felt selfish you couldn't enjoy it with me.'

She smiled again. I finished drying myself and spread my towel alongside her, noticing that her canvas bag lay just behind her head. As I settled back I noticed she was examining me. Her voice was thoughtful.

'It is strange, but you look bigger in your costume than when you are wearing clothes.'

I knew it was true and shrugged. She went on: 'You look very strong. Are you strong?'

'Strong enough for what I have to do,' I said, thinking of mouldering grey walls, commonroom chatter, and the sterile untidy sameness of a bachelor's quarters. I flung off the mood before it could attach itself to me and reached for my jacket. 'What about a cigarette? Will you have one?'

I gave her a light and then lay back. The sky was a brilliant blue, too blue to last, but I was on holiday, living each day as it came, and that day was heaven. Through half-closed eyelids I watched Anna. Twice she glanced at me without moving, the third time she turned and reached for the canvas bag. She spread the towel she took from it on the sand and lay back. I closed my eyes contentedly, feeling I had scored my first victory.

The swim followed by the hot sunlight made me drowsy: the murmur of the sea became a soft carpet of sound on which I seemed to float without weight or substance. I did not actually sleep but entered that idyllic place where reality and fantasy merge into one.

The heat brought me to full consciousness again. The hollow was a sun-trap and I was thirsty. I rose quietly to fetch my grip. Anna's eyelids flickered as I returned but I pretended to believe her asleep by touching her arm.

'Would you care for a drink of lager? I brought two bottles with me. Or would you prefer an orange?'

She sat up quickly. 'Thank you. I would like a drink.'

I filled a cardboard carton with lager and handed it to her. 'You've brought me good weather,' I smiled, lifting my glass. '*Sköl* to you.'

She nodded. 'It is beautiful today. I am enjoying it too.' Then, as if she had no right to enjoy anything, she glanced down at her watch.

'It's only 3.30,' I assured her. 'We don't have to leave for another hour yet.'

She nodded, finished the lager, and lay back again with closed eyes. I sat watching her. The warm sun was easing the tension from her, although the faint blue shadows under her eyes remained as testimony of the strain she suffered. Her former wariness had gone, however; she lay passive now, offering her body to the sun as though in immolation to a god. I understood this reversal of behaviour: I had experienced it myself during the war. One kept going without rest for weeks and a numbness to fatigue developed. But once the body was allowed to relax it became as insatiable for rest as a parched man for water.

I lay back myself. Perhaps three minutes passed then she gave a sudden exclamation, sat up, and in a swift movement discarded the upper half of her dress. As she lay back I heard her drowsy, half-apologetic murmur: 'It is so good, this sun. It is like lying in a warm bath...'

I lay very still, staring up at a gull that dipped and soared above me. The sensation of her nearness was acute now but I knew that to touch even her arm at this moment would be fatal. She was exposing her body to the sun god who was bringing her this relief; for me the gesture had only one significance – I was accepted as a friend and not an enemy. With that, for the moment at least, I had to be content.

Another fifteen minutes passed and then I turned quietly to look at her. She was lying supine, long, slender body outstretched in the sunlight, and I could tell by the way her breasts rose and fell, tautening the brassiere straps against her smooth skin, that she had fallen asleep. There was a tiny mole near her left shoulder and I watched its gentle movement as she breathed.

As I turned away I remembered the canvas bag. Pretending to stretch myself I yawned and reached backwards until my right hand was resting on it. Through the thin cover I was able to feel the shape of its contents.

She stirred at that moment, and I relaxed my arms and reached for a cigarette. She sat up abruptly, and fear was momentarily naked in her eyes at her inability to recognise her surroundings. Then she relaxed, only to glance anxiously down at her watch a second later.

'It's all right,' I reassured her. 'I've been keeping an eye on my watch. We've plenty of time to get back to the car.'

Her eyes, still dazzled from the bright sunlight, were full of self-reproof. 'Thank you. I didn't think I would fall asleep. It was very careless of me.'

I made my first positive move, folding my towel to avoid giving it undue emphasis. 'You need to be careless more often. Your nerves were as tight as fiddle strings before we came here.'

She gave me a quick glance but said nothing. I left her dressing as I went around the sand dune for my own clothes.

Five minutes later we were both ready. She gave a backward glance at the hollow as though regretting leaving it. A minute later the woods closed around us, a cool grotto after the heat of the sun.

Her mood was very different now from what it had been earlier. As we made our way back to the car she talked to me of the woodland things we were seeing together. Once she gave a cry of delight, ran off the path, and returned with half a dozen yellow fungi resembling mushrooms. She laughed at my doubtful expression.

'Of course one can eat them: they are delicious. If we had time I would pick more and give them to you for dinner tonight. Those are good to eat too,' and she pointed to a green-spotted fungus growing near the path.

Her knowledge of woodland life, particularly the edible growths, made me curious to know how she had obtained it. This lighter mood of hers lasted until we neared the Stranden where she began showing signs of anxiety again. At the foot of the steps she stopped and turned to me.

'Thank you for this afternoon. I have enjoyed it very much. But now I must go upstairs to Carl – I really ought not to have left him alone for so long.'

'Will I see you later?' I asked, very conscious that she was due to leave the following day.

She paused uncertainly. 'It is difficult to say... At 7.15 I have to catch the bus into Trelleborg. I might be able to see you afterwards but cannot say until after I have been.'

I motioned to the car. 'Can't I run you in? I'll wait until you've finished there and then you can let me know how things stand. It'll be no trouble for me,' I said quickly as she half-opened her lips to protest. 'As I said earlier, I've nothing on today.'

She was gazing at the car, and her expression told me that my offer had another appeal than the mere one of convenience. Yet she hesitated a long time before accepting it. 'Very well, if you wish it. I will meet you downstairs at 7.15.' Halfway up the steps she turned back, her voice urgent. 'You will not be late, will you? It is most important that I am in Trelleborg before eight o'clock.'

I believe that if she had not agreed to go with me into Trelleborg curiosity would have made me follow her. For I was thinking of that canvas beach bag and wondering what her reason could be for carrying an automatic pistol wherever she went.

CHAPTER 3

My curiosity and the sense of urgency Anna had injected into our rendezvous brought me down into the lounge just after 7 o'clock. She came down a few minutes later. To my surprise she was wearing slacks and the black woollen sweater she had worn the previous evening. Over her arm she was carrying a black nylon cape and underneath it I noticed a handbag. The dinner gong sounded as she approached me, bringing a look of concern to her face.

'This means you will miss dinner tonight. I didn't think of it when I agreed to go with you.'

'Neither of us is missing dinner if I can help it,' I said, leading her to the door. 'I'm hoping you're going to have yours with me in Trelleborg when your business there is finished.'

She looked troubled. 'We shall see what happens. But in any case I must return here first. Will you bring me back?'

'Of course.' I was puzzled but left my questions until later. As we went out to the car I asked how her brother was, and her expression deepened into distress. 'He is not well. He has not left his room since this morning.'

I waited until we were seated in the car and then turned to her. 'Don't you think you ought to get a doctor to him? He looked very ill this morning.'

She made a slight shrugging motion of her shoulders, a gesture I was to learn later was characteristic of her. 'He has had doctors – many doctors. There is nothing they can do.'

'What is wrong with him?' I asked, as gently as possible.

She gave a nervous shake of her head. 'Please do not ask me that. It is too long a story to tell tonight.'

I nodded and swung the big Countryman out on the road. On our left the solitary figure of a fisherman was silhouetted on the eastern jetty of the harbour. The glass dome of the small lighthouse gleamed in the sunset. Ahead dark clouds were massing: it looked as if the rain was on its way. We passed a field of stooked corn and its wheaty smell entered the open windows of the Countryman as we gathered speed.

'What part of Germany do you come from?' I asked, trying to sound as if I were making conversation.

'I was born in Innsbrück. But my father found work in Berlin when I was a child and we all moved there. Now Carl and I live in Braunschweig, in the western zone.'

So she was Austrian by birth... For a few minutes there was silence between us. We passed through Boste, the Countryman eating up the miles. I turned to her. 'Where exactly do you want to go in Trelleborg?'

'To the docks, please. I want to meet the 8 o'clock ferryboat from Travemünde.'

I was surprised and showed it. 'Travemünde! Are you expecting someone, then?'

An odd shiver ran through her. I had to wait for her answer, if answer it was. 'Please – if you come to the docks with me – do not ask me questions. Otherwise it is better I go alone.'

A car came round a bend in the narrow road, making me swing over sharply to avoid it. When it had passed I stopped the Countryman and turned to her.

'Listen to me for a moment. By this time you must have realised I like you and want to help you. But I can't help until I know what the trouble is. So why don't you tell me?'

She was taken by surprise and for a moment her expression betrayed her. She wanted to talk but caution would not allow it. I wondered what kind of fear it was that could make her as careful as this.

'It's obviously something connected with your brother,' I argued. 'Why not tell me about it? If I can help him I will. If I can't – if he is wanted by the police or something like that' – as I said it I watched her closely – 'then at least I shall keep my mouth shut. I'm not a policeman, and I don't throw stones at other peoples' houses.'

Although my idiom probably meant nothing to her I think she got the general impression I meant well. But by this time she had conquered her desire to confide in me. Her face was pale and her voice cold. 'Please remember I did not ask you to bring me into Trelleborg. I intended coming alone, by bus.'

'I'm not suggesting you're under any obligation,' I said impatiently. 'Obviously you're not. But be fair to me. You're afraid of someone who may be on that boat and I'm taking you to meet it. That means I'd have to try to defend you if something happened… I couldn't help myself. Surely that gives me some right to know what it is all about.'

Her eyes were wide again, staring at me with an odd intentness. 'Defend me? I could never allow you to do that.'

'Why not?' I demanded. 'What is it you're so afraid of? Tell me.'

She dropped her face, plucked at her nylon cape with a slim hand. 'There is no time now and I must be at the docks before the boat berths. I am hoping these people will not be aboard… If they are not, and you still insist, I might tell you the story afterwards. Let us see.'

'But what if they are on board? What do I

do then?'

She lifted her eyes to me. 'Only what we agreed earlier – that you drive me straight back to the hotel. That is all I want.'

I reached out for the starter key. 'Well; that won't affect my conscience one way or the other. All right. We'll go there now and you tell me what it is all about over dinner.'

The docks at Trelleborg were small and square in shape. The west pier was the berth of the Travemünde ferry. It was flanked by a long red building and terminated in a customs shed, cranes and gantries for the rapid unloading of cars. A small crowd of people and a few taxis were waiting along-side the berth. Half a dozen private cars were parked at the edge of the north quay and Anna asked me to park the Country-man among them. This put the west quay on our left – near enough, I noticed, for us to identify anyone coming down it, but far enough for us to remain anonymously hidden among the cars. Noticing there were sheds beyond and behind the red building, I turned to her.

'I take it you intend identifying the pas-sengers as they come up the quay. What happens if they go round the other side of the red building? There seems another exit there.'

Suspense was already telling on her: her

voice was jerky. 'The only other exit is by train. All other passengers come down the pier. I noticed it when we arrived.'

For the first time it occurred to me she must have been in Sweden at least two days. There was only one ferry a day from Travemünde: it did not arrive until 8 p.m. and it had been only 8.30 when I saw her and Carl at the fishing harbour the previous night. She nodded at my question.

'Yes; we arrived on Monday. We intended to continue the next day and stayed in Trelleborg the night, but when Carl felt one of his attacks coming on I dared not let him travel. So we moved out to the Stranden until he recovered.'

She omitted to explain why they had moved, but in the circumstances it was no longer necessary. 'Last night,' I said. 'If you came in to watch the ferry arrive, how did you get back to Carl so quickly without a car?'

She bit her lip. 'I was given the wrong time for the bus into Trelleborg and missed it. That was why Carl and I were so anxious all the evening...'

There was considerable activity on the quay now, and a few minutes later the black silhouette of the ferry appeared at the harbour mouth. The pound of its diesels came to us, thumping like a frightened heart. It turned a few degrees and headed nose first for the quay. I could see its passengers now, crowding the decks. Its engines were in reverse and water frothed up like yeast about its stern. Bow first it nosed forward. Voices shouted orders, chains clattered, gangways fell with a thud. Then, for a moment, silence came back.

Passengers began jostling down the gangways and the first cars drove off the boat. Anna was leaning forward in her seat, lips slightly parted, her breathing tight and shallow. While I had no idea whom she was looking for, her tension transferred itself to me and made my own heart beat faster.

I saw she was right, that all passengers other than those leaving by train came up the quay alongside the red building. As they came, whether on foot or by car, her eyes checked them carefully.

In fifteen minutes the bulk of them had gone, leaving only a few stragglers. She waited for them to disperse too before finally sinking back in her seat. Her face was still pale, but for the moment the apprehension had lifted from her eyes. She looked like a condemned prisoner granted a day's reprieve.

'So they weren't on it?' I said, breaking the silence.

With an effort she pushed herself up in the seat and turned to me. 'No. We can go back now.'

'Wouldn't you like a drink first?' I asked, noticing how her body was trembling from reaction.

She managed me a smile. 'No, thank you. I would prefer to change my clothes first.'

I started the engine. 'All right, but only on one condition – that you don't take long about it.'

It was good to hear her laugh again. 'I won't be long. I have nothing elaborate with me.'

We were back in under half an hour. Carl was downstairs, sitting in the same window seat that I had occupied the previous evening. He was obviously watching out for us, and there was an air of readiness about him as if he were prepared to quit the hotel at a moment's notice. In the electric light his ailing face was haggard and apprehensive as he watched us approach.

Anna ran ahead of me up the steps, giving him a sign of reassurance as she drew level with him. He sank back in his chair, his eyes closing thankfully. By the time I entered the lounge Anna was already alongside him, whispering words of comfort in his ear.

They separated as I approached. Carl rose unsteadily to his feet and extended his hand. As he was greeting me Anna picked up a newspaper from a chair alongside him. She addressed him in German, her voice sharp with interest.

'Is it a recent one?'

'It is Saturday's,' he told her. 'The receptionist got it for me.'

She opened it. I saw it was the Frankfort *Allgemeine Zeitung*. Her voice was anxious. 'Did you find anything?'

'*Nein, Liebchen.* There is nothing.'

Carl and I made light conversation while Anna paged through the newspaper. Sitting opposite him a second time that day I was able to make a better assessment of him. His condition and behaviour reminded me of something, and quite suddenly I knew what it was. A soldier after months and years of ceaseless action. One or two of my friends had gone that way. Brave men, utterly dependable under fire, and then almost without warning their nerve had cracked. They had become afraid not only of bullets but of shadows too, as if their courage had been a bank and they had drawn too heavily on it. The Services even had a name for it. Moral fatigue.

I eyed him with new interest after that and the feeling grew that I was right. That broad frame of his, emaciated as it was today, had not always belonged to a man who flinched at shadows. I noticed something else too – his deep affection for Anna. It must have been hell for him, feeling as he did, to be forced to let her do the dangerous work. I imagined I saw the tragedy of it in his eyes and felt pity for him.

Anna put the newspaper down and turned to him. 'As Mr Drayton missed dinner because of me, I've accepted his invitation to dine out. I thought you would probably be going back to your room.'

I had the feeling she had already whispered her intention to him before I reached the table. Even so, his eyes seemed to cloud with an expression I could not analyse, although his reply was accommodating enough.

'Yes, of course, *Liebchen*. I only intended staying down here until you returned.'

She touched his arm affectionately. 'You're quite sure you'll be all right? I won't go otherwise.'

'Of course I am sure. Go and enjoy yourself.' With that he rose and held out his hand to me. 'Thank you for taking Anna into Trelleborg, Mr Drayton. I hope we shall see you in the morning before we leave. Good night.'

Anna took his arm to steady him. As they moved away she turned to me. 'I shan't be long changing. Shall we meet here in fifteen minutes?'

CHAPTER 4

When she came down she was wearing the black tailored costume that made her look like a queen. I led her outside and saw the threatened storm was building up in the west. In twenty minutes we were back in Trelleborg. We found a restaurant, with a small orchestra, that served German wines, and we dined well. During the meal we made only light conversation, avoiding the serious topic that I intended should come later. As the atmosphere and the wine took their effect her mood became as light as it had been in the woods that afternoon, but now, knowing her better, I could detect the undertone of strain in her. She too was like a soldier, trying hard but not altogether successfully to enjoy a few hours' reprieve from danger.

After the table was cleared I asked her if she would care to dance. After a momentary hesitation she nodded. It was the first time I had been in any kind of physical contact with her, and I was struck by the firm and yet wonderful resilience of her body. She moved without effort, and although she danced with me only as she might have danced with any man I became aware again of the strong physical desire she aroused in me.

I was tempted to spare her my questions that night, but then remembered she and Carl were due to leave early the next morning. On reaching our table I gave her a cigarette and then came straight to the point.

'Well,' I asked, smiling at her. 'Do you feel like satisfying my curiosity now?'

A furrow appeared between her fine dark eyebrows. Clearly she had been having second thoughts about her earlier confidences and was not pleased with me now for my insistence. She sat very still for a moment, a lovely picture with her brushed-back hair and smooth face and neck, now tinted golden by the sun, rising like a firm flower from the black calyx of her costume. Then she nodded abruptly.

'Very well. But let us go out on the verandah. It is growing too hot in here.'

The verandah extended out on the pavement. There was little traffic in the street and few pedestrians. By this time the storm clouds had taken full possession of the sky, blotting out the last of the twilight. A low rumble drowned the sound of the orchestra as I led her to an unoccupied table. I ordered two martinis for us and as the waiter left I heard the challenge of her voice.

'What exactly do you want to know?'

I chose my words carefully. 'I'd like to know who it is you're expecting to follow you here from Germany. And why you, and particularly your brother, are so afraid of them.'

She was touchy about Carl and sprang instantly to his defence. 'You think he is a coward!'

I shook my head. 'No. I think he is a sick man.'

'That's not true. I saw your eyes this morning. You despise him because you think he gives me tasks he should do himself...'

'Doesn't he?' I asked.

'No! I go myself, often without telling him, because he is so ill. If you knew how he feels the disgrace of it, how he suffers...'

Her anger was an outlet to strain and I made no effort to restrain it. It also made her words flow faster. 'Carl has never been a coward. Never in his life. You have no right to say such things about him.'

I leaned forward across the table. 'And yet there is someone he is terrified of now. You can't deny it.'

A flash of lightning momentarily dimmed the shaded lights around us. Through the gloom that followed her white face stared angrily at me.

'That does not mean he is a coward. You do not understand anything and yet you talk like this... And you keep forgetting he is ill.' She paused, then said slowly. 'Shall I tell you why he is ill?'

I nodded, oddly tensed.

Her voice was deliberate, sparing herself nothing, punishing me for my opinion of Carl. 'It is not a pretty story but you have asked to hear it. It happened in the eastern zone after the war. A gang of soldiers caught me in an alley and tried to rape me. There were six of them, and if it had not been for Carl who saw them and interfered...'

She paused, giving my shocked mind a moment to punish me. The storm was almost overhead: people were rising from tables around us and going inside but neither of us took any notice of them. When she went on her words were like drops of blood falling from a reopened wound.

'Carl struck one of them and they turned on him. *Du mein Gott,* the things they did to him – one would never believe men could be such brutes. I screamed and screamed for God to punish them, kill them, but nothing happened. What made it worse for Carl was that he could not altogether save me...'

Thunder came, a great wild voice. I tried to speak as it died away but my throat was too dry. When she continued her tone had changed.

'It is difficult for us to talk to you of these things... Some might say we deserved it for the things Germany did, and they might be right. But that does not make the pain less... And none of us were Nazis. My parents hated them and so did Carl. He fought for

Germany because he was young and had little or no choice. And because he was a man he fought bravely. In 1944 he won the Iron Cross…'

I had never heard an Austrian or for that matter a German admit he had been a Nazi, but I believed her. Every word had a ring of truth.

'This was during the occupation in 1945. Carl was taken to hospital and my mother fled with me into the mountains. We lived on mushrooms, herbs, berries: anything we could find. I wanted to return to Carl but mother would not let me. When I did go, months later, I was very thin and not worth a soldier's second glance. Carl cried when he saw me. We both cried…'

The rain was falling now, as fast as their tears had fallen. Disgusted at my curiosity, I found my voice at last. 'That's enough… I'd no idea… I'm terribly sorry. Let's forget it and have another drink inside.'

Her grave, blue-grey eyes fixed on mine. 'No. It is better I finish now. You have heard why Carl is a sick man but not yet why he is afraid. I would like you to hear that too.'

I sank back. The air seemed full of static, pricking my skin like a thousand pins as I listened in silence.

'Carl was on his feet by this time although still very weak. He was terribly bitter – not against anyone in particular but against the world. I was afraid of what mad things he might do when he left hospital, and so it was a great relief when he agreed to go back and live with us. There was only mother and I – father had been killed during the war – and now, with Carl's help, we got across into the western zone and found a basement room in Braunschweig. It was very expensive and Carl did everything he could to get work. He would be out all day and come home in the evening looking like a grey ghost, with hardly the strength to lift a cup to his lips. Mother was forced to go out to work with me, sometimes to do manual labour, and that made him even more bitter.

'Then one day he brought some money home. Only a few marks, but it bought us food. He was very thrilled: he said he had got work with a man called Otto Steiner and that if he worked hard it might be permanent. My mother was less happy. Before the war her brother had been a policeman and she had heard him talk of Steiner. He had been one of the biggest and most brutal criminals in Germany, but had always been too clever to be caught. Her guess was that Steiner had chosen Braunschweig because it was conveniently near the eastern zone and that he was using the Black Market as a means of building up his criminal organisation again.

'We both begged Carl to leave him but he refused, saying he wasn't going to see my mother shifting rubble in the streets again. And it was difficult to argue with him – everyone dealt in the Black Market in those days, there was no other way to live, and the only difference in them and Carl was that he was getting regular money. For our sakes he would not give up the work and we could only wait and pray my mother was wrong.

'Eighteen months went by and we were able to afford a flat. Carl was making a good deal of money now but none of us was happy. Carl was working all hours – sometimes he would be away for days at a time. He would never say what he had been doing, but I could see from his eyes how he hated the work. And I began hearing rumours about Steiner – that his organisation was now very powerful and was dealing in worse things than the Black Market. Carl told me not to worry, but I could see he was afraid himself. And this terrified me, because I had never seen Carl afraid of anything before. Then one day I met Steiner and I understood.'

Memory had abducted her into the past and her white face showed all the disgust and fear it had been shown that day.

'One week Carl brought home a parcel he had to deliver personally to Steiner. Because he had been with Steiner from the beginning he was one of the few men allowed to have personal contact with him. But when the morning came Carl was ill – it was the beginning of his nervous sickness – and he could not rise from his bed. Seeing he was afraid of the consequences if he failed to deliver the parcel, and fearing for his safety, I offered to take it myself. At first he would not hear of it, but after pleading with him for nearly two hours he finally told me how I could find Steiner.'

She broke off and held out her hand. 'Please give me a cigarette.' She inhaled on it deeply before continuing.

'I had expected to go into some underground cellar, but instead found myself outside a block of offices that looked like the headquarters of a business concern. I was taken to a waiting room and after a few minutes a man appeared who said he was Steiner's secretary. I learned later that his name was Hacht. He reminded me of the pictures I had seen of Goebbels during the war: he had the same thin body, chinless face and oily smooth hair. And from the way he spoke and acted his mind seemed as twisted as his body...'

'Twisted?' I asked.

She nodded. 'His left leg was deformed, giving him a limp. He took me to an office upstairs. Steiner was sitting at a desk in the centre of it. My first impression of Steiner was his size. He was a huge man, not run to seed but with broad powerful shoulders and a thick, strong neck. I guessed his age at about forty. He was almost bald and had a strong, clean-shaven face. He was staring at some papers on his desk as I entered, but as I came forward his eyes moved slowly up my body to my face. And then I had my first real taste of fear. His eyes were...' She hesitated, one hand moving helplessly as she searched for the right words. 'It is difficult to describe the impression they made on me. They were *teuflisch* ... they gave me the horrible feeling that he was not one of us – not a mixture of the little good and the little bad that we are – but something entirely evil. I was terrified when Hacht closed the door and left me alone with him.'

I could see the scene as though I were there: the huge squatting figure, like a great spider, at his desk, and the young slim, white-faced girl with her parcel.

'I do not know how long he stared at me. But at last he lifted a hand and beckoned me forward. It was huge and covered in thick, golden hairs. As I approached he said slowly: "I find it interesting that Carl keeps secrets from me. He has never mentioned living with such a beautiful girl."

'He had a cultured voice: somehow that made what was to follow worse. I put the parcel on his desk, told him my relationship with Carl, and why he could not deliver the parcel himself. His eyes never left me as I was speaking. They were filthy eyes, stripping the clothes off my body. When I had finished he leaned forward and said with a laugh: "Just the same, my dear, you can tell Carl I shall want to possess you one of these days. Your body pleases me." But he did not say "possess". He used the word the soldiers use. And his laugh was not because he was joking but because he enjoyed using the word in front of me…'

The dead match I was still holding snapped between my fingers.

'I ran all the way home, and although I dared not tell Carl what had happened I begged him to give up the work. My mother pleaded with him too. But I think we both knew it was already too late. Steiner would never allow him to leave the organisation now.'

By this time rain was drumming down on the canvas roof of the verandah. Cold drops occasionally splashed on the table but neither of us took notice of them.

'I only saw Steiner three times more,' Anna went on. 'The first time was at home. He came when Carl was away and asked when I was going to give myself to him. When I told him to get out he laughed and asked me how much I cared for Carl. It was my mother who intervened – she was a brave woman. We had a telephone now: she picked up the receiver and told him if he didn't go she would phone the police and tell them he had broken in and assaulted us. She said she knew they would be only too glad to get a charge against him. He stared at her as though he hadn't seen her before, walked over to the door, and turned. I shall never forget his expression and his words to her. "What a stupid woman you are," he said softly. "To have lived so long and learned so little. You will have to be taught something before you die." With that he left us.

'I was terrified of what Carl might do if he were told and begged my mother to keep quiet. It was a mistake: we ought to have done everything we could to fight Steiner. A week later mother was dead, killed by a car while out shopping. The driver was never found and the coroner's verdict was manslaughter by a person or persons unknown.'

It was a story that held me as rigid as a revolver at my stomach. Yet her face told me it was true.

'Things moved quickly now. For one thing, Carl's nerves had almost gone. He seemed to have no resistance to Steiner, to be hypnotised by him. I did not know what he was being made to do – he never discussed anything with me – but I heard rumours that Steiner was now abducting people and transporting them across the frontiers. My life was a living hell in case Carl was involved in this traffic, particularly when he was away for days and came back looking as if he had sold his soul to the devil. Sometimes he would be sick, as though he were trying to vomit from himself the disgust he was feeling. It could not last and it did not.

'One Tuesday evening in November Steiner and Hacht came round to our flat to see Carl. Steiner seemed unusually restless and I could hear him growling at Carl to hurry up. They all left in less than five minutes, Carl telling me he would not be back until the following day.

'Wednesday came and went and he did not return. On the Thursday morning I had a visit from the police.' She paused, blew smoke out through her nostrils. 'As soon as I saw them I knew it was the end. And I think I was glad.'

I found my voice again. 'They were all arrested. Steiner too?'

'Yes. The police allowed me to speak to Carl and this is what he told me. After leaving our flat Hacht had driven them out by car to a house in the country. There a second car met them, driven by a man called Müller and someone else Carl did not know. Müller was ordered to take a road that led round the rear of the house while Hacht drove along the front road and hid his car in a wood. After telling Carl to stay with the car and guard it Steiner and Hacht made their way to the house.

'A few minutes later another car drove up. Carl, watching from the wood, saw two men get out. After looking around them carefully they went up to the house door and rang the bell. The door opened and they went inside. All was quiet for a minute or two, then there was a succession of revolver shots. The front door was flung open again and Steiner and Hacht appeared, dragging a third man between them. Acting on his instructions Carl drove the car out on to the road and Steiner and Hacht threw the struggling man inside. Carl was told to guard him while Hacht took the wheel. Müller's car did not follow them as they drove away.

'Carl knew nothing about the captured man, whom Steiner called Kleinberg, but from the direction they were driving guessed he was a German political refugee. Halfway to the frontier, however, a police car fastened on them and gave chase. Hacht drove like a fiend – Carl says he has never seen such driving – and managed to draw slightly away from the other car. They were among the forests of the Harz by this time and on a lonely road. Steiner turned to Carl and told him that to get Kleinberg they'd been forced to kill the other two men. If they didn't get rid of Kleinberg now and the police caught them, all three of them would be on a murder charge. When Hacht stopped the car Carl was to jump out with Kleinberg, hide him in the woods until Hacht had drawn the police car away, and then shoot him and hide his body. In that way all evidence against them would be destroyed.

'Hacht braked, Steiner pushed the two of them out, and the car accelerated away. Carl pulled Kleinberg off the road and crouched down among the trees as the police car came racing by. It disappeared round a bend in the road and Carl and Kleinberg were left alone.'

She paused a moment, leaving me, as it were, with a frozen picture of the scene in my mind. The police car, headlights shining on the trees, disappearing down the winding mountain road. The silence it left behind; the dark, waiting woods; the two panting, white-faced, frightened men... Lightning flashing in the deserted street added a bizarre effect to Anna's story as she continued:

'Carl says Kleinberg was almost delirious with fear and made all kinds of wild promises if his life were spared. He offered Carl impossible sums of money, said he wouldn't go to the police, and promised to leave Germany and never return. First he said he would go to Austria, and then, as if that were not far enough, said he would go to Stockholm. "I have relations in Sweden," he sobbed, "Steiner does not know it but my mother is Swedish – her friends will help me."

'The promises were so impossible Carl believed none of them. He was certain Kleinberg would go straight to the police if he were released and that would mean Carl's arrest on a murder charge. But he could not bring himself to kill a helpless man. He released Kleinberg and then surrendered himself to the police and told them everything.

'Knowing all about Steiner's activities, this was exactly what the police wanted. They took down Carl's statement, arrested Steiner and Hacht, and then waited for Kleinberg to come forward. And then the strange, and for us terrible, thing happened. Kleinberg never came.

'The police hunted everywhere but never found him. It was fatal for their case, because Steiner had hidden the bodies of the men he had shot and the police never found them. Without the bodies and Kleinberg as witness Carl's evidence was not enough to support a murder charge against Steiner. All Steiner could be convicted on were lesser crimes for which Carl had evidence. These were few enough because Steiner had always kept as much as possible from his henchmen. But they were enough to get him a sentence of ten years. Hacht was given nine.'

Memory of the trial brought a shuddering breath from her. 'I shall never forget the last day. Carl had been in the witness box and as Steiner was brought forward next it meant they passed on the floor of the court. As they came opposite one another Steiner stopped and looked at Carl with those devil eyes of his. He said nothing, did nothing … but I knew and Carl knew that at least one death sentence had been passed that day…'

Now I understood their fear, and the occasional raindrops that splashed our way were ice-cold on my face.

'Carl?' I asked. 'He wouldn't get away scott-free, of course?'

'No. But his behaviour and his evidence were taken into account. He was sent to prison for three years.'

'And what did you do in that time?'

She was strong, this girl – she dismissed those hard, empty years with an indifferent shrug of her shoulders. 'I worked. I was a shop girl, a receptionist, a mannequin. After all that had happened before it was not difficult.'

'And when did Carl come out?'

'In 1950. I went on working while he opened up a small import agency. But his health was poor – in prison he had started having attacks of weakness – and these grew steadily worse and more frequent whenever he was excited or worried. Doctors told us it had something to do with the head injuries the soldiers had given him, that his whole nervous system was damaged. His only hope of cure was complete rest from worry and this he could never get when every tick of the clock brought Steiner a step nearer to him.

'But we never discussed it until the last year. It was I who broke the silence, and it was strange how it frightened Carl, almost as though he had somehow convinced himself the whole thing had been a nightmare and my words had made it real again. We tried to think of a way of escaping from Steiner, but for months could think of nothing. Of course, there was police protection, but we knew that would not keep him away for long. I made Carl go over the entire story with me again, particularly the things Kleinberg had said to him in the woods. Until now Carl had believed those things nothing but hysteria – he had never bothered to tell them in detail to the police because he believed them worthless – but now I made him remember everything he could. There was precious little to work on – Austria and Stockholm were the only two place names he could remember – and because it was more definite I chose Stockholm. Carl's agency had made us a little money by this time and I went to a private detective and asked him to make enquiries about Kleinberg there.

'The months went by, the cost was terrible, and just when our money had almost all gone and we were going to call off the search a cable arrived telling us the detective had found someone in Stockholm who answered to Kleinberg's description.

'There was little time left – Steiner had

been given a small remission of sentence and although we couldn't find out the exact day of his release we knew it was soon. I went straight to a lawyer, and although he assured me Steiner could be retried for murder if Kleinberg could be persuaded to come forward and give evidence, he strongly advised me to say nothing about our discovery to the police until we had seen Kleinberg ourselves. He was afraid the police might make only a perfunctory enquiry – after failing to find either Kleinberg or the two murdered men they had become sceptical of Carl's story – and the lawyer was afraid that a half-hearted enquiry might only alarm Kleinberg and make him vanish again. He also thought that the fewer people who knew of our discovery the better. For although Steiner was still in prison, Hacht had been out for nearly a year, and there would be others still working for him...'

There was a picture of Steiner in my mind at that moment, plotting revenge on Carl after ten long years, and then suddenly hearing that he and Anna had possibly traced the one man whose evidence could incarcerate him for life... I leaned forward, searching her face in alarm.

'You were careful?' I demanded. 'You made certain no one learned what you were doing?'

Her eyes fumbled for mine and as they met I knew the whole frightening truth.

CHAPTER 5

Her voice was low, fighting back the fear that was within her. 'It happened two weeks ago. A man I've never seen before brushed up against me when I was out shopping. "I've got a message for you, Anna Frandl," he said. "From someone you know very well. He says if you don't want to die an even worse death than Carl Frandl is going to die, stop looking for Kleinberg." With that he vanished into the crowd.'

The pieces of dead match gritted into charcoal between my fingers. Everything was ice-clear to me now, and it was some seconds again before I could speak.

'So that's why you keep looking in German newspapers? You're expecting news of Steiner's release.'

'Yes. He is well known – there is certain to be a paragraph.'

It would have been kinder to have kept the thought that came to me silent. 'You could recognise either Steiner or Hacht leaving the boat – I see that. But what about his other men? You suspected me last night. How can you be certain none of them has already landed?'

One of her slim hands was resting on the table. It jerked spasmodically at my words. 'We know most of them… But it is true that that danger exists. That is why I do not like leaving Carl alone and why we must go on tomorrow…' Then she remembered his illness and her face clouded. 'But it is not easy. He is still very weak and it is a long tiring journey to Stockholm.'

Her hand was still lying on the table and a sudden impulse made me reach out and take it. It was ice-cold to the touch. She hesitated and then gave me an uncertain smile. I think it was the courage of that smile that decided me.

'Listen,' I said. 'I intended going up to Stockholm sooner or later and if it will be any help to you I could leave tomorrow with you and Carl. That should make it more difficult for you to be followed and also it will be more comfortable for Carl.'

For a moment she was silent. Then she looked up at me. 'After what I have told you, would you really do this for us?'

I nodded. 'See how Carl is feeling in the morning and then let me know when you want to leave. I can be ready in half an hour.'

'There is no need to ask him. We would leave as early as was convenient to you.'

'Good. All I have to do is fill up with petrol. Shall we say eight o'clock, then?'

She gave a sudden exclamation of distress.

71

'Wait! Let me think. Whatever happens you must not become involved with Steiner...'

I sat watching the conflict on her white, lovely face. She was talking to herself more than to me. 'It ought to be safe. We do not think Steiner is out yet and even if Hacht or any of the others trace us I do not think Steiner would want them to injure us until he arrived. And yet there is the risk that he...'

I took sides in the conflict. 'Leave me to do the worrying about myself. You and Carl be ready at eight o'clock tomorrow.'

For a long moment she was silent. Then she made that characteristic movement of her shoulders and smiled her thanks at me. 'For Carl's sake I must accept. I cannot tell you how grateful I am.'

My hand was still resting on hers. She pressed it gently and then drew her hand away. 'I think, if you do not mind, that I ought to go back now. It is getting rather late.'

We drove back to the Stranden in silence, each with his own thoughts. I parked the car and led her inside. On the first floor she turned to me. 'I am going to tell Carl of your offer now and he is sure to want to thank you. May he come to your room later?'

I nodded. She did not move away at once but stood facing me, tall, slim, very lovely. I hesitated, then put my arm round her slim shoulders and kissed her. For some reason or other I expected coolness and for a moment her lips were motionless against mine. Then, quite suddenly, they parted and her whole body seemed to surge upwards and press itself against me. Only for a few seconds; then she murmured something indistinct and pulled away.

'We shall meet again tomorrow,' she whispered. *'Auf Wiedersehen,* and thank you.'

With that she was gone, and I turned a little blindly for my room.

Carl came to see me ten minutes later. He was wearing a dressing-gown and his face held a mixture of emotions.

'Anna has told me all that has happened tonight, Mr Drayton. I hardly know what to say to you.'

I tried to make things easy for him as I closed the door.

'There's nothing to say. I intended going up to Stockholm anyway. I shall be glad of your company.'

He shook his head in distress. 'It was wrong of Anna to tell you of our trouble. It has put you in an impossible position.'

'Rubbish,' I said brusquely. 'She did the right thing. She's worried about your health – she knows you're in no condition for a long tiring journey.'

My reference to his health brought an instant reaction, reminding me of what

Anna had said about his feeling towards it. 'This broken-down, useless body of mine. Once it was strong and reliable – now it cracks up every time I need it most...' His self-disgust turned back into concern for me. 'Anna has told you of my past – how ten years ago I was a criminal. This present trouble is a direct result of it and I don't want to get innocent people involved.'

After hearing his story I had a good deal of respect for him. Now, among other things, I liked the way he made no attempt to gloss over his past.

'You're not getting me involved,' I said impatiently. 'Steiner isn't out yet and as far as you know none of his men have traced you here. I'll be in no more danger taking you to Stockholm than the driver of the train you'd have taken. Don't exaggerate the thing, for God's sake.'

He stood undecided a long time before his haggard face twisted into a wry smile. 'All right. If that's the way you feel I should be a fool to refuse. I can only thank you and hope you have no reason to regret it.'

I took his thin hand, feeling again the ague that racked him. 'I shan't have any regrets. It'll be pleasant having you along.'

We chatted a few minutes more and then he returned to his room. I got into bed, but it was a long time before I fell asleep. My thoughts were on Steiner, and I was wondering into just what complications and dangers a protective instinct and a woman's beauty could land a man.

CHAPTER 6

I rose early the next morning and packed my things before breakfast. I then went to attend to the car. It was a fine sunny morning, without the stickiness of the previous day. I drove off to the nearest filling station, had the car checked over and filled with petrol and was back at the Stranden before eight o'clock.

Anna and Carl were waiting for me in the hall. Carl was wearing a brown sports coat, a colour that accentuated the paleness of his gaunt cheeks, while Anna was dressed in slacks and an open-necked blue shirt. She gave me a smile of welcome as I approached and pointed to the desk where a suitcase and a large grip were standing. 'As you see we do not have much luggage. I think it will go easily into your car.'

I showed them a road map of Sweden. 'There are two ways we can go to Stockholm. One is to link up with Highway 1 east of Hälsingborg and follow it through central Sweden, the other is to take Highway 4 along the east coast. I suggest we take the first one – it's a good hundred kilometres shorter. Is that all right with you both?'

Carl nodded and turned to Anna. She hesitated before answering. 'If I thought we were being shadowed I would prefer to take the less likely route. But as things are it is better we take the shorter one – it will mean less travelling for Carl.'

I looked around, then drew closer to them. 'I think it would be a good idea to leave a red herring or two behind us. There is no need for the staff here to know you're going all the way with me. Let them believe I'm only taking you to the station.'

Anna's appreciative glance was less for my suggestion than for the fact I was thinking on security lines.

'I arranged with Carl last night that everyone here should think you are taking us to catch the 9 a.m. train. I was going to ask you to drop a hint of this to the receptionist.'

I had not met many women who knew how to handle situations of this kind and my admiration for her grew. After a brief chat to the receptionist I returned to the Countryman. To get their luggage into it I had to lower the rear seat, but there was plenty of room on the front bench seat for the three of us. Anna sat between Carl and me, and a minute later we were on our way, heading north through the lush, undulating countryside of Skåne.

For the first half-hour Carl, grateful for the lift, did his best to keep up a conversation with me. But he found it an effort to talk over the noise of the engine, and as time passed the conversation became more and more desultory. Anna said little. Since entering the car she had shown a curious reserve to me. She was not unfriendly: she showed me all the conventional courtesy the occasion demanded, but somehow the slight intimacy of the previous evening had vanished. I wondered if Carl's presence had something to do with it, and shrugged. She was not an easy person to understand.

We had a break for coffee in Eker and reached Ljungby just after 12.30. By this time Carl was looking very drawn and Anna threw me a pointed look. 'Perhaps it might be a good idea to stop here and have lunch.'

I found a pleasant restaurant on the out-skirts of the small town, built of Swedish pine with an open-fronted verandah overlooking a flower garden. We ordered a *smörgås* lunch. The sun was warm and brought a spicy, resinous smell from the pine planks.

Anna asked the proprietor if he knew any-where in town where a German newspaper could be bought. He thought a moment, and then called a small boy from the rear of the house and said something to him in Swedish. The boy ran off, to return five minutes later with a newspaper which he handed to Anna.

In their anxiety to search the paper both of them lost interest in the meal. Their tension transferred itself to me and it was a relief when Carl shook his head at last and laid it aside.

'Nothing?' I asked.

'No. But it is three days old. Perhaps we can get a more recent one in Jönköping.'

Before we started off again Anna drew me aside, 'Carl is looking very tired. Do you mind if we give him an hour's rest? Somewhere in the country where he can sleep.'

I nodded and we pulled away. It was hot in the car now – my own shirt was clinging to my back – and Carl's gaunt face became more and more drawn. About twelve miles north of Ljungby we found ourselves running alongside a lake. I found a suitable spot and drove off the road among some trees. Going around the back of the Countryman I pulled out my tent.

'He'll be able to get a proper sleep in it,' I told Anna. Carl protested at the trouble I was taking, but the tent was up in three minutes. I slid my rubber mattress into it and then turned to him.

'Get your head down for an hour. Then, if you feel up to it, we'll go on to Jönköping before calling it a day. That will leave us only 200 miles to do tomorrow.'

Carl continued protesting about the delay he was causing, but it was obvious he needed the rest. Anna made him comfortable and then returned to the car. There was a ground sheet lying there, and, refusing the camp stool I offered her, she sank down on it.

I do not know how long we sat there in silence. It was a peaceful place, with the blue lake shining through the trees and the birds singing their hearts out around us. I found myself watching Anna. She had her arms around her knees and from the way she was staring at the lake it seemed her thoughts were far away. She was good to look at, with her bare tanned arms, disciplined thoughtful face, and sleek glossy hair.

Then, as though I had been wrong and she had been aware of my gaze the whole time, she turned towards me. Our eyes met and it seemed neither of us could look away. The air suddenly became hushed as if my other senses had become aware of her gaze and surrendered to my sight their powers of attention.

It was she who broke the spell, turning her head sharply away and making an exclamation that had protest, fear, and self-reproach all jumbled up in it. Embarrassed now, and oddly restless, I rose to my feet.

'I'm going for a walk,' I said. 'Do you feel like coming or would you rather stay here?'

Something in the look she gave me made me think of a hunted deer I had once seen hiding among gorse in the Cornish moors. She hesitated, then rose reluctantly to her feet. Her face was almost sullen as she folowed me through bushes and willow, over outcrops of rock, until we came to a small inlet fringed with white pebbles. A promontory of moss-covered boulders flanked it at one side: we climbed the boulders and came to a hollow ringed with pines and thickly carpeted with brown pine needles. Here I paused and turned to her.

'Do you want to go on any further? Or should we turn back?'

She did not answer. She was standing between me and the lake, staring out across it. I gazed at the lovely lines of her and felt my throat suddenly contract. Reaching out I caught hold of her arm.

'Anna,' I said. 'You're very beautiful, Anna.'

She turned sharply towards me and again I saw fear tugging at her eyes. I sank down on the pine needles, pulling her down after me. She was trembling and turned away as we lay there.

The pine needles were soft and yielding and gave off a scent that mingled with the hot smell of summer. I lay still for a long time, watching the bowl of blue sky above the pines. A dragonfly appeared and hovered over us, the sunlight splintering off its wings in shafts of dazzling colour. For a moment I was a child again – back to the day I had gone fishing with my father and seen my first dragonfly. I had cried with joy at the sight of it: a magic creature of glowing colour, the most beautiful thing I had ever seen. But the years had taken away the dragonflies until I had believed them gone forever. But now one was back – magic was abroad in the world again...

'Anna,' I murmured, drawing her towards me. 'Anna...'

I listened to her resentful voice. 'Two days ago I did not know you existed... Then you come out of nowhere. At first I believed you our enemy. But instead you are kind to me. You are kind to Carl. You put me in your debt...'

The dragonfly trembled and was gone.

'There's no debt,' I said, sinking back. 'And so there's nothing to pay.'

Her body surged towards me as it had the previous night. 'No. You must not misunderstand. I am just talking ... talking because I do not understand these feelings. I have not come with you to pay a debt – if that were all, it would be easier. It is something else – something I do not understand. Oh; all this talk. There is too much talk...'

Her lips kissed me as though they were parched for love. Holding her was like holding a white writhing flame. Once she cried out: *'Carl! Versteh, mich!'* and a moment later her lips, as if to deaden their protests, were searching for mine again. The earth shuddered under our warm bodies as though eager for its own dissolution. Storm-tossed we clung together, waiting for the end. It came in a great soundless explosion that flung us to a far place where passion had gone and peace closed our eyes.

It was Anna who awoke first. She shook my arm. 'John; wake up. It is nearly half-past four.'

I sat up, to see her eyes bright with alarm. 'I do not like leaving Carl for so long, not in the open like this. Please hurry.'

She was ready in less than a minute and hurried off, leaving me to catch up with her. We found Carl stretched out on the ground-sheet alongside the car. He rose to his feet as we approached, and his expression told me he had been anxious about us.

Anna went straight up to him and kissed his cheek. She spoke to him in German. 'I am sorry we have been away so long, but it was very beautiful beside the lake. When did you wake up?'

'About half an hour ago,' he told her.

'And you feel better now? Your headache has gone?'

In her attention she was like the mother of a sickly child who for two guilty hours had found clandestine pleasure in the activities of a healthy one. Now, ashamed of her disloyalty, she was making an even greater fuss of her invalid. She barely spoke to me, as though bitterly resenting what had happened alongside the lake.

As Carl had already packed away the tent and mattress we were able to leave almost immediately. Carl may have noticed Anna's silence, for he made an extra effort to make conversation with me, but after half an hour fatigue overcame him again and the last part of the journey to Jönköping, over an undulating road flanked with dense woods, was covered mostly in silence.

On the outskirts of the town I slowed down and turned to them. 'I take it you do both want to stay here tonight? With an early start tomorrow we can be in Stockholm just after lunch.'

They both agreed, and I found a small hotel on the hill up to the Folksparken. I chose a small one because by this time I was certain they were travelling on a limited budget. It was now seven o'clock, and as we stood at the desk signing the register guests were already entering the dining room. Carl, who looked extremely tired and drawn by this time, was eyeing them apprehensively and Anna drew him aside. After arguing half-heartedly with her for a minute or two he capitulated and came over to me.

'As we shall be making an early start tomorrow Anna thinks I should retire now and have dinner in my room.' His gaunt face grimaced wryly. 'You know what women are like, the fuss they make. Will you forgive me? Perhaps tomorrow I shall be better company.'

I assured him I understood. He then asked me what time I wished to leave in the morning. I shrugged.

'It's entirely up to you, but if you want to reach Stockholm in the afternoon we ought to leave no later than eight.'

He held out his hand. 'I shall be ready. And thank you for your help today.'

Anna took his arm. As they reached the lift she turned and made a gesture for me to wait for her in the lounge. She joined me at a table five minutes later, refusing the cigarette I offered her. She spoke without meeting my eyes.

'It was necessary for Carl to have dinner upstairs – when he is so tired he cannot bear to be among a crowd of people. I think it is better I dine with him tonight.'

I nodded, trying to force her eyes into meeting mine. 'Do as you wish. But what about the rest of the evening? Aren't I going to see you again?'

She had risen and I thought she was going to refuse. The look she turned on me was full of defiance. 'Do you want to see me?'

I stared at her. 'Why shouldn't I? What has come between us all of a sudden?'

I don't know whether I sounded hurt, resentful, or just puzzled, but at any rate her sullenness seemed to fall away. She stood biting her lip, then suddenly reached down and brushed my sleeve. It was an oddly nervous gesture for her, but it pulled down the strange barrier that had come between us.

'I will look for you after dinner,' she said in a low voice. 'Where will I find you?'

'I'll be in my room. I have two letters to write.'

By the time I'd had a shower and changed my clothes there were only four guests left in the dining room. The waiters, impatient to finish the meal, wasted no time in serving me and I was back upstairs in my room within twenty minutes. It was a warm evening and I opened my casement. With the streets below falling away down the hillside there was a fine view over Lake Vättern. Night clouds, massing over its eastern shore, were soaking up the twilight.

I looked down at the shadowy road below. Private houses made up most of its length, but there was a block of three shops at the nearest street corner. As my eyes grew accustomed to the twilight I saw there was a man standing in the darkened doorway of the first shop. At first I did not give him a second glance, but after I finished my first letter something brought me back to the window and I saw he was still there. Paying more attention to him this time I saw he was small in height and bare-headed. He was too distant for his features to be distinguishable but I thought he had smooth black hair. Impatient with myself, I was about to leave the window when he moved a few paces along the pavement. The movement stiffened me. He walked with a limp, dragging one leg as if it were deformed. For a moment my heart-beats quickened. Then I drew back, telling myself it was nothing but coincidence. Yet when I looked again three minutes later he was still there.

A tap on the door made me start. I pulled the curtains across the window before opening the door to Anna. She was wearing the black costume I liked so much. As she entered the room she caught sight of my open writing pad on the desk and paused. 'I'm sorry. Haven't you finished your letters yet?'

'I've done the one that matters. The other one can wait.'

'I want to see if I can get a more recent German newspaper,' she said. Her hand rose, fanning her face. 'This heat! I thought the storm last night would have cleared the air more.' She was moving forward to draw aside the curtains when I stepped in front of her.

'I'm ready,' I told her. 'We'll ask the receptionist downstairs to try to get us a paper while we have a drink.'

To my relief the curtains were drawn when we entered the lounge downstairs. It was typically Swedish in its decor, with modern light-oak furniture and decorative plants. A radio playing Grieg stood in one corner of the room. A party of six middle-aged people were clustered around a table near it. On a settee by the window a young man was lost to the world with a teen-age blonde. I took Anna over to an armchair, ordered two martinis for us, and then went outside to the desk.

The receptionist told me he had no newspapers but that some Germans were staying at the hotel and he would enquire if any of them could oblige me. Leaving him telephoning upstairs I returned to Anna. My mind was on the lame man, fretting whether I was doing the right thing in not telling her about him. Matter-of-fact reason assured me his presence outside was only coincidence and to talk of him would only give her unnecessary anxiety. But reason can be poor comfort when one's sense of danger is aroused, and mine was prickling like a needle at that moment. I decided to ask Anna more about their plans on reaching Stockholm.

I gave her a cigarette, sat in an armchair opposite her and picked up my glass. 'I've been going to ask you to tell me more about Kleinberg. What exactly has your agent discovered about him?'

She hesitated, and I wondered if a last doubt of me still lingered in her mind. If it did she dismissed it.

'He owns a small shop in Gamla Stan, the

old part of Stockholm. A girl called Inga Norgren manages it for him. He is not married and our agent thinks the girl is his mistress.'

'Has he changed his name?'

'No.'

'I wonder why not?' I asked slowly.

She gave a nervous shake of her head. 'Perhaps because Kleinberg is as common a name in Sweden as it is in Germany. Or perhaps just because he did not bother. Until we know more about him we cannot say.'

I put my next question as kindly as possible. 'If Kleinberg is a fairly common name in Sweden, what makes you and Carl certain your agent has found the right man?'

She nodded and rose. 'Wait here and I will show you.'

She came downstairs a few minutes later and passed a photograph across to me. It was a picture of a wiry, bare-headed man leaving a shop. It was not easy to make out his features, the snapshot had been taken from the side – probably from another shop doorway – and only the man's profile showed. In addition the print suffered from over-enlargement. I got an overall impression of a bony, rather foxy face, but little else.

I could feel her gaze on me. I looked up. 'And Carl can recognise him from this…'

My voice broke off. My sudden glance had caught her by surprise and the fear in her eyes that Carl might be wrong was naked. She nodded jerkily. 'Yes. As soon as he saw it he recognised Kleinberg. You know how these things are … sometimes the first impression is enough…'

The undertones in her voice were pathetic. *Don't destroy his hopes,* they pleaded. *And please, don't destroy mine either…*

I nodded and handed her back the photograph. I had to ask her one last cruel but necessary question.

'When you find him, what makes you believe you can persuade him to come forward and witness against Steiner this time?'

Her low voice was barely audible over the sound of the radio. 'There are a number of reasons. He was panic-stricken then – now he has had ten years to think about it. And he must fear Steiner's release himself, in case Steiner finds out where he is. Then there is Carl. Surely he cannot refuse to witness when he knows a man's life depends on it…'

I could not allow myself to strain the thin thread of hope to which she and Carl were clinging so desperately. I nodded and raised my glass. 'Here's to it. He'll certainly have to be tough to resist you.'

She was thanking me with her eyes when the receptionist came across the lounge towards us. He handed me a newspaper. 'It is the latest one I can get, *min herre:* one of our guests bought it in Malmö yesterday.'

I thanked him and glanced at the date. It was two days old. I handed it to Anna who rose immediately. 'If you will excuse me I'll take it upstairs to Carl. He won't sleep until he gets it.'

I sipped at my martini and waited for her to return. On the settee opposite the youth appeared to have entangled his wrist watch in the blonde's hair and was struggling to free it to the accompaniment of her titters. As I sat there my thoughts went back to that afternoon by the lake and to Anna's odd behaviour afterwards. A sudden thought made me start violently. I fought against it but as I remembered back all the pieces suddenly seemed to fall into place. I glanced impatiently at my watch. She had been away over five minutes and I wanted urgently to question her. Ten minutes passed and I could wait no longer. I rose and went upstairs. As I reached our landing I saw her coming out of Carl's room. Her face was chalk-white.

'Anna,' I called, alarmed. 'What's the matter?'

She saw me and made in my direction. Halfway down the corridor she broke into a run. I caught hold of her, held her tightly. 'What is it? What has happened?'

She buried her face in my shoulder. I could feel her whole body trembling. 'It is the newspaper. There is a short paragaph… Steiner was released three days ago.'

CHAPTER 7

I drew her into my room and closed the door. She was fighting to hold back her tears and I left the room in darkness. After a few seconds she recovered and lifted her head. 'John. I must talk to you. Now that Steiner is out everything has changed.'

'Go on,' I said quietly.

'He is quite ruthless. If you help us he will consider you as much an enemy as ourselves. And that will put your life in terrible danger. You must get away from us at once.'

'And Stockholm?' I asked. 'What about that?'

Her voice had a flat, hopeless sound. 'We shall have to go there by train, as we had planned to do before.'

I could see nothing in the darkness but the white blur of her upturned face. 'Never mind about Steiner for the moment. I want to talk to you about Carl. He's your husband, isn't he, Anna? Why didn't you tell me that before?'

She started and then her whole body seemed to sag in my arms. There was a long silence, then she gave a sigh, a low distressed sound in the darkness. 'Lies, John –

they are criminals like Steiner. Once you have dealings with them they will never let you escape. I first lied to you about Carl because I thought you were an agent spying on us. Afterwards, when I began to trust you, it became difficult to explain away and I did not try.' The blur of her face turned squarely to me. 'I will be quite truthful with you now. When I saw you had a car I had the hope you might offer to help us. And so I may have used my sex a little... Perhaps I did that ... it is so difficult to be sure...'

I had not known this kind of honesty in a woman before, nor had I seen such devotion and loyalty as she gave to Carl. Yet there was her behaviour that afternoon, so oddly incompatible... As though reading my thoughts she went on quickly:

'There is something I want you to under-stand. When I made Carl marry me in 1946 I knew we could never be physical lovers – the injuries he had received defending me had been too crippling. But I knew he moved me and I felt it might be the one thing that could save him from himself. It was easy to make the gesture then – he was my hero and I was only eighteen and idealistic. I did not know how the body could burn for love, how it can torture you until you hardly know right from wrong. I married him gladly and was proud of my sacrifice.'

The struggle of her emotions was easier to

detect in the darkness. Through it I saw the bright moist challenge of her eyes.

'They say to be unfaithful means one has lost one's love… It is not true – one loves with the mind, not the body. The thing itself is nothing and yet it is so demanding. Oh, *du mein Gott,* why are we made like this…?'

I stood in silence, listening to the sound of a war that could never be won.

'It has only happened once before, and then I felt such disloyalty to Carl. But for five years all has been well and then you come along… This afternoon – I do not know what happened. I was grateful to you – very grateful for Carl's sake – but that was only part of it. There was that shining lake, the sunlight … even the shadow of Steiner … and there was you, strong-looking and healthy and wanting me as I knew you did. All those things were there and other things that I do not understand…'

She paused, then said quietly: 'For a while afterwards I almost hated you. That was wrong of me and I am sorry. For obviously I was to blame for everything that happened.'

Moral courage of this kind is a beautiful thing in itself. It made her more desirable to me than ever and tightened my arms around her. She lay in them for a moment, then gently drew back. 'I must go back to Carl now. This news has upset him very much.'

I put my hand on the door, checking her.

'Tell him not to worry about getting to Stockholm. We'll go on tomorrow as arranged.'

She stood very still.

'And when we get there I'd like to help you find Kleinberg. With Carl as ill as he is you'll need another man to take the weight off your shoulders.'

Her hushed voice was unsteady. 'Would you really go as far as that?'

'If you'll let me, yes. I'd like to help.'

'And you understand the dangers, the risks you will be taking?'

'I think so. You've made them pretty clear.' I stood aside from the door. 'Go and see how Carl feels about it.'

I could feel the conflict in her: the yearning for my help, the fear for my safety. My mention of Carl strengthened her resistance.

'Carl won't agree. He is ashamed enough that his past has brought me into danger. He will never agree to an innocent man becoming involved too.'

My voice roughened. 'He hasn't any choice. He can't give you any protection against Steiner – he's almost helpless. If you don't remind him of that, I shall.'

She flinched at my words. Her tone had a sudden frightened ring. 'John; why do you offer to do this for us? Tell me.'

I felt a sudden awkwardness. 'I don't know. Perhaps because I don't like bullies. Why?

Does the reason matter so much?'

Her intensity startled me. 'Matter? It is everything. Until now I have let you believe a lie – perhaps let you hope for something that could never be. Now, if we allow you to share this danger, I must be certain you know the truth...'

I remembered her honesty and understood. 'It's all right, Anna. I know how you feel towards Carl. And I know you'll never leave him whatever happens. In other words I'm not going into this thing with any illusions. Now go and tell him he must let me help. I'll come and see him in ten minutes.'

At the door she paused. She reached out, touched my cheek, and a little sob broke from her. Then she turned and ran down the corridor to Carl's room.

Instead of putting on my bedroom light I went over to the window and drew the curtains aside. A street lamp threw a shadow over the shop doorway but a darker shadow inside it told me the man was still there. My heartbeats quickened again: it began to look as if they had found us and the hunt was on. I watched for over ten minutes, but the man made no movement from the doorway. I drew the curtain closed again and went to see Carl.

His ailing face had not yet recovered from the shock of the news and the nervous tic

96

was tugging at his eyes like an invisible wire. But he fought me as Anna had said he would, stressing the dangers, protesting it was madness for me to risk my life for him, an ex-criminal. I could tell both from his words and from Anna's distressed expression that she had not used the weapon I had given her, and I listened mostly in silence, waiting for his protests to exhaust him.

'You must not get involved in this thing,' he panted. 'You do not know Steiner – he is a devil. What is happening to me is a result of my past and probably I deserve it. But I don't want anyone else involved.' His tormented eyes were on Anna. 'Already I have dragged one innocent person down with me... I cannot drag another.'

It was my opportunity and I didn't let it slip. 'Exactly. Anna is in the same danger as yourself. That's why you must accept my help. From all I hear Steiner himself is a match for two men, and there may be Hacht and others too. You haven't a chance against a crowd like that, particularly in your present state.'

Once again my reference to his health brought a reaction, this time a violent one. 'You don't have to keep reminding me what a wreck I am,' he gritted. 'I know how my body breaks down and cringes every time there's a crisis... God knows, I hate it enough.'

There was no time to mince words – I was thinking of the lame man outside. 'Hate it or not, you've got it. And it puts too much of a load on Anna – she must have extra help. I'm offering you that help and for her sake you can't refuse it.'

It almost defeated him, as I knew it must. But he made one final protest. 'You may become involved unnecessarily... The fact Steiner is out of prison doesn't mean he knows where we are. The danger may only start when we return to Germany with Kleinberg, and we couldn't expect you to come all that way with us.'

Sooner or later they had to be told and this seemed the best time to do it. 'If my guess is right you're going to need help from this moment onwards. A man has been watching this hotel from a shop doorway for at least two hours. A small man with a limp...'

Before my eyes Anna's face went ashen. *'Oh, Gott, nein!* With a limp... It could be Hacht.' She ran to the window. I shook my head.

'Your rooms face the side street. He's at the front.'

I called after her as she ran outside. 'Don't turn the light on. Be careful.'

Carl was trembling with shock at the news as I turned back to him. 'You can see now that you must have help,' I said quietly. 'So don't let's argue about it any more.'

He dropped his face into his hands. Mixed up with my respect for him there was now a fair share of guilt. I went over and dropped an awkward hand on his shoulders. 'Stop worrying,' I muttered. 'I know the risks: I'm going into this with my eyes open.'

He lifted his pain-wracked face at that and took my hand. 'All right, John. I'd be a liar if I said we didn't need your help.'

So, in that deceptively quiet room, the decision was made for me. That it held danger I knew. But the agony, the bone-sapping terror, the despair … those things were hidden in the mists of the future and perhaps it was as well…

Anna, tight-lipped and pale, returned. She nodded at my enquiry. 'I could see his shadow although he did not move… But if he has a limp it must be Hacht.'

'We must get away early tomorrow,' I said. 'Before dawn if possible. There's just a chance we might surprise them that way.'

They both nodded. Carl's anxious eyes were on Anna. 'You must stay in my room tonight, *Liebchen*. It is no longer safe for you to be alone.'

I backed his suggestion. 'And as it is next to yours and has a communicating door I think it would be a good idea if I took over Anna's room.'

Both of them agreed and I went to the door. 'If you'll take out what you need tonight I'll move into it,' I told Anna. 'In the meantime I'll go and settle up for our rooms so we can make a quick get-away in the morning.'

When I went downstairs the lounge had emptied of guests and the hall was deserted except for an old porter at the desk. His English was poor and I had to speak to him in German. After muttering it was not his job to write out accounts or to take money he finally produced a bill for the three of us. I paid him, asked him to give me an early call, and then went out into the street.

My heart was thumping hard as I made for the three shops on the corner. A motorcycle passed me, followed by a car. They left a heavy silence behind them. I was perhaps thirty yards from the first shop when the small figure of a man left its doorway. His limp was noticeable, making me think of a crippled spider disturbed from its vigil. He was visible for only a few seconds before vanishing round the street corner – too short a time for me to be absolutely certain he was hurrying away from me. When I reached the corner the narrow side street was empty.

Deciding that if the man was Hacht it was better to leave him in doubt whether he was observed, I walked straight past the street and round a block of flats before returning to the hotel on the opposite side of the road.

When I passed the side street it was still empty, as was the shop doorway.

I collected my pyjamas and went to Anna's room, where she was waiting for me. I told her I would give her a call the next morning as soon as the porter awakened me. 'Don't forget to lock your door securely,' I warned her. 'From now on we mustn't take any chances.'

I don't know what my expression was as I watched her preparing to go through the communicating door into Carl's room, but she suddenly took two quick steps forward and kissed my cheek.

'Don't lie awake tonight thinking, John,' she whispered. 'Close your eyes and sleep.' A moment later the door closed softly and she was gone.

I locked the outer door, undressed and switched off the light. Before getting into bed I opened the curtains. Enough light came in from the side street to illuminate the room faintly. As I lay there her faint, elusive perfume came to me. It was so real it made me start and look around, believing she had returned.

I lay back, eyes staring at the ceiling. She had told me to sleep, but that perfume gave me no rest. It reminded me she was lying only a few feet away, her long white body alongside Carl. At this very moment his hand might be touching it for warmth and comfort, and she would press nearer to him, giving him every pleasure it was in her power to bestow. It was no consolation for me to remember his impotency – I had my first feeling of jealousy for him, and I understood the misgivings that had been in Anna's mind as she left me.

It was well past midnight when I fell asleep. What awakened me I do not know – perhaps the moonlight that was now shining through the open curtains. I looked at my watch, saw it was two-fifteen, and was just turning over when I heard a faint sound in the corridor outside.

It brought me upright with a start. As I listened I thought I heard soft footsteps. Uneven footsteps, one foot dragging a little behind the other...

They came softly nearer, to my door. For a moment my body was paralysed. Then I threw back the bedclothes. They must have caught the hanging light switch, for it swung against the wall with a sharp click. Only once – I caught it before it could swing back again – but the movement outside the door ceased at once.

I badly wanted a weapon but could find nothing suitable. By the time I unlocked the door and pulled it sharply open the corridor was empty. I ran down the dimly-lit staircase and a cold draught on the lower landing led me to an open window. It faced the car park at the rear of the hotel, but all was dark and still when I peered out.

I went back upstairs and made certain Carl's door was locked before returning to my room. There I lay sleepless, watching the shift of the moonbeams as I waited for dawn.

CHAPTER 8

I rose just after 4.20 and slipped down the corridor to my room. I didn't turn on the light, dragging on my oldest pair of slacks in the bleak grey light that was soaking through the window. I had a quick shave, packed my suitcase, and slipped a small torch into my trousers pocket. Then I returned to Anna's room and tapped quietly on the communicating door.

She must have been awake because she answered me immediately. 'You can dress in here if you want to,' I told her. 'I'm going down to the car for a few minutes. Whatever you do, don't put the lights on. Don't forget to warn Carl.'

I took a look at the outside of Carl's door, saw nothing suspicious there and then went downstairs into the hall. A small light over the desk gave an illuminated picture of the old porter, head on arms, fast asleep. I had to shake his shoulder twice before he awoke.

His grizzled head rose heavily. One eye, its lashes crusted together, had difficulty in opening as he peered at me.

'I want go to outside into the yard,' I told him in German. 'Will you please unlock the side door?'

He grumbled something unintelligible and pointed to the front door which could be unlatched from the inside. I shook my head and repeated my question. After giving me another stare and another grunt, he went to a drawer, produced a key and shuffled down the hall to the door.

It was still shadowy in the yard and a mizzling mist made it chilly. I went over to the Countryman and paused alongside it. I wasn't looking forward to the task ahead of me and my heart was beating heavily. It took a real effort of will to pull the small torch from my pocket and set to work.

I couldn't see anything wrong with the door, so I unlocked it and pulled it gingerly open. I shone the torch around inside, fumbled about under the seats, and then took a look at the controls. Then I took a screwdriver and removed the dashboard. Nothing suspicious there either.

I went round to the front and gingerly lifted the bonnet, shining my torch on the electric leads, checking for any suspicious wiring. Then I went to the wheels to see if the brake drums had been tampered with. Finally I lay down on the wet ground and dragged myself underneath, playing my torch upwards about the chassis.

I heard the hotel door open as I lay there. As I wriggled out I saw Anna approaching.

She was wearing a windcheater, slacks, and a scarf over her head.

'Hello,' I said. 'Are you ready to go?'

She motioned at my wet and oily clothes and then at the car. 'What are you doing?'

'Just making a few adjustments,' I lied. 'I noticed my brakes were pulling me over a bit to one side yesterday. I'm just going to run her up the street to make certain she's all right, and then we can go. I shan't be more than five minutes changing my clothes.'

I climbed into the car, expecting she would go back into the hotel as the drizzle was quite severe. Instead she stood staring at me.

'Go back inside,' I called. 'You're getting wet.'

She came alongside me. 'I know what you are doing,' she said quietly. 'And I do not like you having to take such risks. At least let me share them with you.'

I loved this girl's courage. I leaned out and took hold of her arm. 'Now look,' I said. 'If we want to beat Steiner we have to be rational about everything we do. And sharing risks isn't rational: it's downright stupid. You go inside like a good girl and I'll be back in a few minutes.'

She didn't say a word after that. She just nodded and went inside, her back as straight as a soldier's. That was another of the things

I learned to love about her: how, in a critical situation, she would never argue against an order if that intelligent mind of hers saw a good reason for it. It wasn't a particularly feminine attribute, but I found it a most attractive one.

I felt myself sweating slightly in spite of the morning chill when I slipped the ignition key into place. As I saw it, this was a test case. The car had been unguarded all night, and if Steiner simply wanted Carl killed, without waiting for him to give away Kleinberg's whereabouts, this was as good an opportunity as any for a booby trap. I'd checked on everything visible but knew that didn't mean very much. A skilled operator knew a thousand ways of planting explosives, and it was my guess that Steiner, Hacht or one of their men, would have a working knowledge of them. The real test would come when I got the car moving.

With my heart beating somewhere up in my throat, I switched on the key and pulled the starter. The engine coughed, grumbled, but did not fire. I gave it more choke and pulled the starter again. This time it caught. I let it warm for a moment while I got my nerves under control. Then I put her in reverse, let out the handbrake, and with a deep breath took my foot slowly off the clutch.

The moment she began to roll I felt all was well. But I ran her up and down the back street a couple of times before returning to the yard. Anna, white-faced and tensed, was waiting for me at the hotel door. She said nothing, just touched my arm as I went inside, and it was better than words. I couldn't see anything of Carl, and she told me he was ready and waiting in his room for us.

'As soon as I've changed I'll help you downstairs with your luggage,' I told her. 'In the meantime, will you keep an eye on the car? Don't go out and don't take any chances. If you see anyone enter the yard, close the door and run straight upstairs to me.'

Again she made no argument. In less than ten minutes I had washed, changed, and was ready to go. Carl, wearing a dark overcoat, was looking very wan. I guessed neither he nor Anna had succeeded in getting much sleep, although, as neither mentioned it, I took it they had heard nothing unusual during the night.

At my request Anna had kept a thermos flask out of her grip – I intended getting coffee for us on the way – and I put it with mine in the locker on the dashboard. We packed the rest of our luggage in the back and started off. I drove out through the rear entrance and kept off the Västra Storgatan as long as possible. We passed one or two open cafés but I dared not stop to fill the

108

flasks yet: there was just a chance we had got away undetected and I didn't want to do anything to prejudice that chance. It was broad daylight now, although the sky was overcast and the drizzle still coming down.

In less than fifteen minutes we were out in the country. We passed through Huskvarna and turned north. Below us on our left was Lake Vättern, around us lush, undulating farmland. I took a glance at Anna and saw the tension on her face. We were all feeling it – all very much aware that we had two hundred miles still to cover with some pretty lonely stretches on the way. For the first time since having her I wished the Countryman were an ordinary car. Her square lines would make her an easy object to follow in this undulating countryside.

Assuming he was already in Sweden and had detected us, I tried to guess what Steiner would do. Logic said he would bide his time and wait until we had led him to Kleinberg, when he could kill two birds with one stone, although there was always the possibility he might try to capture us before-hand and get Kleinberg's address by more violent means. We had to guard against both contingencies, and to do that I felt we had to know for certain we were being followed. After driving for the best part of an hour I turned and made this point to Carl and Anna.

'I feel we're too much in the dark as things are. Let's take the initiative for a moment. It's the only way we can plan our moves in Stockholm.'

Carl was fighting his apprehension. 'What do you want to do?'

We had just topped a hill. I pulled up and pointed back. Far away, on the thin ribbon road that ran alongside the lake, were the tiny shapes of three cars, well strung out from one another. The sky had broken now and the cars, slowed down by distance, were crawling like beetles among the cloud shadows towards us.

'They might all be harmless,' I said, pulling away again. 'Just holidaymakers making an early start – after all, it has gone 6 o'clock now. But equally, one of them might belong to Steiner. I think we ought to find out one way or the other.'

By this time we were hidden from the cars, running down the hill into a rocky, wooded valley. I found what I wanted, a timber track that ran off into the woods, and swung the Countryman down it. There were plenty of bushes here and I manoeuvred the car until we were hidden behind a clump of them but still able to make the main road in a hurry. Then I switched off the engine.

I tried to make my voice more reassuring than I felt. 'I think it's safe enough. After all, if they meant us immediate physical harm,

110

this would be the time to be chasing us, not trailing us miles back. If they spot us I can be away in a flash, which will make things no worse than at present.'

Carl, poor devil, was having a hard battle with his nerves. Anna, concerned for him, shared her attention between us. 'What exactly are you planning to do?'

'Watch the cars as they go by,' I said, opening the car door. 'You might see someone in them you recognise. Even if you don't and one of them comes back after reaching the next hill top,' – and I pointed further down the road – 'we can be pretty certain we're being shadowed.'

The cars could not be heard yet and I went out on the road to check on our cover. It was difficult to be certain we couldn't be spotted from the top of the hill, but I thought it unlikely. We were among trees as well as bushes, and the green Countryman blended well. Again, anyone trailing us would have their eyes on the road as they came over the hill.

It was pleasant out there. The stiff, early-morning breeze was rolling the clouds away and rushing zestfully through the pines. After the heat of the last few days it was fresh and exhilarating and difficult to believe danger might be close at hand.

Anna came around the bushes to meet me. She was pale but keeping herself under

111

tight control.

'We should be all right there,' I said. 'Look for a suitable place where we can hide and watch them pass.'

Efficient as ever she had not been wasting time. She led me to a gap in the bushes where Carl, lying on my ground sheet, was watching the road. His sharp breathing was audible and his body shivering as though with cold. We lay down alongside him and waited. Behind us a wood pigeon was cooing, a tranquil sound against the distant tumult of the wind. A movement across the road caught my eye. A hedgehog, like a little fat man in a brown overcoat, emerged from the grassy bank and started towards us. He had progressed no more than three feet when he turned ponderously around and vanished again in the grass.

It was then I heard the hum of the first car. Almost immediately it appeared on the hill top and started down towards us. I felt Carl stiffen and pressed his shoulder reassuringly.

CHAPTER 9

I pushed the leaves aside. The car was a Swedish Volvo. As it drew nearer I saw it had two occupants. The driver, a man, was wearing a panama-style, cream hat; the woman alongside him was fair and bare-headed. As they came level with us she said something to him and laughed... Then they were gone, climbing up the distant hill.

Carl sank back heavily on the groundsheet. Anna caught hold of his arm, her expression more hopeful... 'Perhaps we have been wrong,' she murmured, meeting my eye.

I said nothing, waiting. Half a minute later we heard the second car, a deeper, more powerful hum. It had a bigger silhouette on the skyline, and as it came down the hill my own muscles tensed. It was a black Opel Kapitän, a big German car, and I could see it contained five men.

It was travelling at speed, and as it thundered past stones from its tyres were flung into the bushes. A sudden convulsive start from Carl distracted my attention and I received only a blurred glimpse of its occupants. The driver, crouched low behind the wheel, appeared to be a small man: the passenger alongside him, wearing a hat and fawn mackintosh, to be broad and huge. I saw little more than the back of the other three men's heads as the car sped by.

I turned to Carl. His eyes were closed and his thin chest rising and falling painfully.

'Steiner?' I asked grimly, glancing at Anna. She found difficulty in speaking herself. 'Yes. In the front, alongside the driver.' With a sob she threw herself on Carl, her arms tightly around him.

I leaned forward to watch the car. It was climbing the hill, rocking with speed. As I watched, it reached the crest and plunged from sight, the deep hum dying with it.

Anna was pressed close to Carl as though she were trying to give some of her strength to him, and yet her fear was almost as great as his own. I waited for them to recover.

'Who was in the car?' I asked gently when Carl opened his eyes. 'Did you know them all?'

His ashen face stared at me dully. 'Hacht was driving, with Steiner alongside him. And there was Müller at the back. I did not recognise the other two men.'

Life returned to Anna first. She swung round to face me. 'It was a mistake to stop. Now they are between us and Stockholm.'

'We had to know the truth,' I said quietly. 'It was the only way.'

'But what happens now? What can we do?'

'Wait here. They'll have to return along this road. And when they've gone past we'll drive on again.'

'But if they see us? What then?'

'I don't think they can, coming from the other way. And in any case we'll be ready to drive away immediately.'

I persuaded them both to get into the car so we could make a quick get-away if the worst happened. I waited in the bushes – I wanted to be sure I could recognise all five men again. Slow minutes passed and then the Kapitän came back into sight, moving slowly as Hacht searched for the side road he believed we had taken. The car reminded me of a huge jungle cat that had lost its prey and was now casting about for scent.

It came level with the bushes and the breath was tight in my chest as I peered out. Hacht I recognised at once from Anna's description: small, rat-raced, dangerous. Steiner, to whom I gave most of my attention, was looking in the other direction as they passed, but I had a glimpse of a smooth, solid jaw and powerful features. With his massive shoulders almost monopolising the front seat he looked every bit as ruthlessly formidable as I had been led to believe. I had time for only a cursory glance at the three men behind him, but I saw one was middle-aged and burly with a low forehead and beetling eyebrows, the second a younger man with closely cropped fair hair, and the third a slim, dark-haired man in his thirties. He turned his eyes in my direction as the car passed by, and for an unpleasant moment I believed he had spotted me.

But the Kapitän continued up the hill and vanished over the crest. I gave it a minute and then jumped into the Countryman and drove off. I knew they would spot us – my guess was that they had returned to the hill top to scan the surrounding countryside – but as they wouldn't see our actual starting point I was hoping they would remain in doubt as to whether we had detected them. By this time I was sure they hadn't intended to make any attempt on Carl's life until he led them to Kleinberg, and I didn't want to provoke them into changing their plan. For this reason, while keeping a close watch in my mirror in case they gave chase, I drove no faster than before, even though Carl repeatedly urged me to do so.

As I hoped they were quite content to trail us from a distance. I kept catching glimpses of them, coming around the shoulder of a hill, skirting a lake, always far enough away to look innocent, but near enough to prevent our escaping for long. By this time they must have guessed we were heading for Stockholm

By ten o'clock I decided it was time we broke our fast. In spite of his obvious need for a stimulant Carl would have continued right through to Stockholm without stopping, but I thought that unnecessary. 'We've got five minutes on them,' I told Anna. 'At the next town I'm going to draw up outside a café. You run in and get the flasks filled with anything they have ready, hot milk if there's nothing else, while I stay with Carl. And buy some rolls. You can prepare them on the way – I've got butter and a tin of meat at the back of the car.'

I found the café I wanted in Nyköping. Anna ran into it while I remained with Carl. He was twisted round in his seat watching the road, and I could feel tension building up in him like a tightened spring. I alternated my gaze between Anna in the café and my rear view mirror.

I caught sight of the Kapitän just as Anna came out with the flasks and a bag of rolls. Hacht saw us and drew up some two hundred yards down the road. 'It's all right,' I told Carl as I helped Anna into the car. 'They don't intend to come any closer until we reach Stockholm.'

To Carl's immeasurable relief we drove off. I watched the mirror and a few seconds later the black car also pulled away. I motioned to Anna to take the map from the car locker. 'Before you prepare the rolls, take a look and see if there are any side roads we can take. It's about time we tried to shake them off.'

I was acutely conscious of the problem we would have in making safe contact with Kleinberg while Steiner was so close behind us. Anna found me a road branching off at Svarta that did not rejoin Highway 1 for nearly fifty kilometres. I decided to try it and increased my speed. Fortunately the road was well wooded here, hiding us from the Kapitän. I found the branch road, swung left down it, and for fifteen minutes gave the Countryman its head. On the next hill top I paused, and although we stared back for over a minute we could see nothing of the Kapitän. Carl, unstable because of his nerves, was almost jubilant. I was less excited: I couldn't see us throwing Steiner off as easily as this.

The road surface was poor compared with the one we had left, and it was well over an hour, during which time we ate the rolls, before we rejoined Highway 1 a few kilometres south of Södertälje. There was no sign of the Kapitän here; I drove fast, and as Stockholm drew nearer I began wondering myself if Steiner had fallen for our trick and was wasting his time searching the side roads.

It was just before we reached the bridge at Fittia that I learned differently. The road was busy here with traffic both entering and leaving the city. As we passed a side street my

118

mirror gave me a glimpse of a huge black car that swung out like a shark and fastened itself on to the line of cars behind me.

I guessed what had happened. Having missed us on the Highway, Steiner had wasted no time in a search. Instead he had taken the bold course, driving on straight and fast, and then waiting near the bridge which he guessed we would cross sooner or later. It brought home to me with emphasis the tenacity and quality of our pursuers.

For the moment I said nothing to Carl and Anna and drover deeper into the city. We crossed the west bridge on to the island of Södermalm and I drove down Hornsgatan, a busy main road lined with shops. I saw what I wanted, a police station, and stopped opposite it. A hundred yards behind me the Kapitän drew unobtrusively into the kerb. I turned to Carl and Anna.

'We'll have to decide now what we intend doing for accommodation. Personally I'm in favour of another hotel.'

Anna said nothing, waiting for my explanation, but Carl protested immediately. 'No; that will make us too easy to trace. Our best chance is to get rooms in some quiet back street.'

'I'd agree with you but for one thing,' I said. 'How do we get into that back street without them following us?'

They both stared at me. 'Don't look

119

round,' I said quietly. 'They're a hundred yards behind us: they came out of a side street a mile or two back. At the moment I don't think we have a chance of throwing them off, so the best thing is to get into a decent-sized hotel where we are reasonably safe, and where we can have a good meal and rest. It'll give us a breathing space to work something out.'

I think that had Carl been less tired he might have argued. As it was he looked to Anna for advice.

'I think John is right,' she said. 'It will be very hard to escape from them now: we are all too tired. Later on, when we look for Kleinberg, it will be different.'

I waited to hear no more and drove off. I gave Hacht plenty of work before I found what I wanted, a large hotel on Ringvägen with its own underground garage. It was an expensive-looking place and the way Anna bit her lip as I turned towards it reminded me of their dwindling resources. However, neither of them made any comment and I drove straight down into the garage.

After our essential luggage was removed and the car locked I had a word with the attendant, who spoke reasonable English. I told him I was a salesman with valuable samples in my car, and it was most important no stranger approached it. My seriousness, plus the ten-*kronor* note I held out, seemed to impress him and he gave me a solemn assurance the car would receive his full attention.

A lift at the rear of the garage saved us having to go outside the hotel again. The receptionist at the desk told us we could have two adjacent rooms on the third floor. We viewed them first: they were without fire escapes or any other alternative form of entry, and we took them for one night. Wishing to save Carl the expense, and also feeling it better to be prepared for a quick getaway, I went downstairs and paid the account in advance. Then, after ordering coffee and *smörgås* to be sent upstairs, I turned for the lift.

The hall was spacious, with luxurious grey armchairs on either side. A man was occupying one of them, hidden behind his newspaper. As I approached the lift he rose and stood before me. I caught a glimpse of a fawn mackintosh and I froze.

His voice was casual and his English excellent. 'Good afternoon, Mr Drayton. I would like your attention for a moment.'

CHAPTER 10

His smile gave an illusory impression of joviality. 'My friends are certain you have not yet noticed us, Mr Drayton. But I, after analysing your movements carefully, think otherwise. So I have come to you to put my cards on the table.'

I am not a small man, but he completely dwarfed me, both in height and the width of his massive shoulders. His bald head and hairless face gave him a powerful, even brutal appearance, and yet his smile and manner were almost avuncular. It was not until I met his eyes that I fully understood what Anna had meant when she called him without soul. Ice-cold, pale-blue, they stared at me with the impersonal interest of a collector about to pin another living insect to his board.

'What do you want?' I asked tightly.

He pulled a gold cheroot case out from his inside pocket and held it out to me. I noticed his hands, square, covered in thick blond hair, immensely powerful. He lifted an eyebrow at my curt refusal, selected a cheroot himself and lit it with some care. There was no suggestion of nerves in this operation:

every movement was as controlled and calculated as his words.

'Mr Drayton; there is an English proverb – from John Rays's collection, I believe – that goes as follows: "Scald not your lips in another man's pottage…" To me this has always seemed excellent advice and I am offering it to you now with my compliments.'

There were a hundred things I wanted to tell this man, but at the moment I could find tongue for none of them. He blew out the match, dropped it carefully into an ashtray, and then turned back to me with an amused voice.

'You know, Mr Drayton, I never fail to be astonished at the way men like yourself allow attractive women to make fools of them. It is a reversal of a natural law and offends my sense of propriety. Three days ago you were a carefree man on holiday. Now, because of a pair of pleading eyes and a good figure, you are here, trying to protect a married woman and her treacherous husband from me, and getting yourself rather frightened in the process. Why don't you go on with your holiday? You will find it much safer and much more enjoyable.'

There was no point in wasting words in abuse. I went straight to the point. 'What if we go to the police, Steiner? Have you thought of that?'

He lifted an amused hairless eyebrow.

'The police! Here in Sweden? You think they will give protection to a broken-down stool-pigeon from another country who is so obviously afraid of his own shadow? And for something that happened nearly ten years ago? No, Mr Drayton; I'm afraid not. Mind you they will appreciate your giving them Frandl's case history. Swedish police always like to know which of their tourists have criminal records.'

'They'll be interested in yours, then, won't they?' I countered, knowing he was right. 'All five of you.'

He nodded readily. 'Oh, yes; even more so. Only they would probably have more difficulty in tracing us than in tracing Frandl. Our passports, you see, are all under pseudonyms.'

Every point anticipated and covered... His confidence was frightening. I gritted my teeth and took a step nearer to him. 'Listen to me, Steiner. If anything happens to either Carl or his wife, I won't rest until you get what you deserve. I'll go to the German police and tell them everything; I'll work day and night to get you. I mean it, Steiner.'

He released a balloon of blue smoke and watched it float upwards in the still air of the hall. He did not lift his voice as much as a semi-tone, yet the menace of it was like an icy hand at my throat. 'Mr Drayton; Carl and Anna Frandl are like two people with a deadly and infectious disease – nothing on earth can save them. If you continue trying, if you mix with them for one more day, you will have the disease too. And then it won't be long before you are incapable of telling anybody anything. Think it over, Mr Drayton, because I shall not warn you again. Good afternoon.'

With that he turned and walked down the hall. Cheroot in hand he looked like an industrial tycoon: massive, self-confident, radiating power. For a moment his great bulk darkened the entrance and then he was gone.

I had a cigarette before going upstairs. Anna was unpacking and Carl was at the window. I knew from his expression that he had not seen Steiner enter or leave.

'I've ordered coffee and *smörgås* to be sent up,' I told him. 'Sorry I couldn't order a hot meal but mid-afternoon is an awkward time.'

Anna's eyes were searching my face curiously. I turned for the door. 'I'll go and unpack while the food's on its way. Give me a shout when it comes. I'm as hungry as a wolf.'

There was a false ring in my tone and I wasn't surprised when Anna entered my room a few minutes later. She came straight up to me.

'What's the matter, John? What has happened?'

I hated telling her but it seemed right that I should. I took her hand and did my best to sound casual about it.

'I've just met our friend, Steiner. We had a chat in the hall.'

The blood left her face as if her heart had faltered in its beat.

'Don't be frightened,' I said. 'We're all safe enough up here. Anyway, he left as soon as we had finished talking.'

Her fear showed itself in her instinctive movement towards me. For a moment we were very close again and I knew why. The woman in her was in command, the primitive woman that feared the rapacious, despoiling Steiner, and it drove her against her loyalty to find protection where she could.

Yet her unsteady voice was in conflict with her fear. 'You mustn't go on, John. It's not your fight...You must go away before something terrible happens to you.'

Her cheek was pressed tightly to mine as she spoke and I couldn't help thinking of Steiner's words. Was he right? Was I only doing it because she was attractive? I hoped not – I wanted to believe that somewhere in me there was sympathy for the weak and the sick. Yet it was the nearness of her, her physical body, that drove back my fear of Steiner at that moment.

'Don't talk like a fool,' I muttered. 'We're in this thing together and we'll stay together until the job is finished.'

'But it is not fair to you… You have nothing to win and everything to lose…'

I made it sound very altruistic and could only hope to God it was true. 'There's supposed to be a certain satisfaction in just helping people. Let's leave it like that, shall we?'

For a moment her lips were fierce on mine. Then she pulled away with an exclamation and went over to the widow. She stood staring out a moment, then turned back to me.

'What are we going to do? How can we possibly get to Kleinberg without Steiner following us?'

'It's not going to be easy,' I admitted. 'But I think we have a chance. Much depends on Carl, for he must go with us to identify Kleinberg. Do you think he is well enough to do a good deal of walking and possibly some running too?'

She shrugged her shoulders, a brittle, helpless gesture. 'He seems very tired – I have told him to lie down until the sandwiches arrive. But if the moment were desperate enough he might find the strength – I cannot say. What have you in mind?'

I took a map of Stockholm from my suitcase and spread it out before her. 'The thing I'd like to do most is to take a preliminary look at Kleinberg's shop to see how the land lies. But obviously we can't afford to make any unnecessary visits. Equally, however, we don't want to arrive and find him out. So I propose phoning him to make an appointment.'

She looked doubtful. 'Isn't that risky? We don't know how he will react when he knows our reason for coming. Surely it would be better to tell him in person.'

I shook my head. 'I don't intend giving anything away over the phone. I shall make out we want to see him on business – something to his advantage. And I'll try to make the appointment for this evening.'

She was listening intently now. 'Yes; I understand. But how shall we be able to keep the appointment without being followed?'

'I think we might just manage it if Carl is fit enough to keep up with us. This is my idea. I want us all to leave in the car but you and Carl to crouch down as though hiding. They'll spot you, of course, but that's all right – I want them to. I shall drive off in the opposite direction to Gamla Stan and try to build up a short lead on them. As soon as we find a convenient side alley I shall pull up for a second, and you and Carl will bolt into it. I shall drive on and if we're lucky they'll think you're still with me. You'll keep out of sight in the alley until they've gone by and then you'll take a taxi here,' and I put a pencilled ring around a point north of the island of Gamla Stan. 'I remember from my last visit there's a café here called the Drotten – it's on the corner of Barnhusgatan and Drottninggatan. Go into the rear room and wait there until I arrive. Then, if we feel certain we've shaken them off, we'll go on to Kleinberg. If we're not certain we'll come back here and think up something else.'

'But you cannot come in your car to this café or they will follow you,' she said quickly.

'I shan't come in it. I shall abandon it somewhere and pick it up later.' I paused, eyeing her anxiously. 'What do you think? Will you be all right? For God's sake don't agree if you think it might be too much for Carl.'

She hesitated. 'It shouldn't be. But in any case you will be taking the greater risks. There are five of them, you will be on foot, and if they should catch you...'

I folded up the map and handed it to her. 'I don't think that's likely. On my own I shall be able to move pretty quickly and I shall keep as near as possible to busy streets. Just the same we'd better be prepared for the worst. If I don't arrive and don't phone – say within an hour of your arrival – then you'll have to decide yourselves on your next move. If you decide to go on to Kleinberg, for God's sake be certain first that none of them have traced you.'

I didn't need to tell her why. The cold war with Steiner would end the moment he discovered Kleinberg's whereabouts and all hell would break loose. Knowing this I think all of us found it a real effort of will to begin the business of making contact with Kleinberg.

Anna broke the apprehensive silence that had fallen between us. 'You will take the pistol,' she said. 'I will fetch it for you.'

I had expected this and shook my head. 'No. I want you and Carl to keep it. Please,' I went on firmly as she began to protest. 'I wouldn't feel happy otherwise. Go and ask Carl to come in, will you. If he agrees to all this I'll telephone the shop right away.'

Apprehensive though Carl was on hearing my plan, he made no serious protest and gave me Kleinberg's address and telephone number. The address was 12 Tullgrand, Gamla Stan. I dialled the exchange and put the number through while Carl and Anna stood anxiously at my elbow.

There was a click, a high-pitched buzz, and then a woman's voice. *'Ja. Vad är det ni vill?'*

Feeling that if Kleinberg was our man and the woman on the phone his mistress she ought to have picked up German from him, I would have liked to have tried her in German first. But thinking Kleinberg might still be sensitive to echoes I tried it a different way.

'Good afternoon,' I said in English. 'I would like to speak to Mr Kleinberg, please.'

There was a pause, and then: '*Sprechen Sie deutsch?*'

This was what I had hoped for. '*Ja,*' I said. '*Ich spreche deutsch.* I want to speak to Mr Kleinberg.'

'Mr Kleinberg is out. What do you want?'

'I'm a business man and have a proposition I think might interest him. Do you think you could make an appointment for me this evening? I'm only in Stockholm for two days.'

Her voice was curious and, I thought, a little suspicious. 'What's your name?'

'Drayton,' I said, on safe ground here. 'John Drayton.'

She was obviously puzzled. I went on smoothly: 'I think you can be certain Mr Kleinberg will want to see me – I've a good offer to make to him. What time do you expect him back?'

Her voice had the sullenness of indecision. 'He's usually home by 6.30. I suppose you could call round then.'

I was thinking fast. 6.30 – that meant we would be travelling during the tea-time rush hour. A good time for us...

'Yes,' I said. 'That will be quite convenient. By the way, I take it Mr Kleinberg speaks either German or English?'

'German,' she muttered.

I gave a silent wink of relief at the tensed Carl and Anna. 'Good. Then I'll see him at 6.30 this evening. Please give him my compliments.' With that I put the receiver down and turned to the others. 'He speaks German and we've got an appointment with him. So far so good.'

Carl was looking drawn and anxious. 'How did she sound? Was she suspicious in any way?'

I shrugged. 'Not exceptionally. She was curious as to who I was but that was all.'

He looked relieved. 'What time do you think we should start?'

I gave it careful thought. Ten minutes of driving before Carl and Anna jumped out ... another fifteen minutes before I abandoned the car. Then I had to take a taxi to the Drotten and from there we had to go to Gamla Stan... Say a round total of ninety minutes. Probably an exaggerated estimate but it was better to play safe. I looked at my watch and then at Carl. 'I think we should leave at five o'clock prompt. That gives us a free hour, and if I were you both I should spend it resting.'

CHAPTER 11

Anna stayed with Carl until we were due to leave. At ten minutes to five she tapped lightly on my door. 'We are ready when you are.' She was wearing her black sweater and slacks and looked pale but resolute.

I drew her into my room for a moment. 'Carl,' I asked. 'Is he all right?' When she hesitated I went on urgently: 'If he isn't, for God's sake tell me now before it's too late. I don't want to drop the two of you right into their hands.'

She made a great effort to shake off her fears. 'I think he will stand up to it, if only because he wants to meet Kleinberg so desperately. And after all we haven't much to do. Yours is the dangerous task.' Unexpectedly she reached forward and kissed me full on the lips. 'Be careful, John. Be terribly careful for all our sakes.'

A few minutes later the three of us went downstairs. I could see no one suspicious in the hall as I handed in our room keys, and we took the lift down to the garage. The attendant assured me no one had approached the Countryman since we arrived and we climbed in. I drove out on to the tarmac apron in front of the hotel and here, at a sign from me, Carl and Ann a ducked as low in the seat as they could.

With observers as keen as those shadowing us I had little fear they would go unnoticed as I turned and drove east along Ringvägen. I watched my rear mirror and sure enough, a few seconds later, the black shape of the Kapitän nosed out of a side street and slid into the traffic stream behind us.

Although traffic was quite heavy, Ringvägen's tree-lined thoroughfare was broad enough to carry it comfortably, making it difficult for me to gain any distance on the Kapitän. I was further handicapped by being on Södermalm, the largest of Stockholm's central islands. To drive too far east would mean crossing the Danviksbron, the only eastern bridge, which would make a dangerous bottleneck on our attempted return to Gamla Stan. I followed a tram that branched off to the left, overtook it, and made thirty yards on the Kapitän before I had to stop at a pedestrian crossing. I swung right and then left again, came out in a quieter street and put my foot down. I caught sight of a narrow lane on my left and was braking when in my mirror I saw the Kapitän skid into sight at the other end of the street.

I remembered now what Anna had told

me about Hacht's driving, and realised the task I had set myself. Sweating freely I zig-zagged in and out of the side streets, trying desperately to gain the thirty unobserved seconds that we needed. From the corner of my eye I saw the upturned white faces of Carl and Anna waiting for my signal.

Stockholm's famous one-way streets made things even more difficult. I half-turned into one. It was empty, the red traffic signals at its far end explaining the reason. I noticed the red disc with the horizontal yellow band in time and was about to turn away when the idea struck me. Gritting my teeth I swung into the street and put my foot down. Forty yards behind me the Kapitän turned and followed. A pedestrian stared and waved at me. I kept going, watching the traffic lights. They changed to green and a wall of cars, like a charge of cavalry, came straight at me. I waited until the last moment and then swung left into a side street. A piercing squeal of brakes told me the Kapitän had been caught.

I drove like a madman, right, left, and then right again. Here I found what I wanted, a narrow side alley flanked by tall houses. I braked sharply, leaned over and threw open the opposite door.

'Keep out of sight until they've gone by and then get a taxi for the Drotten,' I panted. 'Hurry, for God's sake.'

I should have driven on the moment they were out of the car but I couldn't. Halfway across the street Carl stumbled and my heart leapt in agony. Somehow, with Anna's help, he recovered and made his trembling legs carry him into the alley.

I accelerated away down the street. Near the end of it I heard the high-pitched squealing of brakes and caught sight of the Kapitän skidding round a corner behind me. They had come out higher up the street, and I knew with relief they couldn't possibly have seen Carl or Anna.

For a few minutes I made no attempt to pull away, content to keep just far enough ahead to prevent them noticing Carl and Anna had gone and to draw them well clear of the alley. At the moment I was somewhere in the north-east corner of the island; I wanted to get right to the other end before abandoning the car. I turned left, found myself in Ringvägen again and drove west along it. Our hotel appeared, then flats, and finally a park. The road suddenly narrowed and I guessed I was nearing the water-front. There were plenty of side streets here and I turned among them, trying now to shake off the Kapitän. I was improving at this hide-and-seek game now, learning to use traffic lights and pedestrian crossings to my advantage. I made a few seconds for myself and came into a cobbled street lined with apartments and warehouses. I caught sight of the entrance to a warehouse yard on my right and on a sudden impulse swung over and drove into it. There I braked, and with beating heart turned and watched through my rear window.

I heard the Kapitän's gears changing as she swung into the street. A moment later she passed the entrance. I turned with relief, only to see two men in overalls waving me angrily to clear the way. Gesturing that my only intention was to reverse the car I backed as slowly as possible into the street again.

To my relief the Kapitän was out of sight. Deciding to leave well alone I parked the Countryman alongside the kerb and started down the street. I had gone a hundred yards when the Kapitän appeared again, nosing back like a bloodhound. I leaped into a shop doorway but the change of its engine note told me I had been observed. I ran down the street, watching them over my shoulder and wondering what Steiner was thinking now he saw Carl and Anna had gone. I could see him, half-turned in his seat, giving terse instructions to his men. The car drove towards me and braked twenty yards away. A rear door was flung open and two men leapt out. Then the door slammed, the Kapitän swung round in the street, and accelerated away.

I watched it go with mixed feelings, relieved

I wasn't to have the attention of all five of them, apprehensive as to what Steiner's departure meant. Reason told me he couldn't hope to pick up Carl and Anna now but a vague uneasiness started nagging me.

But my own problem soon occupied my full attention. The two men Steiner had dropped were coming after me fast. One was the beetle-browed Müller, the other the fair, close-cropped younger man. I saw it was not going to be easy to escape them. By this time most workpeople had gone home and the pavements were almost deserted. In addition the surrounding streets were narrow and lined with wooden apartment houses that offered practically no cover.

I turned down Torkel Street. The waterfront lay directly ahead and below – I caught a glimpse of it between two houses. I came to a long flight of wooden steps and ran down them. In the silence my footsteps sounded alarmingly loud and hollow. There was a wooden house on my left, on the right the steep bank was covered in tangled grass and weeds. As I reached the roadway below I heard the double clatter of footsteps as the two men came down after me.

Fighting back a desire to run I crossed over to a handrail at the other side of the road and looked down. The waterfront lay below, utterly deserted. A flight of stone steps led down to it and on an impulse I ran down them.

It was a mistake. I had hoped there might be a road tunnel allowing me to double back into the city streets, but apart from an occasional flight of steps the side of the embankment was unbroken.

I turned my attention to the waterfront. The road that ran along it was deserted, but the edge of the waterfront was lined by huge piles of sand and pebbles. Among them were a few cranes and huts. Realising that I would be seen the moment the two men reached the handrail above, I ran for the nearest pile of sand. I had almost reached it when a shout told me I was spotted.

The pyramids of sand were close enough together to screen me, and I ran behind them towards Slussen, the bridge I wanted to cross to meet Carl and Anna. I ran fifty yards and then stopped. The piles of sand ended abruptly, leaving no cover all the way to the bridge.

I paused, wondering what I could do. A glance at my watch showed me time was running out fast and a sudden frustrated anger took hold of me. I took a quick glance round a crane and saw the two men had split forces in their search for me, the younger man moving in the opposite direction and Müller making his cautious way towards me. Discovery was only a minute or two away.

I noticed a watchman's hut a few yards

back, and, waiting my chance, slipped back into it. Apart from a cold brazier and a table and chair it was empty, and I backed inside. Badly needing a weapon I found a two-foot metal bar alongside the brazier. It was thin and light, but would have to suffice. Gripping it tightly I waited for Müller.

The wind, blustery all day, was blowing from the water directly into the hut, making hearing difficult. I edged a few inches forward. The planks were weatherworn and shrunken near the entrance and through a gap in them I saw Müller, beetle-browed, heavy of shoulder, making his cautious advance. He was now about twenty yards away and gripping a cosh in one hand.

The seconds passed slowly. Opposite me, on Kungsholmen, I could see the tiny figures of people walking beneath the great red pile of the Town Hall. The distant sound of the traffic and the rush and slap of the water against the quay made the situation seem unreal.

I watched Müller through the crack. He was as careful as a grizzly bear as he came around a crane, stepping forward and then quickly back again in case I leapt out from a blind spot at him. He took another look to make certain I had not broken cover at the other side of the sand and then started towards the hut again.

I waited until he was six feet away and

140

then went out to him, thrusting my foot against the hut to give me greater impetus. I caught him by surprise but even so he managed to get his arm up to block the iron bar I swung at his head. The blow made him grunt with pain and drop the cosh. I swung again but this time he ducked and kicked viciously, catching me just below the knee. Pain blinded me but I managed to grab him as I dropped. He was as strong as a bear and for a moment I could do nothing but hang on. Then pain turned to anger and anger to strength. I got on top of him and tried to hammer his head against the hard ground. He countered by jabbing blunt, vicious fingers at my eyes. I saw the cosh from the corner of my eyes and grabbed it, but the effort lost me my grip of him and he threw me off. He was on his feet in a second, trying to kick me. I hooked a foot around his ankle and kicked hard with my other leg. He went over backwards like a log thrown in the Highland games. He was half-stunned as he rose to his knees but it was no time for niceties. He turned into my first blow and caught the cosh right across the face. The second landed on the back of his head and he sank with a grunt and lay still.

Gasping for breath I took a quick look down the quay. There was no sign of Müller's companion and I guessed the interposed cranes had hidden our fight from him. I slipped around the other side of a pile of sand and took another look. After a few seconds he appeared, glanced down the road and then vanished behind another heap of sand. I gave him a couple of seconds and then ran for the nearest steps.

I sheltered behind them while he took his next precautionary look down the road, and then ran up to the road above. Two minutes later I was walking swiftly down the narrow streets towards the nearest thoroughfare.

With the pressure off me at last I was able to pause and glance at my reflection in a shop widow. I looked a mess, hair dishevelled, face dripping with sweat and clothes covered in dust and sand. I tidied up as best I could and went on down the street. In the distance I heard the grind and clatter of a tram and made in its direction. I came out in Hornsgatan and had to wait some minutes in a doorway before I caught an empty taxi. I sank back with relief in the seat, still trembling slightly from the effects of the fight.

Feeling safe from pursuit now I took the nearest way to the café, over Slussen and across the island of Gamla Stan. Fifteen minutes later the taxi pulled up outside the Drotten. It had a self-service counter on the left, coffee tables along the window and a second room screened off from the window by a glass-panelled partition. Pushing by

142

two tubs of indoor plants that flanked the door I made my way into the rear room. To my inexpressible relief Carl and Anna were seated there. When Anna saw me it was as if a light had been switched on behind her eyes.

'We were growing anxious... It is good to see you are safe.'

'Did everything go all right?'

'Yes. It took us a little time to get a taxi but we saw nothing more of them.'

My voice was anxious. 'Did you keep a sharp look-out? Steiner didn't stay on my heels as I'd expected. When he saw you and Carl had gone he dropped Müller and another man to follow me and then drove back.'

She flinched at my words and I guessed she'd had to pay more attention to Carl than to happenings outside the taxi. The strain on him must have been intense and still showed on his drawn face. But although I again felt a twinge of uneasiness there seemed no possible way Steiner could have picked up their trail so quickly. I dismissed the fear and said: 'It's nearly twenty-past six. Shall we go now?'

At the doorway I made them wait while I took a careful glance up and down the street. I could see nothing suspicious and we hurried into the taxi. Carl turned to me in surprise at the address I gave the driver –

15, Eriksgatan Gamla Stan – but Anna, quick-witted as ever, pressed his arm warningly and he sank back.

For the next few minutes I was kept busy, trying to keep myself from being too conspicuous at the rear window of the cab and yet trying to keep an eye on the traffic behind us. There was a good deal of it about and it was impossible to check all the cars and taxis that followed us. But at least I was certain the Kapitän was not in sight.

We crossed the Vasabron. On our right the Town Hall rose magnificently from the shimmering Mälaren, its bricks russet-red in the evening sunlight. Ahead of us was the old town, and its cobbled streets grew progressively narrower as we threaded deeper into it.

We stopped at the end of a picturesque alley flanked by ancient shuttered houses. I paid the driver and waited until he had driven away before pulling a map from my pocket.

'I thought it wiser not to give him the exact address,' I told Carl. 'Tullgrand isn't far from here.'

I remembered the old town from my last visit to Stockholm, genuinely mediaeval, with streets no more than three yards wide and six-storied, shuttered houses hiding the sunlight. During the day its old curio shops did good business with tourists, but when we arrived the tourists had returned to their hotels and the place was deserted.

We hurried down the narrow alleys, the hollow echo of our footsteps following us. A nearby church bell sounded the half-hour, then the silence flooded back again. The shadows were thick, and I saw Anna give a shiver as though she were suddenly cold.

We found Tullgrand without difficulty, a narrow cobbled alley, and turned into it. Number 6 had a fresco over its doorway, denoting its one-time genteelness. Below it were two small windows. I don't think any of us were surprised to find it was a souvenir shop. Behind the thick astigmatic glass we could see bits of Småland glassware, Lapp embroidery and wood carvings. The house above, pitted and weatherworn, had narrow casement windows and huge old-fashioned drainpipes.

The shop door was locked. I saw a brass bell chain and tugged at it. There was a muffled clang deep inside the house and then silence.

Alongside me Carl's breathing was harsh. He was as tensed as a man going over the top, face shiny with sweat, staring eyes fixed on the door. Beside him Anna looked little better. They had gambled everything on Kleinberg being the right man and their very lives might depend on the outcome of the next few seconds. The tension made my own throat dry and stomach muscles tighten.

The distant hum of traffic added weight to the silence. The only movement came from a cat, slinking furtively out from a distant doorway. The narrow alley, with its tall gaunt houses, was like a deep ravine, the evening sun only reaching the high slate roofs above. Where we stood it was thick in shadow: a little chilly, a little sinister.

I pulled the bell chain again. This time there was a movement inside the shop. I heard Carl suck in his breath, and then the rasp of a withdrawn bolt occupied my whole attention.

CHAPTER 12

The shop door opened and a girl appeared. She was an ash-blonde with full red lips and swinging, gypsy-style ear-rings – handsome in a bold, aggressive way. Her figure was full and generously displayed in a tight-fitting, low-necked linen frock. This, I guessed, would be Inga Norgren.

I spoke to her in German. 'I'm John Drayton. You made an appointment for me to see Mr Kleinberg this evening.'

Her stare moved from me to Carl and Anna. She had a sulky, petulant voice. 'You didn't say you were bringing anyone with you.'

'They're business friends of mine. I'll explain when I see Mr Kleinberg.'

My eyes were growing accustomed to the darkness inside the shop and I could see there was a man standing a few yards behind her. Carl had also noticed him, and in his anxiety to take a closer look almost pushed me from my position in front of the door. The girl looked puzzled and turned to the man behind her. He muttered something in reply and she stood sullenly aside. 'All right. Come in.'

We entered the shop. It had a damp, musty smell. Kleinberg, if the man were he, was walking over to the light switch and all I could see of him was that he was of average height, was wearing a flannel suit, and had a bald patch on the crown of his head. Then yellow light flooded from a table lamp on one of the counters. He turned towards us, and I saw he had a sallow, bony face with a prominent nose and fleshy lips. His sleek black hair was thin down the middle and he had a large mole on the left side of his jaw. I guessed him in his late forties. Then my attention, like Anna's, switched to Carl.

For a seemingly endless moment, although it cannot have lasted more than a second or so, he looked hesitant and fearful as if all his bright hopes had come to naught. Then, like a film changing focus, his expression blurred, only to return transformed. He turned to Anna with a cry of excitement. *'Doch, er ist es, Gott sei Dank, er ist es!'*

She clutched his arm, her white face thankful with relief. Carl swung round on me. 'He's changed so much I didn't recognise him straight away. But it's him – I can see it now.'

Kleinberg drew back, his curiosity turning to sudden alertness. Yet he showed no recognition as he stared at Carl. I wasn't surprised. Carl must have looked very different ten years ago.

Kleinberg turned to me. His eyes were sharp and I thought I saw an uneasy fear in them. *'Vad är det? Vad talar Ni om?'*

'Please talk in German so we can all understand one another,' I said. 'We know you speak it – your girl told us this afternoon.'

The fear in his eyes sharpened. He threw Inga, who was an interested spectator behind one of the counters, a look of dislike. 'What if I can speak it?' he muttered. 'Who are you? What's your game?'

Eyeing his foxy face I wondered what significance he could have had to warrant kidnapping and transportation. One thing seemed certain – it was going to be as difficult to get his co-operation as we had feared. For, although he didn't recognise Carl, the fact that Carl was a German who claimed to have known him in the past was enough to put him very much on the defensive.

I tried to sound reassuring. 'There's nothing to get upset about. My friend here just wants to have a chat with you about old times.'

His suspicious eyes struggled to identify Carl. Baffled, he turned back to me. 'What d'you mean – old times? I've never seen any of you before in my life.' His voice had an apprehensive ring. 'Why did you lie to my girl and say you were comin' here on business?'

'We are on business,' I told him. 'If you'll listen we have a proposition to make to you.'

That calmed him a little. 'Proposition,' he muttered. 'What kind of proposition?'

I gave Inga a pointed look. 'I think it'd be better if we talked in private.'

He was weighing it up, trying to guess what we wanted. At last he turned and muttered something to Inga. The sour glance she threw him and the way she hesitated before flouncing out into the room behind the shop confirmed that theirs was no ordinary owner-shop-girl relationship. She left the door a few inches ajar. Kleinberg noticed but made no immediate move to close it.

Thinking it best to get the thing out quickly now I said: 'My friend wants to talk to you about something that happened ten years ago in Germany.'

That did it: his mind's escape-mechanism could no longer fob him off with implausible excuses for our visit. His sallow face went the colour of old parchment and he drew back against a counter as if a knife was being pressed at his stomach.

Carl, keyed up with nerves, could contain himself no longer. 'You remember now – that November night on the forest road to the frontier. You begged me to spare your life and I let you go... You remember me now – I can see you do.'

Somehow Kleinberg shook off his paralysis and closed the door Inga had left open. He had the look of a man at bay, desperately afraid. His tongue came out, licked his fleshy, colourless lips. 'Germany!' he muttered. 'You must all be crazy. I'm a Swede; I've never been to Germany in my life.'

His response, feared by us all, brought an immediate protest from Carl. 'That's not true. You're the man Steiner and Hacht picked up in the country house and were taking to the frontier. I remember you. I remember that mole on your cheek...'

Anna, who must have had the same thought as myself, intervened quickly here. 'You've nothing to fear from us, Herr Kleinberg. After what my husband did, he and Steiner are enemies now – that is why we have come to see you...'

Although he remained frightened it seemed to me the sharper edge of his fear left him at that assurance, convincing me he knew all about Steiner and his imprisonment. He listened motionless while Anna went on to explain the purpose of our visit. Not knowing anything about him it was tricky, suspenseful work, particularly as she had to hide from him the fact Steiner was already out of prison. We had agreed on this concealment beforehand, afraid that if Kleinberg did not already know the shock might make him run away again.

As she talked I watched Kleinberg's bony, frightened face, trying to guess what was going on behind it. 'For years my husband

and I have dreaded what would happen when Steiner was released,' Anna finished. 'You were our only hope and we've gambled everything on finding you. Now we've succeeded you can't refuse to help us, not considering that my husband spared your life at the risk of his own.'

Kleinberg's tongue came out again, licked his dry lips. 'How did you come to get this address?'

'We employed a private detective. It took him months to find you.'

The light glistened on his sweating forehead. 'Who else knows my address?'

'No one other than the detective and the three of us here. For our sakes as well as yours we have kept it a secret.'

He wasn't going to talk; I could see that from his expression. At the same time I felt certain now that he didn't know Steiner was out. After a short, tense silence he turned sullenly to Carl.

'Sorry, but you're wasting your time. You've got the wrong man.'

Carl was white to the lips with this rea- lisation of his worst fears. 'But you must help – it means everything to us. We'll pay your fare to Germany and all your expenses – we have kept money aside for that. And once you've identified yourself the police will give you protection...'

Fear of Steiner was like a brand on Klein-

152

berg's face. 'I tell you, I'm not the man you want. You're wasting your time.'

Carl had a blind, helpless expression now. 'But it is a matter of life and death to us. Surely you can see that.'

Something drastic was needed to break the impasse. Arguing to myself that while Kleinberg might not know of Steiner's remission of sentence, he must know the ten years term was almost over, I provided it.

'It might be a matter of life and death to some other people too if this address gets known,' I said quietly.

He went rigid as if a knife had been pressed into his belly a second time. He turned slowly to face me, his voice hoarse. 'What are you gettin' at?'

He had to be frightened enough to make him co-operate but not enough to make him run away. I stepped out as gingerly as a cat on a hot tin roof.

'I said other peoples' lives might be in danger if your address became known. This man Steiner is quite ruthless – you must have gathered that from your experience that night – and you are the key witness to his murder of two men. Steiner must know that while you're alive he's never really safe. So it seems to me you've just as big an interest in keeping him behind bars as my friends here. And time is running out fast.'

He was breathing as tightly as a man with

asthma. 'I keep tellin' you I'm not the man you want. Why the hell can't you believe me?'

My voice was hard. 'You're the man all right. It's written all over your face. You dodged your duty ten years ago when Steiner murdered two of your friends: you're not going to dodge it again when two more people are in danger. This time you're going to talk.'

His frightened voice was as repetitive as a cracked gramophone record. 'You're wrong – all of you. I'm not the man. I've never been to Germany in my life.'

I tried it another way. 'It's not as if we were asking you to do it for nothing. We're prepared to pay you well.'

From the corner of my eye I saw Carl and Anna turn and stare at me. Kleinberg brushed a hand across his sweating forehead. 'Pay me?' he muttered.

'Yes. Your expenses and a thousand *kronor* for giving evidence.'

I heard a muted gasp from Carl. At the same time I noticed that the door behind Kleinberg was a few inches ajar again. I didn't know how much Inga had already heard but I made certain she heard what followed.

'A thousand *kronor*,' I said. 'For doing a job that'll help you to sleep safely at night. You've taken us the wrong way, Kleinberg,' I went on, making my tone more conciliatory. 'The last thing we want to do is get you into trouble. But there's no denying you are in the same boat as my friends here. If you help them you help yourself at the same time. And get paid good money for doing it.'

For a moment he seemed almost tempted. Then his fear of Steiner rushed back, making him shake his head violently. 'It's no use. You're wasting your time, all of you.'

At that moment Inga appeared in the doorway. 'Can I come in?' she yawned. 'I've left my cigarettes on the counter.'

Kleinberg took no notice of her. She picked a cigarette packet from the counter and then leaned back against the wall, eyeing me with a thoughtful, speculative stare. I didn't let the opportunity slip.

'I might even consider going higher if you change your mind. If you do, phone me at the Hotel Skandia in Ringvägen. Don't come in person,' I went on, keeping my voice free of all suggestive undertones. 'We don't want to take the slightest chances with your safety.'

Kleinberg was opening his mouth to give his final refusal when Inga touched his arm and muttered something in Swedish. He answered her angrily, but made no further comment to us as we made for the shop door. There I turned, my eyes on the girl more than on him. 'You're being offered good money, Kleinberg, for a chance to rid yourself of a nightmare you've had for years. You'll be the biggest fool in Stockholm if you turn it down.'

The expression on Inga's face satisfied me, and I opened the door. Carl hesitated, and for a moment I feared he was going to spoil everything. Then Anna took his arm and led him out into the silent, empty lane.

The shadows were thick around us as we started down it. Carl kept a pace or two ahead of us and it was not until he stumbled that I saw the reason. Disappointment and reaction were taking their toll: his body was shivering as though from malaria and his facial nerves were twitching grotesquely. Shame that his condition made him keep his face averted and it was not until he had stumbled twice more that he allowed us to take his arms.

I tried to bring him some comfort. 'I don't think it went too badly for the first attempt. After all, we've seen from his conduct that he knows what happened to Steiner and that he's afraid of him. In one way that's greatly in our favour. When it sinks home that his hide-out might be discovered by Steiner as well as us, he's going to become much more co-operative, particularly now there's money in it.'

I wished I could believe my own argument. Something told me it was going to be very hard indeed to get Kleinberg to talk. My hope lay in the girl. Whatever else happened I felt she was going to work hard on him.

My reference to money made Carl turn his ailing, distressed face towards me. 'You should not have offered him so much money. We cannot afford it and it is not right that you should pay it yourself.'

We had reached the end of the street. There was an intersection here, four narrow roads radiating out like the spokes of a wheel. Over the end of one a gilded church belfry was still reflecting the setting sun. It was the Storkyrkan and we made our way towards it. A boy on a bicycle came out of the shadows and passed us, followed a few seconds later by two pedestrians, a man and a girl.

'I shouldn't worry about the money,' I told Carl. 'It's as much my fight as yours now.' I was thinking wryly of my skirmish with Müller. It had been the first musket-ball in my own personal fight with Steiner, and I had fired it. Steiner would not have overlooked that.

It was quiet in those narrow streets with their shuttered houses and dark alleyways, and we were all glad to reach a busier quarter. Here I used a public telephone booth to call a taxi and less than half an hour later we were safely back in the Skandia.

I saw them upstairs to their room and then

turned to Carl. 'I'm going to slip out again to fetch my car. I'll be back as quickly as I can.'

Although by this time he could barely stand he wanted to accompany me. I knew his fears. We had shaken Steiner off for a few hours – he would guess how we had used the time. That guess was more than enough to make him commence the violent measures we all knew must come. Difficulties were in his way while we stayed in the hotel, but the car was a perfect bait to draw the fish to him. It would have been wiser to have left it – certainly for the night – but this I did not want to do.

'I'd rather go alone,' I told Carl. 'I won't take any unnecessary chances. But I want the car back – we may need it tomorrow.'

Anna followed me to the lift. 'I know you can't take Carl in the condition he's in to-night. But let me come with you. It may make all the difference to your safety.'

I took her hand and pressed it. 'I'd rather do it on my own. You look after Carl and I'll be back in half an hour.'

Her anxious eyes followed me into the lift. Downstairs I phoned for a taxi and waited in the hall until it arrived. I noticed no one following me on my way to the Countryman, and, deciding Steiner must be waiting near it, I made the driver stop at the street end. Seeing nothing suspicious I let him drive right up to the car. Ignoring his puzzled expression I stared up and down the gloomy street. Still I could see nothing, but instead of relief I felt apprehensive. In some odd way this sudden neglect of attention captured back for Steiner the initiative we seemed to have won that afternoon.

Then it occurred to me that the car might have been tampered with. Wanting the taxi to stand by but not wishing to involve the driver in any unsuspected risks, I motioned him to wait for me further down the street. Then I took off my jacket and checked the car as thoroughly as I had checked it in Jönköping.

It was an unpleasant few minutes, particularly when I lay helpless under the chassis. But nothing happened and I could find nothing wrong with the car. Puzzled, I paid off the cab driver and a minute later started back to the Skandia.

Carl was asleep when I got back. He had been worrying about me so much Anna had been forced to give him a strong sedative. Knowing she had been even more anxious I tried to spare her further worry by minimising the strangeness of Steiner's conduct.

'They probably didn't feel it worth while watching the car when they know we're staying here,' I said.

It was an answer that convinced neither of us, but it had to suffice for the moment. To avoid disturbing Carl she went with me into my room. There she turned to me.

'You're not very hopeful about making Kleinberg talk, are you? But I saw you watching the girl, Inga. Are you thinking she may have some influence on him?'

I nodded. 'Yes. Money usually means a good deal to her type and Kleinberg didn't strike me as having much. I think there's a good chance she'll tackle him, although whether he'll play is another matter.'

A sudden shiver ran through her. 'What if he doesn't, John? What is going to happen to us then?'

It was one of the few times I ever saw her courage falter, and for that reason it touched me deeply. I put an arm around her shoulders and lifted her face to mine. 'We'll make him talk – one way or another. Don't worry about that.'

She tried to smile and I kissed the bravery of her lips. Her body trembled and surged up to me for a moment. Then she moved restlessly away, only to return with a sob and press her cheek against my shoulder. Her voice was low, frightened. 'If one could only see the future, John. If one could only know what will happen. Everything seems so jumbled … so full of terrible difficulties. What is going to happen to Carl? What is going to happen to you and me…?'

CHAPTER 13

The next morning passed slowly and not without some tension. Carl wanted to visit Kleinberg again, while I wanted to wait and see if Inga would make the first move. With nothing to support my case but my impression of Inga, I would probably have been unable to restrain Carl had not Anna intervened.

'John is right, Carl. It is better they come to us. In any case, Kleinberg may not be at home and we do not want to make unnecessary trips to the shop – it is too dangerous.'

Carl was edgy, fretful. 'We don't know what effect our visit yesterday had on him. While we're sitting around here he might run away again.'

'We couldn't stop him doing that wherever we were,' she pointed out.

'We might at least be able to trace him. But by waiting around here we give him time to cover up his tracks.'

There was a good deal in what Carl said, and had it not been for the difficulties and dangers involved in making the trip I would probably have given in. As it was we compromised.

'Let's give the girl until lunch-time to phone,' I said. 'If she doesn't, then we'll phone her to see how the land lies. After that we can decide on our next move.'

Carl reluctantly agreed and the slow, restless hours passed by. At 12.15, just as I was about to give in and phone the shop, the telephone in my room rang. To my infinite relief it was Inga, saying she would like to see me. I tried to persuade her to meet me in town but without success.

'I can't,' she muttered in her low, sullen voice. 'There's no one else here to look after the shop.'

I then asked her if Kleinberg had agreed to talk. She hesitated a long moment. The distant clang of the shop bell seemed to make up her mind. 'I can't talk now. I'll explain everythin' when you come.'

I had to be content with that and gave Carl and Anna the news. Carl was excited and I had to warn him against disappointment. 'She may be doing this without Kleinberg's knowledge. But at least it is a move and it has come from their side. The one thing I don't like is having to go to the shop again.'

Anna guessed what I wanted and made the suggestion for me. 'I think it is better John goes alone. He will be less conspicuous than the three of us.'

Carl was disappointed, but to his credit made no protest. I wasted no time and in

162

ten minutes was on my way. Although again I saw no evidence of pursuit I covered my trail by taking three taxis and felt confident of being unobserved as I made my way down the narrow lane to Kleinberg's shop.

This time the shop door was ajar. As I pushed it back the bell jangled somewhere back in the tall cliff of a house. The damp, musty smell came to me again as I stepped forward. The thick, astigmatic windows allowed little daylight into the shop and an electric lamp was burning over one counter. Furry seals winked at me with their glass eyes from shadowy corners; colourful Lapp dolls watched me with a curiosity that even their slant-eyed stoicism could not conceal. The silence had the thick quality one finds underground. It was like entering a cave and finding it the cache of a mountain sprite.

The illusion vanished like a burst bubble as Inga, as modern as a champagne cocktail, entered the shop. She was wearing a different, although equally low-necked, linen frock, and was sex from her dagger-heeled shoes to her piled-up, ash-blonde hair. I wondered how Kleinberg found the money to keep her.

She motioned me into the living room at the back of the shop. I paused in the doorway. 'I take it you're alone this morning. That Kleinberg is out?'

There was both suspicion and fear in the

look she threw me although she tried hard to conceal the latter. She nodded curtly and went back into the shop to bolt the door. Then she returned and sank into the armchair opposite me, crossing her nylon-sheathed legs. She was trying hard to be casual but I could see her tension.

'Well,' I said. 'What's your news? Has Kleinberg agreed to do the decent thing and witness for us?'

Her sullen eyes lifted to mine, a stare of dislike. I understood why a second later. 'Max hasn't agreed to anythin'. He's gone.'

It was like a blow in the face. 'Gone!'

'Yes. He phoned me a couple of hours ago and said he was gettin' out before you landed him into trouble.' In spite of herself her voice roughened. 'You see what you've done. Why the hell had you to come an' spoil things.'

There was sweat in my clenched hands. I was thinking of Carl and Anna, wondering how I could break this news to them and damning Kleinberg viciously under my breath. Somehow, anyhow, I had to get his whereabouts from this girl.

'Where has he gone?' My voice was urgent. 'Did he tell you?'

She sneered. 'Wouldn't you like to know that?'

I fought off panic and allowed reason to take over my mind again. 'All right. He's gone and you phoned me to come here. Why? What do you want?'

She pulled a cigarette from a packet and lit it, her movements nervous and jerky. Her eyes avoided mine as she answered.

'I thought you might have a proposition to make. That was why.'

My breathing came easier. 'You mean, you'll tell me where he is if I give you money?'

Her voice was hard, defiant. 'Maybe. If you make it worth my while.'

I paused, thinking hard. Finding Kleinberg was not enough: he had to be made to talk and act. I made my offer with that in mind.

'I'll give you a thousand *kronor* too. But not until you've persuaded him to help us.'

'What makes you think I can do that?' she muttered.

My eyes moved over her meaningly. 'I think you could. If you used the right kind of threats, that is.'

She blew smoke out through her nostrils. There was a pause, then she said abruptly: 'How much danger would there be for him if he did talk?'

In spite of what the cynics say there is nearly always some attachment in these liaisons and I wondered how deep hers went. I decided to twist the question round in my favour.

'Far less danger than if Steiner were to

trace him. He was the only witness to his murder of two men, and Steiner knows it. Work the risks out for yourself.'

'You're sayin' Steiner would try to kill him?' she said, watching me.

'I believe so, yes. And you would be in just as much danger for having associated with him.'

That seemed to decide her. She inhaled deeply on her cigarette again, then turned to me. 'All right. Give me the thousand *kronor* and I'll tell you where he's gone.'

I shook my head. 'A quarter now, another quarter when I find him, and the balance when you've persuaded him to talk.'

Again the look of dislike crossed her face. 'All right,' she muttered, holding out her hand.

I took two hundred and fifty *kronor* from my wallet – almost all the money in my possession at that moment – and passed it over to her. She stared down at it a moment and then said sullenly: 'He's gone up to Kiruna in Lappland.'

I stiffened. 'Kiruna!'

'Yes. He thought he'd get well away from you up there.'

He wasn't far wrong, I thought grimly. Kiruna was two hundred miles inside the Arctic Circle, nearly a thousand miles north of Stockholm... 'What's his address?'

'He couldn't tell me when he phoned.

166

Friends of his have a business there – he's goin' to look them up and then leave their address at the Post Office for me to collect when I arrive.'

So in any case he had arranged for her to follow him… The knowledge confirmed my belief that he was well under the spell of her voluptuous good looks.

'What are you going to do about the shop?' I asked.

'We've got a chap who looks after it when we're away on holiday. I'm to contact him this afternoon and give him the keys. Then I'm to catch the 17.00 train tonight.'

I had to make a snap decision, and could only hope Carl and Anna would agree to it. 'All right! You go tonight and we'll follow tomorrow. That'll give you time to work on him.' I leaned forward in my chair. 'This is what I want you to say. Tell him it may not be necessary for him to come back with us to Germany if he can tell us what Steiner did with the bodies of the two men he murdered. With them as evidence we might not need him at all. If you can persuade him to tell us that I'll give you the rest of the money.'

The idea had come to me on the way to the shop and I was excited about it for more reasons than one.

'An' if he refuses?' Inga asked sullenly.

'Meet us at the station just the same, give us his address, and you'll get the other 250 *kronor* I've promised you.'

'How will I know when you'll arrive?'

'That depends on the trains. How do they run up there?'

She crossed the room with that affected, voluptuous walk of hers, picked up her handbag and pulled a slip of paper from it. 'There's one in the mornin' at 7.12. And there are two in the evening: one at 17.00 and another at 20.30.'

I thought quickly. We would have plenty of preparations to make and our trail would have to be covered... 'We'll try to catch the 17.00 train tomorrow – the same one you're catching tonight. That'll give you twenty-four hours alone with Kleinberg. When does it get into Kiruna?'

She studied the slip of paper again. 'At 14.32 the following afternoon.'

I rose to my feet. 'Very well – that's when you meet us. Wait in the restaurant so we don't miss you.'

She walked with me into the shop and unbolted the door. I turned to her in the entrance. 'Work hard on Kleinberg,' I said. 'Both of you are in far greater danger than you think.'

Again that curious expression of both dislike and fear came into her eyes. 'Don't worry,' she muttered. 'I'll meet you in Kiruna.'

With that I had to be content as I made

my cautious way back to the Skandia.

As I had feared Carl was intensely upset at the news, which he took as final proof that Kleinberg would not help us. Even the fact that Inga had told us where he had gone brought him no consolation. He lifted his grey, shocked face up to me.

'You talk as if he'd only gone to the other side of the city. Kiruna is as far from here as Warsaw or Prague.'

'It's still in Sweden,' I pointed out. 'And only twenty-one hours away by fast train. I don't see any great problem there.'

He gazed at me hopelessly for a moment, then shook his head and turned away. Anna answered for him. 'It's the cost of it, John. Already we've had to draw on the money we were keeping for Kleinberg's expenses. If we go up there we shall have nothing for him even if he agrees to return with us. And we can't go on borrowing money from you.'

I was getting worried about the money side of the affair myself, but there could be no turning back now. I went on to tell them what I had said to Inga about the bodies of the two murdered men. 'If Kleinberg can tell us where they are hidden and we find them, the German police will be forced to believe your story, and my guess then is that you won't have to pay Kleinberg's fare – the police will want to subpoena him and will apply for extradition. Inga might get him to talk – provided, of course, he doesn't know Steiner is already out. At all costs he mustn't learn that.'

There was hope again on Anna's face, but Carl was inconsolable. 'The very fact he's gone so far away shows he has no intention of talking. That isn't going to change his mind.'

I clapped an encouraging hand on his bowed shoulders. 'You're forgetting Inga, Carl. She's good-looking, very sexy, and half his age. He won't want to lose her and if she threatens to go he might do anything.'

He stared at me. 'But why should she make a threat like that?'

In the circumstances I didn't want to tell him, but there was no other way of reviving his hope. 'Because I've offered her a thousand *kronor* if she can make him talk. And she seems pretty keen to get her hands on it.'

His despair turned to self-reproach. He rose unsteadily and gripped my hand. 'My friend, I'm sorry. While I wallow in pessimism you spend your money and risk your life trying to help us. I am more than ashamed of myself.'

'I suggest we start making our plans to leave right away,' I said. 'As I'm not taking the car the suitcases are going to be our Achilles' heel – we haven't a chance of dodging pursuit while we're carrying them, and if we forward them there's too great a risk Steiner might make enquiries about their destination. So I suggest we use them as red herrings. We'll pack the barest essentials we need into a single grip, leaving the rest of our things in the car, and we'll forward the suitcases, weighted with rubbish, to a fictitious destination.'

They both nodded their agreement to the idea. 'And we leave on the 17.00 train tomorrow evening?' Anna asked.

'Yes, but not from Stockholm – it's far too risky. My idea is to make a diversionary journey during the day and connect up with the 17.00 train somewhere along the line – perhaps at Uppsala.'

We spent the rest of the afternoon making our preparations. First I made telephone enquiries regarding bus and train schedules. Then we began packing the kit we would need for the journey. This had to be selected carefully, as we were taking no more than Anna's grip would hold. The suitcases we weighted with rubbish, locked securely, and after dinner we prepared to take them down to the station. I could have arranged for the hotel to dispatch them, but this was one time I wanted to be followed. Carl wanted to accompany us but because of the amount of travelling to be done the following day Anna urged him to retire early.

After making certain his door was locked

Anna and I started off in the Countryman. The few precautions I took on the way were designed to avoid suspicion, not to throw off pursuit, but in spite of this we saw nothing of the black Kapitän. At the station, uneasy in case our precautions should be in vain, we had the suitcases taken over to the forwarding bay, where I paid for them to be sent on to the Grand Hotel in Göteborg.

It was then I caught sight of the man standing alongside the magazine kiosk some distance down the station hall. I had no more than a second's glimpse of his face – the moment I turned he lowered his face behind a newspaper – but I believed him to be the third of the three men I had seen in the car with Steiner – the dark-haired, slim one.

Wishing to be certain, I told Anna to stay where she was and started casually towards the kiosk. As I approached the man turned away, folded up his newspaper, and walked unhurriedly towards one of the exits.

Satisfied, I bought a newspaper and returned to Anna. 'I'm almost certain that was one of them,' I told her. 'And if it was he's seen everything we've done, which is just what we want.'

On our way back to Carl I turned down the Söder Mälarstrand, the waterfront where I had fought Müller. I wanted to find out if the slim man were following us, and the long, quiet road here was ideal for the

172

purpose. I drove a few hundred yards down it and then pulled into the kerb. The road behind us remained empty of traffic right back to Slussen bridge.

'He must have stayed to find out where the suitcases were routed,' I told Anna. 'It couldn't be better.'

Her face was pale, anxious. 'But where are the rest of them? Why have they suddenly given us this freedom of movement?'

I didn't say it, but felt they must be devoting their attention to the hotel, making certain Carl did not escape. In a sense that covered us too, because they knew we would have to return for him. It left other questions unanswered, as I was well aware, but I could think of no better explanation.

Anna turned to me. 'What is it like in the far North, John? Have you ever been up there?'

I shook my head, glad of an opportunity to take her mind off Steiner. 'No; but I'm told it's a marvellous place – hundreds of miles of tundra and heather and rock plants. And this is the right time to go. Late August is autumn there and the colours are said to be fabulous.'

'Hundreds of miles of tundra and heather,' she repeated slowly. 'It must be a lonely place, John.'

I followed the stare of her eyes. Across the water the sky was slashed like a great crimson wound. Against it, as sharp and erect as daggers, were the black spires and towers of Kungsholmen. On our right the superb pile of the Town Hall seemed to be drawing the colour into itself, its bricks glowing like uncut rubies. The red stain ran into the water, dyeing it like blood.

I felt a shudder run through her. I turned, and instantly she was in my arms. It was always the same whenever she sensed danger or fear, and there was fear running in her now. She was thinking of the great northern wilderness where the old pagan gods of Hel and Loki still held sway, and of what would happen to us if Steiner discovered our plans and followed us there.

It was a thought that reminded me again of the infinite care we would have to take the following day. One slip and our excursion would be as foolish and suicidal as a stag breaking cover before a pack of hunting hounds. It was this knowledge that drew our bodies and lips together, each searching the other feverishly for a palliative to the brutal demands of life and duty.

It was a distant carillon of bells, tumbling over the water from the Tyska Kirkan, that reminded us of our obligations. Apart now, avoiding each other's eyes, we left the hushed crimson Mälaren and drove back to Carl.

CHAPTER 14

The next morning was fine and sunny. After breakfast I went to the desk. I cashed my emergency traveller's cheques, paid our account, and made provisions for my car to be kept in the hotel garage until our return. I gave the receptionist our forwarding address as the Grand Hotel, Göteborg. Then I went upstairs where Carl and Anna were waiting for me. Anna was wearing her slacks and black sweater; Carl was dressed in flannels and his brown tweed jacket. Anna had packed the grip; the rest of our kit we took down into the garage and locked it in the Countryman.

By ten o'clock we were ready. The receptionist offered us the hotel car, but I asked him to phone for a taxi. We waited for it in the hall. My mouth was dry and there was a hot, hard lump in my stomach. Anna's disciplined face was pale and her voice curt, always a sign of nerves in her. But my attention was on Carl. If he were to crack in the next few hours we would never make the train undetected.

He looked as if he had spent most of the night gearing himself for the supreme effort he knew he must make today. His smile was stiff, his face haggard, and he moved jerkily, as if every muscle in his body were tensed and waiting for the forthcoming battle with his nerves.

A porter entered the hall, signalling to us that our taxi had arrived. My eyes met Anna's and then I picked up the grip and we went out.

The broad, tree lined Ringvägen was carrying its usual heavy flow of traffic but I could see nothing of the Kapitän as our taxi pulled away. Remembering how the slim dark man had succeeded in following us the previous evening, however, I took no chances. We went east almost as far as the Sofia church, then took a tram into the Folkungagatan, a busy shopping thoroughfare. Here we pushed our way through two crowded stores before taking a second taxi across Gamla Stan into the city centre. We next took a tube, waiting in the exit until the last of the passengers went out. It was nervous, exhausting work – murder on Carl. Our ultimate destination was the bus terminus: to cover our tracks as thoroughly as possible we had decided to take a bus to Enköping and then a local train to Uppsala. In distance it was no more than fifteen minutes from our hotel, but because of the diversion we had to make I had allowed us two hours, and we used up every minute of them.

No one we recognised followed us into the bus, but we had a nerve-racking ten minutes before it pulled away. Carl, able to rest at last, sank back and closed his eyes. His drawn face was twitching as if he were in great pain and both Anna and I watched him anxiously.

He made no complaint, however, although the two-hour journey in the hot coach must have been an ordeal for him. In Enköping I would have liked to take a taxi direct to the railway station, but felt I dared not relax. We hid for half an hour in a large store, and then went to a cinema matinée, leaving by a back entrance a few minutes after the film commenced. By the time we reached the station I was feeling tired myself. Carl was grey and stumbling along like a man in a nightmare. I could feel nothing but admiration for him.

He was able to lie down in the train to Uppsala: our compartment was empty and Anna persuaded him to put his legs up on the seat. He obeyed her but I could see from his twitching face and limbs that his revengeful nerves were allowing him no rest.

We arrived in Uppsala a few minutes before 5 p.m. Making Carl as comfortable as possible in the restaurant, Anna and I took it in turns to have coffee and to keep an eye on the platform. We saw no one we recognised and at 5.50 the long, sleek North

Arrow, the Stockholm-Narvik pulled into the station. It consisted almost entirely of sleeping coaches, but we managed to find a lounge compartment and helped Carl into it. While Anna was attending to him I went off to look for the guard. He was a little, bent man, very courteous, and with a fair command of English. He confirmed he had no spare sleepers but when I told him I had a sick man with me he went off to speak with one of his attendants. He returned a few minutes later and led me to a two-berth cabin near our compartment.

'There is only one man in here, *min herre*. Your friend can have the other berth if he wants it.'

I put one or two innocent-sounding questions to him and then had a word with Anna.

'What do you think? He's going to need all the rest he can get and he should be safe enough if he locks his door tonight. I've checked on the man with him – he's a Swede going on a fishing holiday.'

Like me, she was uncertain, but after seeing the berth was near our compartment she reluctantly agreed. 'I think we must take it. Otherwise he may have a breakdown before we arrive.'

The guard gave me a ticket for the berth, refusing the tip I offered him. Five minutes later the electric train, as smooth as a cat's fur, slid forward and out of the station. We were on our way to Lappland.

Carl was able to close his eyes until 6.45, when second dinner was served. Thinking I would take the opportunity of seeing who was on the train I wandered down the corridors, but with most of the cabins sleepers with windowless doors I had little success. After twenty minutes a middle-aged man wearing a leather windcheater came down the corridor. He excused himself in Swedish as he pushed by me and entered the cabin. Satisfied, I returned to our compartment where I told Anna about him.

'I think he's genuine enough. Certainly he's no one we know.'

Anna nodded, her eyes on Carl. Exhaustion had finally overcome his nerves and given him sleep, but from the way he kept jerking and groaning it was a sleep without rest.

'I'm worried about him,' she murmured. 'He keeps complaining of a pain in his left side and a feeling of weakness. That is how his serious attacks usually commence.'

The dinner gong sounded a few minutes later. Reluctantly Anna awoke Carl and the three of us made our way into the restaurant car, where we saw no one we recognised. As we sat there I saw Anna was right about Carl. He kept pressing a hand under his heart and he seemed to have barely the strength to lift his fork to his mouth. I noticed, too, that in this condition he appeared to find the presence of strangers around him a great strain. It was obviously hell for him to be there – I was sweating myself at the strain of it – but somehow, in spite of Anna's whispered entreaties, he saw it through. Back in our compartment he sank into his seat with a groan of relief. I offered him a cigarette when he opened his eyes and he took it with a grimace of gratitude.

'Feeling bad?' I asked gruffly.

He tried to smile. 'Ghastly, John. Like death itself.' He turned his eyes down at himself with aversion. 'This damned body of mine – it always lets me down when I need it most. God only knows why I bother to keep it out of danger.'

In his bitterness he had forgotten Anna. She turned to him protestingly. 'You mustn't talk that way. You've done wonderfully well to-day – far better than you expected. It's not strange that you're tired tonight – we're all tired.'

I observed then the depth of his affection for her, how it immediately neutralised the acid of his bitterness. 'I'm sorry, *Liebchen,*' he said, very gently. 'It was only a mood and has gone already. You mustn't let it upset you.'

Their eyes met and held. It was not a glance of hot desire such as lovers give one

180

another: it was a much purer thing than that. There was understanding in it, friendship, compassion: all the things learned from self-sacrifice and suffering and from years spent living together. It was something in which I had no part whatever and yet – and I was glad of this – I felt no jealousy. Only a deep desire to help them both.

I left the compartment, walked a short distance down the corridor and stood gazing from the window. Large stretches of grassland were sweeping by, dotted with conifer woods. Occasionally a farm-house would come into view, mostly wooden buildings painted the popular *falun*-red with white doors and window frames. Their quaint roofs, rounded and turned to shed the winter snow, reminded me of women's tight bonnets.

After five minutes Anna came out of the compartment and approached me. Her hand reached out and gently touched my arm. That was all, but I understood. We stood in silence for a minute or two, then she turned to me.

'Do you know if the attendants have made up the sleepers yet?'

I shook my head. 'I don't think so.'

'Carl must get some rest. I think I'll go and ask them to make up his bed now.'

I was turning to go myself when she stopped me. 'No; you've done enough today.

'I'll see to this: you go and talk to Carl.'

She slipped away before I could argue. As I entered the compartment Carl gave a start. He turned his head quickly but I could see the expression on his face. I took the seat opposite him and leaned forward.

'What's the matter, Carl?' I asked quietly. 'Don't you believe we've given them the slip?'

My question made him start again. He hesitated and did not answer.

'Why not, Carl?' I insisted. 'What makes you think not?'

He sighed and gave a helpless shrug of his shoulders. 'Because I know Steiner, John, that is why.' His apologetic eyes lifted to mine. 'Forgive me, my friend. I am not being critical of you. You have been most thorough and it's difficult to see how anyone could have trailed us today. And yet…'

'And yet you still think Steiner has managed it?'

He nodded. 'I must, John. I must because I know him so well. For him to trail us all the way to Stockholm and then lose us like this – it is out of character. He is like the devil's general at this kind of thing, working out every move his opponent can make and planning counter moves to combat them. It is unthinkable he should fail now when his very existence is threatened.'

His words shivered an alarm bell in my

182

own mind, but my reason fought against the warning. 'You must admit we've seen no evidence of anyone trailing us today. Even if a stranger had followed us we couldn't have failed to notice him.'

He nodded, but seeing he remained unconvinced I felt an illogical and unfair impatience at his pessimism.

'He might be clever but he isn't infallible. Don't forget he's been in prison nearly ten years – that'll have taken the sharp edge off him. And he can't have as many followers to call on now as he had in the old days.'

The sun had set and shadows were entering the carriage. We were running through a series of lakes joined together by rocky, scabrous hills. A house appeared, tiny and courageous in that inhospitable landscape. Then it was gone, torn away by the great wild sweep of the hills.

Carl's voice was barely audible above the singing of the steel wheels – he seemed to be talking to himself more than to me. 'It's not just his cleverness that makes him such a terrifying enemy. It is his implacable desire for revenge on anything or anybody who gets in his way. There's a perversion in it that demands more from his victim than even death. I saw it demonstrated one night in Hannover, in the early days when he used to work with us. It was night time and we were unloading a lorry. We'd been tipped off that the police were keeping a special watch for us and we were working as quietly as possible. As Müller dragged off the first bale a terrier ran towards us from some ruins. It was a moonlit night and I could see it was a puppy with bright, excited eyes and perked-up ears. It thought we were playing a game and barked and wagged its tail and ran around us.

'I tried to shoo it away but it kept coming back. Müller threw a stone at it but it only barked louder. Steiner showed no sign of anger. Instead he patted his knee and called softly to it. It wagged its tail and came nearer... Steiner leaned forward as if to pat it, and then suddenly kicked out with all his strength.'

The train siren sounded, a shocked, futile cry in the wilderness of lakes and hills.

'The puppy lay beside a wall, whimpering slightly. In the moonlight I could see Steiner's face as he stood over it, smiling as the devil himself might smile. He eyed it for a moment and then kicked again...' – for a moment Carl's voice faltered – 'he didn't stop when it was dead. Once he had started he couldn't stop – I saw the bloodlust on his face. I wanted to kill him and knew I was too frightened to speak. Müller, who has beaten up more men than he has fingers and toes, looked as if he were going to faint. Only Hacht laughed...'

The compartment had suddenly grown very cold. I found myself sitting on the edge of my seat, every muscle tensed. I heard Carl again, musing now.

'The slaughter of the war sickened me and for a while after it I became a pacifist. I argued that if men would only learn meekness they could teach it by example to their enemies. I knew it could only work if all men had a little of God in them, but I believed they had. Then I met Steiner and soon knew that a few devils still walk in the world.'

We sat there, each with his thoughts. Then Carl glanced back at me, his voice apologetic. 'I don't know why I've told you this – it's a bad time to choose. Perhaps it's because I want you to believe that Anna and I aren't being afraid of shadows when we fear him so much.'

I met his eyes. 'I've never thought that, Carl. Otherwise I'd hardly be here tonight.'

He gave me a smile of gratitude. An awkward yet companionable silence followed. High in the fading sky outside I saw a night hawk suddenly plummet downwards into the shadow of a hill. With the sombre mood of the moment still on me I wondered what manner of victim lay torn and bloody in its claws.

CHAPTER 15

Anna returned shortly afterwards. 'Everything's ready now,' she told Carl. 'Your sleeping pills are under your pillow and I have had the thermos flask filled with hot milk. But don't take any pills until the other man is in his bunk – you must make certain the door is locked on the inside before you go to sleep.'

Carl rose unsteadily. His laugh could not hide his bitterness. 'It's a fine thing, John, when a man has to take the only bed and leave his wife sitting up all night.'

Anna hushed him and led him outside. At the door he turned back to me. 'Don't leave her alone tonight, John.'

I shook my head and then I was alone, listening to the singing wheels below me. Anna returned a few minutes later. She didn't switch on the light but came over and sank into the seat alongside me.

'Tired?' I asked.

She gave a faint smile. 'A little, yes.'

'You're worrying about Carl, aren't you?'

'Yes. He's so ill and depressed tonight.' A thin shiver ran through her. 'He has a feeling of danger – I can tell it.'

186

'You have it too, haven't you?' I said, watching her.

She threw me a quick glance, then shook her head defiantly. 'No. We've seen nothing of them today: we must have thrown them off. Let's not talk of them any more.'

We sat in silence for a long time, watching the arrival of the night. We were still travelling through lakes and rivers, and wooded islands rose from their steel-grey waters like grim castles. As they faded behind us into the mauve-ash dusk it was easy to imagine the last guarded frontier to the northland had been crossed.

Just after eleven o'clock there was a clatter of doors and a clumping of footsteps as the buffet car closed down and the last of the passengers went to their sleepers. I waited ten minutes, then walked down the corridor where I found Carl's door safely closed and locked. At that moment the train slowed down and pulled into Ånge. I lowered a window and stared out. Only a few passengers were embarking and I could see no one I recognised. I waited until the train pulled out and then returned to Anna.

All was quiet again until just on midnight, when we pulled into Bräcke. Seeing there was more activity here I told Anna to stay in the compartment and I jumped down on the platform. Although the sky was clear and the moon full the night air was already perceptibly colder than in Stockholm. About thirty passengers were clustered round two coaches at the rear of the train and I walked towards them. Again seeing no one I recognised I returned to Anna. All those embarking must have had reserved sleepers because she was still alone in the compartment.

I shook my head at her enquiring glance. 'No, nobody we know. It looks as if we've definitely shaken them off.'

She nodded but made no comment. We had a cigarette and sat watching the platform while the porters finished loading. We noticed no one else enter the train and there was a slam of doors followed by a whistle. A moment later we began moving again.

The station lamps slipped past faster and faster, alternatively lighting and shadowing Anna's face. They gave way to darkened houses whose roofs glistened silver in the moonlight. These clung to us a moment as though begging us not to leave, and then we were alone again in the vastness of forest and plain.

In spite of her denials I knew Anna was unable to feel we were out of danger. And, although reason provided me with un-answerable arguments against it, a similar premonition was growing in me. Yet paradoxically it was that very premonition that gave the night ride on the train a fascination I shall always remember. My mind, untethered on the brink of sleep, wandered back to the war to provide me with a reason.

Jumbled romanticised thoughts came to me. A bomber going out on a mission, droning high along the path of the moon... There was a suspension of danger there – an impossibility of death with the moon and the stars and the white clouds so lovely and compassionate all around you.

Or in the desert before an attack. Tomorrow you know all hell was going to break loose, and yet as you sat there with the sand running like molten silver through your fingers and listened to the awesome message of the desert, you felt as wise and immortal as a god.

Or a ship going out to a battle rendezvous in the tropics. The loveliness of the waves in the moonlight, the way they cascaded into white fire as your bows cut through them. Nothing could die in such a magic world. Nothing ... nothing ... nothing...

And yet all the time a little hard voice inside told you otherwise. And so you learned the old eternal truth that life is never as precious and beautiful as when danger and death are close at hand: that the man who lives only for safety is the man who never lives at all.

Anna must have felt something of this too, because sometime during the night I felt her turn towards me. I saw her eyes, white and shining in the darkness, and then, just as in the car, we were drawn together.

Only those who have known such desire can understand and forgive it. My lips could not drink in enough of her soft, warm skin. After a long, wild moment she took my hand and cupped it tightly over one of her breasts.

'*Es ist schön,*' she murmured, her voice low and throaty, '*dir so nah zu sein.*'

I drew her even closer and kissed her again. But this time, running a hand gently down my face, she took control of us both.

'*Wir müssen nicht,*' she whispered. 'But keep your hand on my heart. It is good to feel it there.'

Although no longer ignorant of her relationship with Carl I could not fight my desire and I knew I would love her again whenever the time and place permitted. At the same time a small hard voice left me with no illusions. With Carl treating me as a friend, every stolen kiss was another link of steel chaining me to him. That chain would make me stay with him to the end, no matter what that end should be. In no other way would I be able to live with myself.

She slept beside me, dark head in my arms, firm body pressed into my hand, and I had no wish for the dawn to come. Once I felt her stiffen and knew she was dreaming. Her breast rose and fell quickly under my hand, and under it I could feel the sudden pounding of her heart.

'*Nein,*' she moaned. '*Oh, Gott, nein!* Leave me alone.'

I wished Steiner in hell at that moment. Her body gave a convulsive jerk, awakening her. She must have thought I was he, because for a moment she fought like a tigress to pull away. Then she fell against me with a sob of relief. '*Ich habe geträumt,* John! Thank God it was only a dream.'

I comforted her and then went out to check Carl's cabin. The door was still locked and all seemed well. I went back to Anna and this time she fell asleep almost immediately, her slender body relaxed in my arms. She did not awaken again until the train jerked sharply round a bend on the track. I heard her sleepy voice. 'How strange it is, John. A week ago I didn't know there was such a person as you in the world. Now I depend on you and need you so much...' Her dark head snuggled closer into my arm. 'So very much,' she repeated drowsily and a second later was asleep again.

We were passing through the great northern forests now and were still in them when dawn came. I watched the sky lighten and wondered what the day had in store for us. Just after 5.30 Anna stirred and I kissed her gently on the lips. She brushed her cheek against mine and then sat upright.

'Where are we?'

I told her. She asked what time we crossed the Arctic Circle and I pulled a timetable from my pocket. 'According to this, about 11.45. We arrive in Kiruna three hours later.'

There was no sign of activity in Carl's sleeper and as soon as possible I took Anna to breakfast. There we made arrangements for Carl's breakfast to be taken to him at eight o'clock.

On our return we hung around in the corridor outside his sleeper. Just after 7.30 the door was pulled aside and the Swede, dressed only in shirt and trousers, glanced out. He recognised us as friends of Carl and motioned us to enter the cabin. His urgency gave us both a shock – Anna's face went chalk-white – but although it was serious it was not the thing we most feared. Carl was sweating and shaking in his bunk like a man with malaria. Anna diagnosed his condition at a glance.

'It is one of his bad nervous attacks – I thought last night it was coming.'

I tried to help but in the tiny cabin only succeeded in getting in her way. I went back into our compartment and after ten minutes she joined me. She was pale and upset.

'How is he?' I asked.

'Very weak. He says he'll manage but it is quite impossible. We shall have to find him a room where he can rest.'

'A hotel in Kiruna?' I suggested.

She bit her lip and I knew what she was thinking. With Steiner hunting for spoor she would have preferred a helpless Carl anywhere but near Kleinberg. I pulled out my timetable again and studied it.

'There are quite a few sidings past Kiruna. Why not go beyond it and find accommodation in one of them? It has one big advantage. At a small siding it'll be much easier to make certain no one is following us off the train. I know we can't be certain we're not being watched from it, but I don't think they would dare to go on and return later – for all they know we might be making yet another diversion and in that case they'd lose us altogether.'

'But what about the girl, Inga?' she asked. 'You mustn't miss seeing her. Everything depends on that.'

'I won't miss her. The train stops at Kiruna for at least ten minutes. I can jump off and tell her to meet me there later. Once we've decided which siding to get off I can find out from the guard how the trains run back to Kiruna.'

Her expression was anxious. 'Wouldn't it be safer if you went with her to Kleinberg now and left me to look after Carl?'

I knew she was right. With Inga a doubtful ally of such critical importance to us, anything that disturbed our existing arrangements was to be avoided. But I dared not leave Anna the dangerous task of finding safe shelter for a helpless Carl on her own.

'I'm sure it will be all right,' I said. 'She's keen to get the money, and after all it's no great hardship for her to return to the station later. Of course, if she refuses we may have to change our plans. But let me talk to her first.'

With this decided we had next to choose a destination. None of the names in the time-table meant anything to us, and we didn't want to find ourselves stranded on some isolated siding that had no accommodation to offer Carl.

'Wait here,' I told Anna, going to the door of the compartment. 'I'll be back in a few minutes.'

The old, bent guard was my objective. On a run like this one, with the railway the only link between the northern hamlets, I felt certain he must know some of their in-habitants. I found him in a luggage van in the rear of the train, talking to one of the stewards. He broke off his conversation on seeing me. *'Ja, min herre.* Can I help you?'

I told him my sick friend was worse this morning and wanted a quiet place in which to rest for a few days. 'One of those log cabins you people spend your holidays in would be ideal. Do you know anyone in any of the hamlets beyond Kiruna who might rent us one for a few days?'

He shook his head doubtfully. 'Only railway workers live up there, *min herre*, and the hamlets are very small. Some are no more than half a dozen huts. I don't know anyone who owns a spare one.'

'Then do you know anyone who would rent us a room?'

'Most of the huts have only a kitchen and a living room, *min herre*. The men up there work shifts and don't often take their wives with them – it is too lonely...' Then his expression changed. 'Wait, there is Engestrom, the supervisor at Torneträsk. One of his men was sick when I passed through two days ago and Engestrom had moved into his cabin to cook for him. He might lend you his cabin for a few days.'

'Torneträsk. How far is that beyond Kiruna?'

'Just under an hour by train, *min herre*.'

'And is this cabin of Engestrom's far from the station?'

'Not too far. Perhaps one and a half kilometres through the woods. It is on the side of Lake Torneträsk.'

'And it is secluded – there aren't many other houses about?'

He smiled at the question. 'There is nobody at all, *min herre*, except a handful of railwaymen who work at Torneträsk siding. It is lonely country up there.'

It sounded exactly what we wanted. 'Will you have time to speak to Engestrom for us? I'll pay him well for the loan of it.'

He agreed to do this. I then checked on the time of trains between Torneträsk and Kiruna. I found I could catch one at Torneträsk at 6.6 p.m., which would get into Kiruna about 7.30, and return on the only evening train, the 9.45. It would give me only two and a quarter hours to find Kleinberg and do business with him, but it would have to suffice. Thanking the guard, and paying him for our extra journey, I hurried back to Anna. She was standing at the window, staring out at the passing forest.

'It seems we might be lucky. The guard thinks a railway worker at Torneträsk may lend us his cabin for a few days...' Then I caught sight of her face and pulled her around. 'What's the matter? Why have you been crying?'

Her voice was low, upset. 'It's Carl. He has been so sad these last few days, so conscious of his illness. I think it is because of you, John... I try to give him heart but it is no use.'

I stood in silence, not knowing what to say.

She raised her face. 'I've just told him what we intend doing. He didn't like it. He said he wanted to go with you to Kleinberg and that we should all get off at Kiruna as planned.'

I was a little impatient. 'But what if we find out we're still being followed? Surely he must realise the handicap he'd be to us.'

She turned her face sharply away. 'I'm sorry,' I said, more gently. 'I know how he hates being helpless. But the stakes are high, Anna. We've got to face the facts as much for his sake as our own.'

She nodded wearily. 'I know. He would be in our way. That is what I had to tell him to make him agree. But it hurt, John. It hurt very much...'

CHAPTER 16

We had a passenger enter our compartment in the mid-morning, a small man dressed in knickerbockers and a brown velvet jacket. He was middle-aged, with a face as brown and wrinkled as a monkey's. From his clothes I judged him native of the northern provinces, but nevertheless kept a wary eye on him. At first he made no attempt to enter into conversation, but after hearing me talk to Anna in English his attitude changed and he became quite talkative.

Learning that he lived in Gällivare I took the opportunity of learning all I could of Kiruna, which was only sixty miles further north. He proved interesting, taking even Anna's mind off her troubles. As we sat there the train siren gave a triple hoot. He turned to Anna and wrinkled his monkey face into a smile.

'That is the signal that we are crossing the Arctic Circle. Now you are in the Witch-north.'

The Witch-north?' she said, puzzled.

'Yes. Don't you know that once you come here you are lost for ever?'

Anna's cheeks went pale and my own

198

muscles tightened. His voice ran on. 'Our Witch-north uses her beauty to trap you. Once you have seen her you will always want to return, no matter where you live. Soon, when we leave these forests, you will understand.'

We both relaxed as the meaning of his chatter became clear. After another quarter of an hour he rose. 'We shall be in Gällivare soon – I must go and pack my things. Have a good journey and enjoy yourselves.'

'I think he's harmless enough,' I told Anna. 'But we'll keep our eyes open for him.'

Alone again, we gazed through the window. The trees had been thinning for some time and also shrinking in height. Suddenly, with no warning at all, they fell away and we were in the tundra.

Anna gave a gasp of unbelief. After the shadows of the evergreens the sight was almost overwhelming. All around us lay an enormous rolling plain, a fantastic combination of grey lichen, purple heather, huge rocks, yellow bushes, and great patches of scarlet ferns that gave the illusion the ground was bleeding. Lakes, burns, and swamps were everywhere, and rolling hills, covered in drifting cloud shadows, swept away to bold horizons. It was a wild and exciting land, stirring something deep in my blood.

Anna's voice was low, incredulous. *'Es ist wunderbar,* John. *Unglaublich!'*

After a while trees began to appear again, smaller now and less dense. Some were only just beginning to change colour, autumn leaves glowing like golden fruit among their green foliage. Others were completely transformed into every shade from bright yellow to flame-red. In the slanting sunlight they glowed like dazzling angels among the dark firs.

Houses were rare, and the few we saw were huddled alongside the railway track. We passed one, little more than a shack, separated from its kind by miles of forest and swamp and plain. Fifteen minutes later we caught sight of another, built alongside a lake. Anna gave an exclamation of surprise and pointed. There was a small plane on floats moored to a jetty alongside it. I made a quick calculation and found we were already more than six hours' flying time in such a plane from Stockholm. It brought home vividly to me the vast distances of this northland.

The tiny house and plane were swept away like leaves in a wind as our train rushed on. The colour outside grew brighter. At 12.45 we began slowing down and pulled into Gällivare, a rail-junction. The town of cowled wooden houses was built around a lake. Lowering the window I looked down the platform. The only person I recognised was the wizened Swede, making for one of the exits with a huge suitcase in his hand. I pointed him out to Anna. Five minutes later we plunged off again into the sea of colour.

Anna paid one of her many visits to Carl and then I took her to first lunch.

'Do you think he's going to manage to walk to the cabin?' I asked her. 'According to the guard it's about a mile from the station.'

She shook her head anxiously. 'It's impossible to say yet. I shall help him to dress half an hour before we're due in Torneträsk and we'll see how strong he is then.'

Just after 2.30 a large lake appeared on our left. Behind it rose a black mountain with a cleft down its centre like an enormous axe-bite. I pointed it out to Anna.

'That will be Kiruna Vaara, the iron-ore mountain the little Swede was telling us about.'

I watched it with interest as it drew nearer, remembering its importance during the war. The statistics given me by the Swede had been impressive. Punctually every hour, summer and winter alike, a freight train left it for Narvik, each one heaving a load of sixty wagons containing a thousand tons of ore. Black and forbidding, dominating the tundra for miles around, it was the sole reason for the existence of Kiruna, Narvik, and the fabulous single-line rail track through the mountains that linked the towns together.

Then my thoughts turned to Inga and all else was forgotten. Would she be there? If she were not, what could we do next? There seemed no answer to that question, and I saw from Anna's face that she too was feeling the strain. Silent we watched the town taking shape and definition as it emerged from the tundra. It was on the opposite side of the lake to the mountain and in view of its northerly latitude was a fair size – over twenty-five thousand inhabitants. We passed a notice board that gave its particulars. 1,143 kilometres from Stockholm and over 1,500 feet above sea level. With the sun warm in our compartment it was difficult to believe we were further north than Iceland or the utmost reaches of the Yukon river.

Little passed between Anna and me as the train entered the station: there seemed nothing to say. I pressed her hand encouragingly, told her to stay in the compartment, and was on the platform before the train stropped moving. In spite of the bright sunshine there was a bite in the air. I could only see two buildings of importance: a block of booking offices and a hotel restaurant further down the platform. Compared with earlier stations down the line it was relative busy, but again I saw nothing of Steiner's men.

I ran to the hotel and found myself in a small hall with the restaurant on my right.

Pushing back a glass-panelled door I caught a glimpse of empty tables, and my heart skipped a beat. Then I saw her, half-hidden behind a cluster of shrubs in the far corner.

She showed no surprise as I approached her, and I knew she had seen me through the window. She was dressed in a flattering green woollen frock, and with her piled-up, ash-blonde hair and nylon-sheathed legs, she looked as beautiful and artificial as a glossy advertisement. She was trying hard to appear indifferent, but she could not conceal the look of dislike and fear that came into her eyes as I reached her table.

I came straight to the point. 'I haven't long – I'm going on in the train. Will you come back and meet me here at 7.30 this evening?'

Surprise showed on her sullen face. 'Goin' on! But why? I thought the whole idea of comin' up here was to see Max.'

'It is. But my friend's been taken ill and I have to get him to a place where he can rest. I'm coming back on the first train I can get.'

A puzzled frown marred her smooth forehead. 'But where are you goin' to? There's nothin' up the line as far as Narvik. Why don't you get him a place here?'

There seemed no point in her knowing, even though I had no reason for distrusting here. 'Never mind where we're going – there isn't time to talk about it now. Will you meet me here at 7.30 or will you give me Klein-berg's address so I can come straight round?'

She hesitated, then muttered sullenly: 'It's a bit tricky to find – I suppose I'd better meet you. Who'll be comin' – you and the girl?'

Relieved at the way things were going, I shook my head. 'No; she'll stay with Carl.' I heard the slam of doors outside and my voice quickened. 'What does Kleinberg say? Did you ask him about the bodies?'

She nodded. 'At first he denied everything, but later on – when I did as you said – he began to come round a bit. He wouldn't actually tell me what happened but he said he might talk to you an' your friend if you made it worth his while. That's all I could get out of him.'

It was more than I'd dared to expect. 'You've done well,' I said. 'Meet me here at 7.30 and if Kleinberg talks I'll see you get the rest of that thousand *kronor* right away.'

I had just time to jump back into the train before it pulled away. Anna rose anxiously to her feet as I entered the compartment. I held out my hands to her. 'I've good news for you. Kleinberg says he might talk.'

For a moment she seemed unable to believe me. Then she gave a low cry of glad-ness and threw herself forward. Holding her tightly I told her what had happened. When I finished she kissed me and then turned away. 'I must go and tell Carl. He will be so excited…'

The train was gathering speed, running alongside a road lined with sheds. On the left stood a long line of stationary trucks filled with grey-black iron ore. Beyond them was the shining lake. Less than a minute later the tundra took their place and all I could see of Kiruna when I looked back was the huge brooding mountain.

There was colour again in Anna's face when she returned. 'Carl's very thrilled at the news. He asks me to thank you.'

'How is he feeling otherwise?' I asked.

'He's very weak. He'll have to go straight to bed once we reach the cabin. When do you think I ought to start dressing him?'

'Torneträsk is about an hour by fast train from Kiruna. I should start around 3 o'clock.'

I went to see Carl a few minutes later. He looked in a bad way but there was hope again in his pain-filled eyes. He held out a hand and gripped mine. Through it I could feel his fever.

'Wonderful news, John,' he said. 'I don't know how to thank you.'

I chatted with him for ten minutes and then returned to Anna. She was gazing at the fantasy of colour outside as though unable to drink her fill of it. As far as the eye could see were ferns, shrubs and rock plants of every colour and shade: grey-brown, yellow, bronze, blood-red. There were bottle-green firs and groves of Arctic birch as red as flames. As I entered the compartment she turned to me. 'It is unbelievable, John. It hypnotises me – makes me feel I am a bird flying over it.'

The track was a single line now, demanding occasional sidings to allow approaching trains to pass. We raced through one of these, surrounded by a few huddled cabins. I caught the name, Rautas. A few minutes later the bright colours outside vanished as if a switch had been thrown and I saw we had plunged among mountains with a lake on our left. All was bottle-green and blue now, like a Mediterranean grotto. We swung round sharp bends, lost speed and pulled into a siding name Rensjön.

We paused here to allow an oncoming train to pass and we saw our first Lapp. She was on the tiny platform, an old woman with a face as brown and wrinkled as a brazil nut. She was wearing an electric-blue beaded jacket and a red skirt. Two other Lapps came up alongside her as the train stopped. One ran away as someone from the train tried to photograph him – I learned later that some Lapps still believe a camera negative imprisons their souls. The old woman, however, bore her loss stoically for a 50-*öre* piece.

A few white hornless cattle were grazing in

a meadow beyond the siding. Two children wearing long hose waved at the train from a gravel road. They vanished from sight as a huge freight train roared past, returning from Narvik with its long chain of empty wagons.

We pulled out immediately it had passed. The mountains retreated for a while, then closed in again on our left. I glanced at my watch.

'I think we'd better get Carl dressed. Would you like me to help?'

'No; there isn't room in the cabin. But I would like you to help him into the compartment when I've finished.'

She gave me a call ten minutes later. Carl, fully dressed, was propped up on the lower bunk. He was shaking from head to foot but on seeing me he tried to rise unaided. I stood aside, but when he slipped and fell back I was compelled to throw one of his arms around my shoulders. He gritted his teeth in shame as I helped him upright. 'This damned body of mine, John. How I detest it...'

In our compartment he sank back with closed eyes. I eyed him doubtfully as Anna wrapped a blanket around him.

'Are you quite certain he shouldn't have a doctor?' I muttered.

'They could do nothing but give him sedatives,' she said wearily. 'And we have plenty of those with us. I'll give him one the moment we reach the cabin.'

We were climbing steadily into the mountains now. Snow drifts appeared among them, and far below on our right a majestic lake slid into view, dotted with bottle-green islands. From our height the scrub birch around it looked like jungle grass. I wondered if it were our lake. A moment later the old guard shuffled into our compartment.

'*Ja, min herre*. That is Torneträsk. When we arrive I will speak to the supervisor for you.'

We stuffed our few possessions into the grip. I lowered the window as we slowed down and leaned out. Like Rautas and the other tiny stations we had passed, it was nothing more than a siding and link in the electrified track that ran from Kiruna to Narvik. Its platform was gravel and contained only one brick building, a curious dome-shaped structure looking as if it might house a transformer. Under it were a couple of offices, one with a bench outside. The other side of the track was pure tundra, a gravel cliff giving way to a wooded hill. I turned to Anna. 'Don't worry about us – I can get Carl down. You run round to the back of the train and make certain no one jumps out at the other side and hides in the bushes.'

She obeyed while I helped Carl down to the platform. To his discomfort the old,

208

sympathetic guard took his other arm and helped him towards the bench. I didn't like the attention we were drawing on ourselves – from the corner of my eye I could see faces staring at us from the coaches – but there was nothing I could do to prevent it.

Carl sank down on the bench and I gave him a cigarette. A few seconds later the guard came out of one of the offices, followed by a cheery-faced stockily-built man in a chequered shirt and railway-issue serge trousers. He spoke to me in German.

'The guard here tells me you'd like to borrow my cabin for a few days.'

I nodded, explaining my reason. He took a look at Carl and his expression changed. 'He looks pretty sick. Wouldn't it be better to put him up in Kiruna or Narvik where you can get him a doctor?'

I told him there was nothing a doctor could do, that it was only a matter of quiet and rest. He shrugged. 'Well; that's something you can get here all right. Isn't it, Eiliv?' he grinned, turning to the little guard.

Eiliv gave his gentle, anxious-to-please smile. 'Yes. It is very quiet in the woods.'

'How long would you want it for?' Engestrom asked.

'No more than two or three days, I hope. But I'd like to rent it for a week to be on the safe side.'

He hesitated, then shrugged. 'All right.

Come into my office and we'll see what we can do.'

I thanked the little guard who then hurried back to his train. I waited for it to pull out, wanting news from Anna. She shook her head as she hurried up to us. 'Nobody,' she told me. 'Unless they jumped out before I got into position.'

Relieved, I left Carl with her and joined Engestrom in his office. He shared it with a slim youth of about eighteen who was filing some papers. He pulled open a drawer and threw me a key. 'Here you are. You'll find clean sheets, blankets, paraffin for cooking, and plenty of firewood. Your only real problem is food. There is plenty of canned food but nothing fresh. I'll phone through to Kiruna for bread, milk, and vegetables, but they won't arrive until the first train tomorrow. But I can let you have a couple of loaves to keep you going – I had a delivery today.'

With the natural hospitality of his kind he was reluctant to accept payment, but I finally pressed him into accepting forty *kronor* to cover the use of food and linen. As I rose he pointed a blunt, tobacco-stained finger at the fair-headed youth at the filing cabinet. 'The cabin's a bit tricky to find. Take Lars, my lad here. He doesn't speak English or German but he'll get you there all right.'

I thanked him warmly. Then, accompanied by the youth who carried the two

210

loaves of bread for us, I returned to Anna and Carl.

'Everything's fixed up,' I told them. 'We've got the cabin for a week if we want it.'

Although as unsteady as a drunken man, Carl said he felt stronger and insisted on walking unaided. The youth led us down a gravel track that ran at right angles to the platform. It took us between four wooden houses and then led us into the surrounding woods.

The brick building, the last thing visible of that tiny oasis of life, sank out of sight behind the trees. The silence was intense, broken only by the sound of our footsteps and the occasional cry of a bird. It brought to me with oppressive intensity the reality of our position. If we had escaped from Steiner we could hardly be in a safer place than this unspoiled wilderness. If we had not, it could be our graveyard. With no roads anywhere, with a long, tenuous railway track our only link with civilisation, we would be entirely at his mercy if he discovered us.

Lars led us down the track for three hundred yards and then forked right up a narrower path. It was flanked with autumn tinted trees and flame-red ferns that brushed our legs. The path was rough with exposed roots and it was only a moment before Carl stumbled and fell. I helped him up and made him put an arm around my shoulders. We topped a rise and I caught a glimpse of the blue mirror of Torneträsk. Then the woods closed around us again, hiding our vision.

Carl's staring eyes were fixed ahead like a sleepwalker's as he fought grimly to keep going. In spite of everything, however, his weight on my shoulders grew with every stumbling step. Anna tried to take his other arm but the path was too narrow. Sweat ran into my eyes, making hot colour of the woods swim in the sunlight.

After half a mile I was forced to take a rest. Carl dropped heavily on a tree stump alongside the path. He struggled to speak but could not get enough air into his gasping lungs.

The youth indicated he would like to help. I nodded to him and turned to Anna. 'When Carl's recovered, let Lars help him for a few minutes. I'll catch you up.'

Leaving them there I walked a few yards back along the path and hid myself behind a high bush. I heard Anna murmuring words of encouragement to Carl and a few minutes later they moved away round a bend in the path. I waited, listening.

It was very quiet. High above me a rough-legged hawk was floating on silent wings, watching for prey. A breeze rustled the leaves around me and then died way. From somewhere near at hand came the peculiar cooing of a blackcock. Dried leaves rustled further along the path and my muscles tensed. But it was only a stoat or weasel shifting its cover.

Ten minutes passed, and no one came down the path. Unable to wait longer I ran after the others. Anna was supporting Carl, and from the apologetic smile the youth gave me I guessed she had been doing so since I left them.

'Why didn't you let the boy help?' I muttered, taking Carl's weight from her.

Under the black sweater her breasts were rising and falling quickly and there was sweat on her bare, tanned arms. 'I couldn't, John. He's not as strong as I am.'

I realised with admiration that she was probably right. Carl's hoarse whisper sounded in my ear.

'How are things behind, John? All right?'

I nodded. 'Yes. It looks as if we've made a complete getaway.'

For a minute or two the news gave him strength. Then his legs began dragging again until soon I was supporting his entire weight. When the path widened Anna made him put his other arm round her shoulders, and in this way we struggled over the last half-mile to the cabin.

It was built of dressed pine and stood on the very edge of Torneträsk. Alongside it, pulled up on the bank and covered by a tarpaulin, was a twelve-foot dinghy. The woods reached up to the cabin door, and a hundred yards to its right the bank swept upwards into a blunt promontory covered in willow and red birch.

We unlocked the door and found ourselves in a small kitchen. There was a stone hearth, with a metal cooking grill on the right, and a sink, cupboard, and small table on the left. It was cool inside and smelt strongly of pine. An open entrance led into the only other room, a combined bed-sitting room. Against one wall was a set of wooden bunks, one suspended over the other. A paraffin lamp stood on a deal table in the centre of the floor. The floor-boards were unstained but covered near the table by a threadbare carpet. A fishing rod stood in one corner of the room, and a few books were scattered on a small table under the far window. The only other furniture consisted of two wicker chairs, a small portable radio, and an oil stove. There were windows on three sides, the far one overlooking the lake. A side door led into a store containing a pile of faggots, cans of paraffin, and a tin of spirit.

Lars helped me to get Carl over to one of the bunks and then signified he had to return to the station. I gave him three *kronor* and thanked him as best I could. He blushed when Anna held out her hand to him: it was clear she had won his adolescent heart. Then he disappeared into the silent woods and we were alone.

I lit the spirit stove so that Anna could make a hot drink for Carl. Then I built a fire in the stone hearth. The burning logs gave off an aromatic smell and sent sparks flying high up the chimney. I drank the cup of black coffee Anna handed me, and then draped the sheets and blankets around the fire. I turned to ask if there was anything else I could do, and paused. Carl was lying with half-closed eyes on the lower bunk and Anna was sitting alongside him, one hand gently stroking his face. Her expression as she gazed at him gave me a sudden urgent restlessness: I had to escape from the cabin for a few moments. Moving as quietly as possible I opened the door and slipped outside.

I walked round the cabin and took a look at the dinghy. The oars were folded inside it, under the tarpaulin, and it appeared in fair condition. The air was as fresh as mountain water and I took deep breaths of it. Still restless, I took a path along the bank of the lake. It led me into the woods and to the top of the blunt promontory. From it I could see the cabin below me, smoke eddying lazily from its chimney. Ahead was the shimmering Torneträsk with its bottle-green islands; across it snow-capped mountains rose like clouds against the blue sky. Far away came the piping call of a curlew and around me the Arctic birch rose like cool red flames. It was a place of great beauty.

Anna found me twenty minutes later. I was sitting on a knoll staring out across the lake and her voice made me start.

'What is the matter, John? Why have you come here?'

The faint trace of defiance in my voice annoyed me. 'Nothing's the matter. I have a couple of spare hours before my train leaves for Kiruna and thought I'd take a look around. How is Carl?'

She came and sat beside me. 'I gave him a sedative. He is sleeping now.'

We sat in silence for a moment, gazing at the autumn fire of the woods, the blue lake, and the distant soaring mountains. Then she turned to me. 'This is a strange, beautiful land, John. I know now what the little man meant when he called it a witch. It gets me here,' and she pressed a hand to her heart, 'almost like a pain. Do you know what I mean?'

I nodded silently.

Her gaze was on the woods again. 'So much beauty and so few to see it. And it comes year after year, as if people do not matter at all...'

'Do they?' I said.

She turned then and looked into my face. 'You are bitter today, John. And you must not be. I cannot help loving Carl ... any more than I can help loving you.'

The ache for her was too much to bear. At

first she made no response when I kissed her, lying with closed eyes in my arms. Then, with a shudder and a tiny helpless shake of her head, she pressed herself against me.

Underneath the sweater her shoulders were brown but her breasts were as white as the flesh of an apple. She pulled my head down and under the swelling roundness came the steady, strong beat of her heart. I heard her voice, distant and sad.

'You must remember what he did for me – why I cannot help giving him love and loyalty. For your sake and mine you must never think it can be different. Promise me that, John.'

I nodded mutely, burying my face in her cool firm skin. Her arms tightened in pain around me. 'And yet it is all so unfair to you. *Oh, wie kommt das,* John...?'

I could not speak. My eyes were tracing out the swelling loveliness of one breast against the blue Arctic sky, but my thoughts were on Carl. Carl, who by risking everything for her had lost the physical power of expressing his love that was the birthright of every man. There was no passion in me at that moment, nothing but a blind resentment that such things should be. Then she took a deep breath, her breast dipped and quivered, and all my thoughts were consumed in the white-hot desire for her that once again swept through me.

She felt it, shuddered, and cupped my hand over her breast in that way of hers. Perhaps it was the thought that our love was stolen and must soon end, perhaps it was the wild strong land around us; whatever the reason it gave a wild abandon to our kisses and a fierceness to the grip of our limbs. We made love as men and women must have loved a hundred centuries ago, with the sun on our bodies and the soft grass beneath us, and I for one could have believed the Witch-north gave us a power of loving beyond that possessed by ordinary mortals.

When it was over we lay exhausted in each other's arms. Her body was trembling and I found she was weeping. *'Ich liebe dich,* John,' was all she would say to me, and I thought it wise not to question her further.

We lay for a few minutes in the drowsy aftermath of love, renewing our strength in the sun and in the silence. Remembering my train was due in the station just after 6 o'clock, I was keeping an eye on my watch, but as I expected, her anxiety for Carl roused her without any prompting from me.

'I ought not to have left him as long as this,' she murmured in self-reproach, dressing hurriedly. 'It is dangerous and very selfish of me.' I made no comment and followed her down the path to the cabin.

Carl was safe and still sleeping when we

reached him. I had no time to waste and prepared to leave at once. Anna followed me outside.

'The train back leaves Kiruna at 9.45,' I told her. 'Whatever happens I intend catching it. So I should be back about 11.15.'

She held out her hand to me as I turned to go. Her small automatic was lying in it. I looked at her sharply.

'I don't need that. Kleinberg isn't going to make trouble.'

Her voice was quiet. 'You know I'm not thinking of him. Please take it, John.'

'But there's no danger, Anna. Steiner's still searching around Stockholm for us.'

Her courageous blue-grey eyes held steady on mine. 'I hope so too. But we're not quite certain, are we? Otherwise why did you leave this gun on the table for us…?' When I hesitated she went on quietly: 'Please take it, John. It is you who are going among people again, not us. I shall feel much happier if you have it in your pocket.'

I shook my head and to avoid further argument started up the path. After a few yards I turned back with a smile.

'Have a hot meal ready for me. About 11.15.'

I turned back once more before rounding a bend in the path. She was still standing in the cabin doorway, her face pale and the gun still half-outstretched in her hand.

CHAPTER 17

I saw no one in the woods and arrived at the station with five minutes to spare. Engestrom saw me and asked how we found the cabin; I told him we were comfortable. I would have liked to have asked him to keep silent about our presence there but felt to do so might make him suspicious.

The local train was punctual and a few minutes later I watched Torneträsk receding into the distance as we swung south through the mountains. The sun had set behind them now and there was a chill in the air. We stopped at most of the small sidings and it was 7.20 before the black forbidding hulk of Kiruna Vaara rose from the tundra. The lake appeared a few minutes later as we pulled into the untidy outskirts of the town. There were sidings here and we pulled into one for a moment. A freight train, dragging its long chain of wagons, heaved its massive bulk past us as it headed for Narvik. I glanced at my watch and saw it was just on 7.30. Sixty great wagons of ore en route for Narvik every hour and leaving as punctually as an express train. It was impressive efficiency and made me glance in respect at the black mountain that dominated the town. Our train moved forward again and a minute later drew into the station.

I found Inga in the restaurant, smoking a cigarette. She was searing a swagger coat over her green frock. 'Well,' she asked sullenly, 'have you got your friend fixed up?'

I nodded. 'Yes. He's quite comfortable now. What about Kleinberg? Has he said anything more to you since this morning?'

She ground her cigarette into an ashtray filled with butts. 'No; but he knows you're comin', and is ready to see you.' She uncrossed her silken legs and rose. 'One of his friends brought me here and is waitin' outside. If you're ready we'd better go.'

I followed her outside the station where a Swedish Volvo was waiting. Inga opened the front door and said something to the driver. He leaned out and nodded at me, a short, round-faced man wearing a windcheater. I tried him in both German and English but he shook his head.

Inga motioned me to jump in the back of the car. 'He only speaks Swedish,' she muttered. 'Don't worry – he knows where to take us.'

I kept a precautionary watch through the rear window as we drove through the centre of the town. It was a prosperous, untidy-looking place, reminding me of an American boom town. Flats and shops of modern design stood cheek by jowl with traditional wooden houses. Roads were often unlaid and yet cafés and bars blazed with light. I saw now the reason for its claim to be the biggest town in the world. It sprawled across the tundra as untidily as a gawky schoolboy on a double bed.

The houses alongside us thinned, straggled, and finally fell away as we crossed a stretch of pure tundra. Confident now that we were not being followed, I turned my attention to Inga. In the restaurant, both at noon and this evening, I had felt there was a good deal of tension mixed up with her sullenness, and I saw now I wasn't wrong. She was sitting forward in her seat, legs drawn up under her, looking as tight as a coiled spring. I wondered what had happened between her and Kleinberg.

'What's the matter?' I said abruptly. 'Has Kleinberg found out you sold his address for money?'

The familiar look of dislike was in her eyes as she glanced at me. 'No,' she muttered sullenly. 'He thinks I cabled it from here after he agreed to see you.'

'Then what are you looking so tensed up about?'

She dipped into her handbag for a packet of cigarettes and I saw her hands were trembling. She lit one and inhaled deeply, giving me the feeling she was searching for the right words to say. At last she turned to me, her voice defiant. 'If you want to know it's because I don't like this set-up. If this Steiner is as dangerous as you say I don't fancy Max gettin' mixed up with him. In fact I'm beginnin' to wish I'd thrown your bloody money right back in your face.'

Thankful that the remorse hadn't struck sooner, I tried to reason with her. 'He couldn't be in greater danger than he'll be when Steiner is released. By helping us he's helping himself, and it looks as if he's at last beginning to realise it.'

She said no more, staring sullenly out of the window. In the twilight the treeless heath we were crossing looked bleak and desolate. Houses stood in isolated groups: it was difficult to believe we were still within the boundaries of the town. Far ahead, on the other side of a wide, shallow valley, the lights of a small village glimmered faintly. I tried to imagine what it would be like in another month when the Arctic winter swept in from the north.

A solitary house, boxed in behind high hedges, stood in the heath on our left, thirty yards back from the gravel road. Our driver stoped in front of it. I met Inga's eye.

'This is where he's staying,' she told me.

We climbed out. There was a bite of frost in the air now. The driver made no move to follow us and I turned to Inga. 'Isn't he coming with us?'

She shook her head. 'He has to get back to town. He'll collect you later.'

'Tell him to be here no later than 9.20. I must get the 9.45 train.'

She turned and addressed the driver. He nodded, turned the car and started back to town. I followed Inga through an open sagging gate into the front garden of the house.

The garden had once been a lawn, now it was thirty yards of tangled weeds. The house behind it was a big, ugly, wooden building with a cowled roof and dormer windows. Its colour, a dirty grey, made it look as if it had only received an undercoat of paint. There were no lights visible and in the grey twilight its small, close-set windows had a dissolute and sinister appearance.

It was built on piles above ground, planks filling in the space between the elevated front verandah and the ground. Some were missing, giving a curious toothless aspect. The only sign of life came from a smoking chimney at the rear.

In the silence I heard the sharp cry of a fox. Our footsteps sounded loud on the weed-grown gravel path and even louder when we climbed the hollow wooden steps to the verandah. I found my heart beating faster as Inga approached the weather-scarred front door. It fell open with a groan.

I could see no one in the shadowy hall as she turned to me.

'Max'll be at the back with his friends. Come on in and I'll call him.'

As cautious as a cat I stepped inside the hall. The damp smell reminded me of Kleinberg's shop in Gamla Stan and for a moment brought me absurd comfort. There was a door and a flight of stairs on my right, two other doors on my left. Inga motioned me to follow her down the hall to the second door. She passed outside it.

'Wait here and I'll fetch him. He's probably playin' cards in one of the back rooms.'

The nervousness in her voice, the look on her pale face: both jangled my mind like an alarm bell. I was just about to catch her by the arm when the front door closed with a hollow thud.

For a moment I was afraid to look, afraid of what I might see. Then I turned stiffly and a bomb of fear exploded inside me.

Steiner, looking gigantic in the half-light, was standing between me and the door. In the echo-carrying hall his deep chuckle had a Mephistophelian quality about it.

'You seem surprised to see me, Mr Drayton. You shouldn't be. I told you we should meet again.'

Two other men had come out of the front room and were standing beside him. One was Müller. His lips and nose were badly swollen and his eyes, little more than blackened slits, were piglike in their hatred of me. The other man, small and misshapen, with a young-old chinless face, was Hacht. Beside the gigantic Steiner he looked a ghastly caricature of a crippled child along-side its father.

But it was Steiner who held my eyes. He was huge, bald, smiling, almost avuncular in appearance, and yet an aura of evil as icy as the Arctic night hung around him.

'You've disappointed us today, Mr Drayton. We thought you were bringing Frandl and his beautiful wife Anna to entertain us.'

His mention of Anna helped me fight off my paralysis. I threw a glance at Inga who was still standing behind me. It must have been a vicious one because she shrank back. Steiner gave another of his deep chuckles.

'You seem to have taken a sudden dislike to your charming guide, Mr Drayton.'

I was struggling to understand. It was obvious Inga had known they were here: I understood now her behaviour in the car, the excuses she had made for it. But then where was Kleinberg? Had she betrayed him too? Somehow I could not believe that.

The preliminaries appeared to be over. Steiner made a sign to his henchmen and stated towards me. 'I think we will entertain you in the back room, Mr Drayton. We have provided a few amusements for you in there.'

I was right in his path. Something obstinate in me kept me from moving aside. He came right up to me, enormous in the half-light. 'Stand aside, Mr Drayton,' he said softly. 'I want to pass.'

Inwardly I cursed myself for a stupid fool but I still did not give way. The regretful smile Steiner gave might have come from a sorrowing uncle driven into chastising his nephew. He gave a slight nod of his head, and Müller, who had been straining like a bull-terrier on a leash, leapt forward, a look of unholy glee on his battered face. As I swung round to face him Steiner moved like lightning. One huge hand caught mine and bent it back agonisingly. His other hand closed over my face, just above the jaw. It tightened with terrifying strength and the pain that ran down my neck made me cry out and stumble back. I lashed out blindly with my free fist. Müller caught my arm and was shaking to break it at the elbow when Steiner stopped him.

'Patience, Hans,' he said softly, letting his huge hand fall away from my face. 'There is plenty of time for that.' Then he turned and entered the rear room.

Müller, still twisting my arm, searched me to see if I were carrying a weapon. Then, kicking my ankle, he pushed me forward.

'Los, verdammter Engländer! Da'rein!'

The room was sparsely furnished with a long mahogany table and a number of straight-backed wooden chairs. A log fire was struggling in a smoke-blackened hearth to keep the evening chill at bay. Under the window, which was covered by a piece of sacking, there was a stained sink and on the draining board alongside it stood an untidy assortment of plates, cups, and other implements whose purpose I could only guess. The floorboards were bare, echoing our footsteps. A naked electric bulb burned from a rusted bracket in the centre of the ceiling. The cobwebs, clustered thickly in the top corners of the room, told me the house had been long empty.

Steiner picked up a chair and planted it in the centre of the long mahogany table. It creaked uneasily as he lowered his great bulk on to it. Hacht, with the swift movements of a crab, scuttered up from behind me and took a seat at his right hand. Müller shoved me down into a chair opposite them and stood behind me.

Steiner lowered his elbows on the table and eyed me mockingly. In the harsh glare of the naked bulb I was able to take in more details of his appearance. He was wearing a charcoal-grey suit with an impeccably white shirt and a maroon tie. His cuff-links were gold, as was the expensive watch on his hairy wrist. Again I thought of a business tycoon, this time presiding over a board meeting.

He pulled out his case of cheroots and selected one. He did not offer the case to Hatch but no resentment appeared on the henchman's chinless face, a fact I thought significant. He lit the cheroot, released a cloud of blue smoke, and then settled comfortably back in his chair.

'That's better, Mr Drayton. Now we can talk in comfort.'

I waited, breath tight in my lungs.

'After all the trouble you have taken to shake us off,' he went on mockingly, 'this must be very puzzling to you. You come a thousand miles to the north, you come voluntarily to his lonely house in a lonely town, only to find us waiting for you.' He cast a sly glance at Hacht. 'You must find it something of a riddle.'

Hacht's laugh had the sycophantic ring of the hyena. Steiner turned back to me. 'Would you like to hear how it was done, Mr Drayton?'

I had already decided the less I said the better. But I could not help throwing another vicious glance at Inga. Steiner saw it and laughed.

'Yes, of course. It was made possible by our charming and beautiful friend here. A very intelligent girl, Miss Norgren.' He had turned his eyes on her, and as they rose from her nylon-clad legs to her frightened face they were like lecherous hands lifting the clothes from her body. Their touch seemed to hypnotise her: she made neither sound nor movement. Something in that stare told me Steiner already knew her body and had possessed it.

He nodded and turned back to me. 'An intelligent girl and also an exclusive one, Mr Drayton. Not one a man can buy for a few hundred *kronor,* as you tried to do.'

I broke my silence for the first time. 'How did you find her and Kleinberg in the first place?'

He lifted a hairless eyebrow, a pained gesture at the naïvety of the question. 'Do you not know? When Frandl and his wife jumped from your car, you had forgotten you were on Södermalm, an island, with only three bridges connecting you to the centre and northern suburbs of Stockholm. It is true I could not know for certain that Kleinberg was not living on Södermalm or even south of it, but reason told me you would not willingly have led us so near to him. So, when I discovered Frandl and his wife missing from your car, I took a calculated risk. I sent one of my men by taxi to cover Västerbron bridge and Hacht and I, each in a taxi to avoid detection, covered the two one-way bridges on Slussen...'

That was it. The nagging fear that had haunted me for days: the single but fatal mistake that had ruined us. I gritted my teeth in self-hatred. Then I swung round on Inga. 'What about your Max, who you're supposed to be so fond of? Have you sold him to them as well?'

She sneered at me. 'What's the use of tryin' to bluff now? Mr Steiner's told me what your game was: how you were tryin' to frame him by frightening Max into givin' false evidence. Well, it's all over now and from what I hear you deserve all you get.'

I understood now the fear in her eyes when I had visited the shop a second time. Steiner had been there first, frightened her with some story about me, and told her to phone me and arrange a visit. I wondered dully what the story had been.

Smoke from Steiner's cheroot drifted between Inga and me. 'It was quite simple, Mr Drayton. I suggested to Miss Norgren that in order to escape from you Mr Kleinberg should go off for a few days to a mountain hut he owns in Jämtland. After that it was just a matter of hanging out the bait that you were so eager to bite. So eager you paid money to get it into your mouth. Nothing, of course, could have made Miss Norgren's task easier.'

I was staring at Inga in unbelief. 'You believed all this? You talked Kleinberg into going alone to a mountain hut?'

My insistence was beginning to frighten her: there was doubt in her defiance now. 'Why not? He was out of your way there.'

I knew she hadn't told Kleinberg that Steiner was near or he would have locked himself in the cellar... Steiner must have worked hard and fast on her, I thought bitterly, both in cash and kind. I was thinking of Carl and Anna, of all their hopes blasted into ruin, and all because of this blind stupid bitch. I knew she was only a dupe, that she had been led to believe she was protecting Kleinberg as well as feathering her own nest, but at that moment I hated her more than I hated Steiner.

'You stupid, blind slut,' I said viciously. 'Don't you understand why they wanted him to go to his cabin? They knew it would be lonely there – they could make murder look like an accident. Kleinberg's dead – his body's already rotting somewhere in the mountains – and you've helped to kill him.'

Her eyes were bright with fear now: her voice high-pitched. 'You're lyin'. You're lyin' just as you lied before.'

I could say no more: my throat was choked with the ashes of defeat. Steiner's triumphant eyes mocked me. He rose and went over to Inga, his voice soft and persuasive.

'Don't take any notice of him, *Liebste*. He is a vicious man and this is his way of trying to get his own back on you. You'll find your Max safe enough when you go home. Now go upstairs to your room and rest. We have some business to discuss with Mr Drayton.'

She hesitated uncertainly. Steiner smiled and ran a hairy hand up her arm from wrist to shoulder. It was a peculiarly suggestive movement and seemed to have the same hypnotic effect on her that a stroking hand may have on a cat. She appeared to regain her confidence, muttered something to him, and left the room.

CHAPTER 18

Steiner waited until the door had closed and her footsteps had died away. Then he gave a deep chuckle and returned to his chair.

'Women,' he said to me. 'How they like to believe themselves enigmas and yet how easy they are to handle.'

'What have you done with Kleinberg?' I asked.

He picked his cheroot up from the table and examined it carefully before returning it to his mouth. He put a match to it and looked at me quizzically.

'You know, Mr Drayton, all of us here have found something amusing in the Frandls' interest in Kleinberg. Find him, get him to talk, and their troubles were over. That is what they have thought and led you to believe. Now I will tell you just how vain all your efforts have been.'

He leaned his great bulk forward across the table. 'Frandl was never an imaginative man, Drayton. When he saw me and Hacht drag Kleinberg into our car on that November night, all he could think was that he was another innocent refugee I was abducting for profit. That was why he was certain

Kleinberg would go straight to the police when he released him and so back up his own story. It never occurred to him that nothing on earth would have got Kleinberg into a police station.'

'Why not?' I demanded. 'You'd just killed two of his friends.'

Hacht let out one of his shrill cackles as Steiner threw him an amused glance.

'His *friends,* Mr Drayton?' Soft though Steiner's words were, they hit me across the face like a bludgeon. 'Those two men we killed were Federal agents going to arrest him. Now do you understand?'

I understood enough to feel sick. I listened to the rest of the story in silence. Kleinberg had been a crook who had once worked for Steiner. Then he had grown ambitious and started work on his own, using some of Steiner's contacts and markets. That had been enough to seal his death warrant, but in addition Steiner had been given warning that two special Federal agents were going out that night to arrest him. Knowing the danger to himself, Steiner had gone to get him first. The Federal agents had arrived while Steiner and his men were in the house, and he had ambushed them. To destroy as many links as possible he had made Müller take away their bodies and hide them while his intention had been to take Kleinberg a hundred or so miles away before killing him.

The subtle change in Steiner's voice as he described Carl's behaviour sent an icy chill down my back.

'He betrayed me, Drayton. He did it because he was certain Kleinberg's evidence would get me a life sentence. You should have seen his face when I was only given ten years. You should have seen his wife's face – that beautiful bitch who had been working on him to betray me. They both knew what would happen when I came out...'

His huge hands were splayed out on the table like hairy spiders. He was thinking what he was going to do with them both, and the ferocity of those unspoken thoughts held us all motionless and hushed. He lifted his devil's eyes back to me.

'So I've had them watched for years, Drayton. Not because I wanted anything to happen to them – I just wanted everything ready and waiting for the day I came out. That was how I heard about his wife's idea to have me re-tried. Next I heard they had traced Kleinberg, and decided to kill two birds with one stone. Hacht, my right-hand man here, was going to shadow them for me, but as fate would have it I was released in time myself. A passport was waiting for me and we went straight after them.'

The stunted Hacht's big eyes were glowing at his compliment. He made me think of an anaemic schoolboy receiving praise from his teacher. I was reminded of Anna's analogy of him – his resemblance to Goebbels.

Steiner's voice was soft and mocking again. 'And then you, Don Quixote, arrived on the scene. At times you were quite ingenious. The trick in the car, for example – it deceived us for a few minutes. But no professional would have forgotten he was on an island, and once we had trailed you to Kleinberg and found he had a stupid and ambitious mistress the rest became only a matter of barter and arrangement. In fact, most of us were able to take rest from trailing you while we came up here and found a suitable address. We gave Inga Norgren her instructions when she arrived, and then all we had to do was sit back and wait to welcome you. We were hoping, of course, that the three of you would come, but that is something that can be arranged later.'

I had never thought to be thanking God for Carl's collapse as I was then.

'You might wonder why we chose Kiruna,' Steiner went on. 'A glance at a good map will enlighten you. From Gällivare there is only one road as far as Kiruna and from Kiruna there is only the single railway track the whole way to Narvik. Hundreds of miles of wild, empty country, Drayton, with only one way in and one way out. The perfect trap – get you in here and I had you. And that is what I have done. I have a man in Gällivare and another in Narvik, straddling the exits if something should go wrong. But nothing has gone wrong, Drayton – don't think that. I've got you, and you know where the Frandls are.'

There was something I desperately wanted to know – now more than ever. 'What did you do with the bodies of the two Federal agents?' I asked. 'Carl says the police were never able to find them.'

The insane, hyena laugh of Hacht sounded again as Steiner threw him another glance. 'Desperate situations call for desperate measures, Drayton, and we're rather proud of the one we improvised there. Braun-schweig is a city, and in cities people are dying every day. I knew of a large cemetery on the outskirts that had no night staff and so on our way out I gave Müller instructions to bury Kleinberg's body in the first new grave he found there. As things turned out it was the policemen he took instead. And they're still resting comfortably there, under another man's monument.'

Fantastic though it was I realised it would succeed if one were bold and unscrupulous enough to do it. The disclosure brought me new hope until I realised Steiner would never have made it if he intended me to live.

'And Kleinberg?' I said. 'In spite of all you've told me, you've killed him, haven't you?'

He lifted his huge hands in mock protest. 'Killed is a harsh word, Mr Drayton. Let us say he has had an accident while out fishing. It is regrettable but these things do happen.'

'You killed him even though he would never have witnessed against you.'

His eyes mocked me. 'Yes, Mr Drayton. In case some busybody managed one day to convince the Federal police of his existence and they tried to extradite him. A precautionary accident, shall we say?'

He glanced down at his watch, then looked at Hacht and Müller in turn. I felt the atmosphere of the room suddenly change. Müller, who had been shuffling restlessly behind me, now stiffened like a wild animal smelling blood. Hacht's chinless face took on the appearance of a schoolboy about to practise an unhealthy and forbidden vice. I could feel both of them hanging on Steiner's next words.

'Now, Mr Drayton. We've gone to some lengths to satisfy your curiosity. Now I want you to satisfy ours. Where have you left Frandl and his wife?'

I had no hope but still played for time as helpless men always do. 'If your organisation is so wonderful I wouldn't have thought it necessary to ask me that.'

He leaned forward on the table again. 'Before you get ideas of making a hero of yourself, Drayton, take notice of this. When

Inga Norgren told us this afternoon that you had gone on with the Frandls, I cabled my man in Narvik to watch out for you. When he cabled back that you hadn't arrived it was obvious you'd left the train at one of the intermediate sidings. So I instructed him to make enquiries about you to all members of the train staff, and if that failed to return along the line and enquire at each siding in turn. I sent that last message off nearly two hours ago and have a man waiting in town for the reply. So your answer will only hasten the inevitable.'

I was thinking of the old guard and Engestrom, and my mouth was dry. In the silence I could distinctly hear the hurried tick of a watch. Behind me Müller's breathing was harsh and anticipatory.

I had the frightening feeling none of them wanted me to talk. Hacht was fidgeting in his chair and the unholy glow in Steiner's eyes seemed to deepen and expand as the seconds ticked by.

'All right, Mr Drayton,' he said softly. 'Now I will show you how I break heroes.'

He made a sign to Müller. Before I could turn a crushing blow on the side of my neck paralysed my whole body. Müller then stepped in front of me. He was swinging a short, rubber truncheon in his hand. With his swollen lips pulled back in a grin from his decayed teeth he resembled a savage ape. His second blow was right in my face, and I felt as if my cheek had been crushed in. Through the blinding waves of pain I heard the high-pitched, excited laughter of Hacht.

The blow threw me backwards. Müller's next blow was across the stomach. I doubled forward, retching for air. The blows came quickly now, raining down on my back in the region of my kidneys. I rolled off the chair to the floor. As I pressed my hands on the floorboards to rise, Müller ground his heel down on my wrist. A boot thudded into my side as I fell back and pain stabbed my chest like a knife thrust. Crushing blows came down on my unprotected body from all angles. One struck me on the back of my head, there was a last explosion of pain and then I blacked out.

The shock of ice-cold water brought my senses back. Müller was holding me up in my chair and Hacht had a bucket in his hands. As I opened my eyes he let out a shrill laugh and threw another icy douche in my face.

I tried to straighten myself. My whole body was aflame with pain. Steiner was still sitting at the table opposite me but I had difficulty at first in focusing my eyes on him. His face and bald head had the appearance of a huge obscene melon floating over the table.

He gave me a full minute to recover. Then he said in the same soft voice. 'Well. Will you talk now?'

I said an unprintable word to him. It was followed by a blinding blow across the face from Müller's truncheon. Steiner laughed and waved him back.

'Müller is keen and a good honest journeyman, as you will admit. But I think this is work for the expert.'

He rose, motioning Hacht to fetch him a towel from the rack under the sink with all the imperiousness of a surgeon about to perform an operation. Hacht scuttled to fetch it with gleeful face. Steiner sent him back for a full pail of water and then approached me.

'It is odd what little attention the fascinating science of torture has received from the world's scholars. As a result the layman has the entirely mistaken idea that a brave man can withstand it. We experts know better, of course. You do realise I am an expert, I take it?'

He might have been asking whether I knew he was a qualified surgeon. I dared not speak in case I betrayed my fear. Hacht fetched rope and they bound me to the chair. Then they tipped it backwards until my shoulders were resting on the floor. Like an anaesthetist giving ether Steiner laid the towel over my face and pressed it down. Blind underneath it I fought the desire to cry out in fear. I heard the clank of the pail and a moment later water began soaking through the towel.

It ran up my nose and into my throat. As I choked for breath it was drawn into my lungs. The more I struggled the worse the agony became. My heart became a great frantic drum threatening to burst; my lungs felt as if they were tearing themselves apart. Blinding stars burst into blood-red embers before my eyes. I went through all the agony of death by asphyxia, right to the moment of unconsciousness. Then Steiner lifted the towel and my chair was stood upright again.

I was a long time recovering, coughing and sobbing for air. I could barely see Steiner through my swollen eyes, only hear his smooth mocking voice. 'Well, Mr Drayton. Are you having second thoughts sitting there? Or do you still have ambitions to save your beautiful Anna from a fate worse than death?'

All my resolution had gone. I was terrified of this devil from hell, and the acid smell of that terror was rising from my body. But there is a substitute for courage, as many men discovered during the war. Hatred. Mine was all-consuming.

'*Du Schwein!*' I sobbed, childishly using every foul German word I knew. '*Schwein-hund!* Unnatural, sadistic bastard!'

For a moment his eyes narrowed. Then he

243

smiled and went over to the sink. He returned and laid a pair of thin, long-nosed pliers in front of me.

He drew his chair nearer the table. 'You force me into bringing the first psychological factor into my persuasion, Mr Drayton. Until now you have believed your discomfort could be immediately ended if you chose to speak. Now that will not be the case. Before commencing I shall give you one chance to speak. Afterwards, no matter what you tell me, no matter how you scream for mercy, I shall complete what I am doing. Is that quite clear?'

Hacht slid along the table and stood in an ecstasy of expectation by his master's elbow. Steiner motioned to Müller, who untied my right arm and force my fingers flat on the table. I struggled to pull away but the water treatment had left me weak. Steiner prised up my second finger, examined the nail and nodded his satisfaction. He lifted the pliers and looked at me.

'You can see what I intend doing. You are going to get one chance to tell me where the Frandls are. If you do not answer I shall rip out that nail as slowly as I can. Now, Drayton – where are the Frandls hiding?'

I was struggling to remember the name of another of the intermediate stations. But fear was choking my wits.

Steiner shrugged and opened the pliers.

'Very well, the operation begins.'

The world opened up and dropped me into a hell of blood-red pain. Somehow, years later, it was over, with me vomiting all over myself and the floor. 'A little rest, perhaps,' I heard Steiner say. 'And a cigarette before the next operation.'

There was no false pride in me now. Pain was still searing up my arm like a white-hot flame. I wiped my mouth with my sleeve and took the cigarette, dragging smoke greedily into my sobbing lungs.

Steiner motioned Müller to swing my chair round. He then went over to the sink and selected a pointed piece of wire with a wooden base that resembled a paper spike. He pushed it among the burning logs in the hearth and then turned to me.

'I congratulate you, Mr Drayton. You make excellent sport. When you have fully recovered I am going to introduce the second psychological factor into your treatment – the knowledge that whatever I do to you now will leave you permanently maimed. I find this treatment usually breaks the strongest men.'

There was a subtle change in his voice and expression, something that brought me an obscure but terrifying warning. He bent over the hearth again, and his face and bald head shone redly in the firelight like some monstrous demon. Frantically I tried to remember the name of another siding. There was one, dancing tantalisingly on the periphery of my memory...

I was too tired ... it slipped away and was gone. In the silence, thick and anticipatory, my tortured mind found escape instead. Nothing of this could be real... The massive, fire-stained figure of Steiner, the hideous little marionette at his side, the ape-like Müller – none of them could exist in a world where the sky was blue and the grass green and women had soft hands like Anna.

Then Steiner pulled the red-hot spike from the fire and reality became more real than I had ever known it. As he rose and turned to me my desperate, scrabbling mind clutched at a name.

'All right,' I stuttered. 'That's enough. They're in Rensjön, sharing a cottage with a railway official.'

Hacht gave me a vicious, disappointed look. Steiner's expression did not change. 'Rensjön,' he nodded softly. 'Yes; that could be. Where is this house?'

'About a hundred yards down the road from the siding,' I lied. 'You can't miss it – it's the only house there built of brick.'

He eyed me for a long moment. Then he bent down and thrust the spike back among the logs. The firelight gave his face a satanic glow. Alongside me Müller coughed uneasily. His battered face was pale as he stared at Steiner, the bruises standing out livid against it. The warning bell rang louder in my mind and suddenly I remembered... Steiner kicking a puppy to death, unable to stop once he had tasted blood... Fear burst in my mind like a grenade as he drew the red-hot spike out again and approached me.

My voice was cracked and shrill. 'I've told you where they are. At Rensjön, in a brick cottage. What more can I tell you?'

His voice was deliberate, relishing the moment. 'You might be lying, mightn't you?'

'I'm not lying. I'm telling you the truth.'

He smiled, and my throat locked in terror. It was a smile straight from hell, and I knew this was how he had looked when he kicked the puppy to death. Nothing, not even the truth, could save me now.

CHAPTER 19

Steiner lifted the red-hot spike and as its heat made my eyes flinch a simper of delight came from Hacht. I was fighting a terror that threatened to turn me into a wreck of a man, and I have never cared to dwell on what might have happened had no interruption come. As it was Steiner threw away the wire spike and drew an automatic as sudden footsteps ran down the hall. Hacht, lightning-fast, already had a gun in his hand. As the door was thrown back I saw both of them relax. A man's voice addressed them in German.

'A message has just come through from Krämer, Herr Steiner. He's contacted the guard who was on their train. It took him some time because the guard had been relieved at Riksgränsen. The Frandls rented a cabin from the railway supervisor at Torneträsk. The guard says it's on the lakeside, no more than a couple of kilometres from the station.'

I was twisting and struggling with the ropes that bound me, trying to see who was speaking. As the man entered my field of vision I saw it was the driver who had

248

brought Inga and me from the station. I wondered dully how many more of Steiner's men were unknown to us.

Steiner nodded and turned back to me. 'So you were lying after all Drayton...' He made as if to pick up the wire spike and then paused. 'No,' he said softly. 'First things must come first. It will be interesting to see how you behave when the beautiful Anna is in our hands.' He turned to Hacht. 'You stay with him, Franz, while we bring in the other two. Keep him locked in the cellar.'

Hacht's expression was that of a schoolboy kept back to do lessons while the rest of his class went out on a picnic. Steiner, amused, put a hairy hand on his shoulder. 'Don't worry, Franz. We shall bring them here first. You shall not miss your sport.'

Müller untied the ropes that bound me and jerked me to my feet. He and Hacht led me to a flight of wooden stairs at the rear of the hall and pushed me down them. An open door with a cold draught blowing through it gaped at the bottom. As I tried to resist a kick caught me agonisingly behind the knee. I stumbled forward and crashed down a flight of stone steps into a cellar. As I lay there, half-stunned, I heard Hacht's shrill, insane laughter. Then the door slammed, a bolt was thrown, and their footsteps retreated up the hall stairs. A minute later a car engine started up at the front of the house.

I lay on the stone floor listening to the receding sound of the engine. Sweat and vomit were icy on my body, and my thoughts bitter beyond measure at the futility of my resistance. Then, as my strength began to return, self-pity lost ground to my fears for Anna and Carl. What had happened to me would be nothing to what Steiner would do to them. The thought of Anna in his hands was like a dagger-thrust, forcing my aching body upright.

By this time my eyes were accustomed to the dim light of the cellar. A dusty, old-fashioned wood stove, elaborately shaped and embossed, stood against one wall. Opposite it was a pile of faggots, covered in dust and spiders' webs. There was nothing more. A tiny window with a cracked pane high up on one wall drew my attention and I limped over to it.

I saw now where the draught was coming from. Its wooden frame was swollen, preventing it closing. But my excitement was short-lived when I realised it was much too narrow to take a man's body.

I stared out through it. It was built only a few inches above the level of the ground outside, giving me a cat's view of the garden. Night had fallen, but a rising moon showed me the dark silhouette of an outhouse. Apart from a few overgrown bushes and the dark, enclosing rectangle of the hedge I could see nothing else. As I stood there the distant sound of a train carried to me. I saw the time was 8.25 and guessed it was an empty freighter returning from Narvik. The sound of its movement across the tundra brought home to me as nothing else the deadly urgency of my position.

Although Steiner had probably not known it when he left, there was only the one local train that night to Torneträsk – the 9.45. He would not be able to leave before that time, but unless I caught the same train and somehow managed to reach Anna and Carl first nothing on earth could save them. So I had not only to escape: I had to escape soon or I could never reach the station in time.

The night air was cold, and the thin draught from the edge of the window stung my eyes. Turning, I made for the door. It was strong and tightly bolted. And beyond it, up the stairs, was Hacht with his thin, unhealthy face, his unnatural desires, and his gun. I dropped on the pile of faggots, trying to subdue my panic, trying desperately to think.

The beating and the pain I had suffered had affected my mind. Mental pictures of Anna in Steiner's hands kept erupting into it, destroying every idea the moment it was born. As the precious minutes slipped by it became harder and harder to keep panic back. One desperate idea kept reoccurring and at last I decided to try it. I would hammer on the door, call Hacht, and try to inveigle him into the cellar. If he came down I would then attack him with one of the faggots. With his gun and his quickness I knew the slimness of my chances, but I dared wait no longer.

I went over to the pile of faggots and selected the strongest one I could find. It was about to hammer on the door with it when the creak of an opening door came to me through the window, followed by quick, light footsteps on the gravel surround outside. Turning sharply I ran stiffly across to the window.

My heart hammered in my throat as I saw the black silhouette of a hand fumbling to open it. I believed it was Hacht, playing some unholy game. Then I heard a whispered voice.

'Mr Drayton. Can you hear me?'

It was Inga. Until that moment I had forgotten her existence. 'Yes,' I whispered back. 'What do you want?'

I could see her indistinct white face now, lowered to the level of the window. 'I must be quick – Hachts thinks I've come out to the toilet. When I go back I'm going to tell him I've heard men's voices down the road – sounding as if they're searchin' for someone. He'll go out to the front to take a look, and while he's there I'll unbolt the cellar door for you.'

I crushed down my wild surge of hope and made myself think of Hacht, planning a piece of entertainment with her as bait.

'Why?' I breathed. 'I thought you were helping them.'

There was no mistaking the vengeful undertone in her whispered reply. 'I could hear everythin' upstairs. I heard what they'd done to Max...'

Her whisper suddenly choked off in her throat. I listened and heard the creak of the door again. 'The toilet,' I whispered urgently. 'Hurry up, for God's sake.'

She ran for the outhouse, the thick grass on the way deadening her footsteps. The door creaked open and Hacht's dragging footsteps sounded on the gravel surround. I tensed against the wall as they paused outside my window. His thin, hateful voice came to me.

'Drayton. Are you there?'

'Where do you think I am?' I said, trying to strike the right mixture of sullenness and defiance. 'What do you want?'

I could hear his relief. 'I just wanted to remind you that it won't be long before your friends will be joining you. And then we shall bring you into the other room again. Don't think we've finished with you.'

I tried to make it easier for Inga. 'Don't be too sure of that, Hacht. Someone might find me first.'

His thin voice sharpened at once. 'What do you mean? Who knows you are here?'

'I'll leave that for you to find out.'

For a moment I could feel his uncertainty. Then he let out his high-pitched laugh. 'You're lying, Drayton. The girl said you didn't speak to anyone on your way here. Nobody knows and nobody can save you.'

I left it at that. When I refused to answer his gibes he gave a last mocking laugh and limped away. A few seconds later the door creaked and closed behind him.

Inga waited in the outhouse for another five minutes. Then I saw her leave it, a silhouette against the luminous sky. She had the sense not to return to my window, making for the door instead. It creaked open once more and then there was silence.

The next minute was pure agony. I had no idea what was happening in the house and was terrified Hacht had grown suspicious of her. Then, quite suddenly, I heard footsteps running down the wooden stairs outside. I ran to the door, heart hammering.

Precious seconds passed as she fumbled with the bolt. I stood helpless, sweat greasy in my clenched fists, praying she could release it before he returned. Then the door swung back.

There was no time for words. I ran up the stairs, dragging her behind me. The rear door of the hall was open, throwing a yellow oblong of light ahead of us. The front door was gaping open.

'How far did he go?' I panted.

'Right down to the road. Then he turned left…'

I wasted a couple of precious seconds whipping my weary mind into activity. I caught hold of her arm and pulled her into the back garden, putting my back to the creaking door. The cold night air bit through my wet clothes. The moon behind us was brilliant now, throwing a dense shadow of the house on the tangled grass.

'The hedge,' I muttered. 'We've got to get through it. He's certain to catch us if we go down to the road.'

She ran with me across the grass. The hedge was high and dense: heedless of scratches I hurled myself into it trying to find an opening. There was nothing: the branches were thick and impenetrable. Sobbing for breath I tore myself away, only to fling myself into it again a few feet nearer the house. Then Inga caught my arm. I paused and heard it too – the distant dragging footsteps on the gravel path in front of the house.

I knew now we could never break through the hedge without his hearing us and having us at his mercy. Neglect had allowed it to grow too high and impenetrable. Instead it was going to be a grim game of Blind Man's

Bluff, with death for the loser. I drew Inga back into the shadow of the house and waited.

Every sound carried in the cold, still air. We heard the footsteps take on a hollow sound and knew Hacht was climbing the wooden steps to the verandah. Then they went from our hearing as he entered the house.

Now I knew the hunt would start. He would see the open door of the cellar and move as swiftly as a crab after its prey. Inga was shivering and panting with fear. I pushed her round the side of the house and followed her. The hedge ran close to the house here: it kept catching our clothes and swinging back with a treacherous hiss of dry leaves.

We reached the side of the verandah at the front of the house. The tangled front garden lay ahead of us, all thirty yards of it silver-rimmed in the moonlight. It was deathly quiet. Sinister, because I knew Hacht had long discovered my escape. He would be like a ferret in his search for us, but he would never take his eyes off that front garden for more than a few seconds. He would know that tangled moonlit stretch of No Man's Land was our only way of escape, and if we let him flush us into crossing it he would pick us off like ducks against a dawn sky.

I struggled to think of a hiding place. Then

I remembered the toothless gaps in the verandah where planks were missing. Motioning Inga to stay still I crept along its base. Five yards from the corner I found what I wanted, a gaping black rectangle. I went back for Inga and motioned her to follow me.

I never took my eyes off the steps ahead as we crept forward, expecting Hacht to scuttle down them at any moment. But we reached the gap safely. I pushed Inga through it and followed myself. It was eerie under there. A spider's web brushed my face coldly as I twisted my aching body round. Strips of moonlight coming through the gaps between the planks gave a dazzling effect to the darkness. Further down, past a column of supporting timbers, a wider patch of light showed where other planks were missing.

I motioned Inga to move nearer the corner of the verandah. When she reached it I lay lengthways to it, my arms within reach of the opening, my eyes staring through a gap in the boards.

The moon-rimed tangled frontage of the house lay before me, ominously silent and empty. For a full minute my eyes never stopped searching it, my ears never ceased listening. Then, inevitably, the pain of my injuries returned, the thudding headache, the dull crushing ache in my back. My body cried for rest and for the second time that night a sensation of unreality made my head swim. Then I heard a low whimper of fear from Inga and it was all back again: the brutal need for me to drive myself on with all haste until I reached Carl and Anna. But I could not hasten here. I had to live, and all the odds were on Hacht.

The priceless seconds ticked by. I felt hysteria mounting in Inga and I gritted my teeth savagely together. Where was the little bastard? What was he doing?

Then I heard him. A scratching such as a rat might make along the side of the house, followed by a faint rustle of leaves. I shifted my position, tried to slant my gaze towards the corner of the verandah. From the corner of my eyes I saw Inga's paralysed white face. Terrified that she would crack, I reached out a hand and touched her reassuringly. As I did so I saw the farthermost strip of moonlight, no more than a foot beyond her, suddenly blink out. Instantly I realised what was happening. He had rounded the corner of the verandah and was creeping along its base. Another moonbeam blinked out, one that had been lying across Inga's arm, and she jumped as if a snake had touched her. I made frantic motions for her to keep quiet: he was now less than three feet from her.

Moving with infinite care I shifted round again until I was within striking distance of the rectangle of light that shone through the gap. Then, with legs drawn up under me

258

and hands poised to grab him, I waited.

Strip after strip of moonlight, blinking out only to reappear again, betrayed his silent approach. The one across my legs went dark, then the one across my body. My heart was thumping so hard now I felt he must hear it through the planking. Then his shadow, like a huddled embryo, lay in the rectangle of light before me.

My hands were waiting like claws to take him. He paused there, and the cosmic clock slipped a full cog or two, turning the seconds into hours. Then, unbelievably, he moved on.

Sick with disappointment I watched the shafts of moonlight blink off and on as he moved silently down the verandah. He reached the second gap and there his shadow suddenly seemed to swell. I gave a frantic warning wave to Inga and dropped flat on my face.

I lay stiff, an earth-smelling tuft of weeds pressed into my cheek, expecting to hear his gloating voice at any moment. But there was still only that devilish silence and the choked breathing of Inga behind me.

I think it was the interposed timbers and the dazzling effect of the moonbeams that saved us. He withdrew as silently as he had entered, his shadow passed round the other side of the steps, and vanished a few seconds later.

Reaction brought hysteria to Inga. She crawled up to the gap and struggled to pull away from me. 'This is our chance... We must get to the road before he comes back...'

I held on to her. 'No; he'll be expecting us to dash across there. We'd never make it.'

Her woollen frock was torn open at the throat, her ash-blonde hair was awry, and there was a streak of dirt across her white face. I guessed how much she was regretting having released me and felt sorry for her.

'Bear it a little longer,' I breathed. 'Sooner or later he's going to take a look through this gap. And then I'll have him.'

There was a faint sound from the far side of the verandah beyond the steps. It moved as I listened and I knew Hacht was creeping back again.

There was no time to get Inga back into the corner. I pushed her down at the other side of the gap, motioning frantically for her to control her sobs. Her eyes were huge and round with fear. To see past her I moved a yard to the left, trying to get an indication of his progress from the shafts of moonlight beyond the steps. At the moment there was no change in them and I knew he was still round the side of the house. Then, quite suddenly, Inga cracked.

She gave a moan of terror and was through the gap before I could grab her. In her high heels she ran awkwardly, stumbling

260

in the silver, tangled grass. I was just going after her when a pencil-thin flame stabbed out from the dark bushes on my left, followed by an explosion. I saw Inga stumble but run on. A small dark figure, as fast as a hunting spider, scuttled out from the side of the house. He must have thought I had gone with her because he ran obliquely across the grass. Bending low I threw myself through the gap after him.

His back was towards me as he fired again. The sound deadened my running footsteps. From the corner of my eye I saw Inga crumple and fall. He was about to fire at her again when he heard me and leapt round. I dived and the flame stabbed over my head. My outstretched arms caught his legs and bowled him over. Then I had my hands on him.

It was like holding some evil, animated marionette that kicked and bit and screeched. There was no mercy in me: they had given me this hate and it seemed right it should be used against them. His thin, twisted limbs were like dried sticks to my strength and as easy to break aside. I got him by the throat and I squeezed until he was dead.

He looked horrible lying there with black face upturned in the moonlight. I had never killed a man with my bare hands before and reaction made me vomit again. I went over unsteadily to Inga. She was badly hurt: there was a black stain both at the front and back of her frock. But she was in no pain and I was glad of that.

Her dazed eyes opened slowly as I lifted her head. 'It's all right,' I told her. 'He won't frighten you any more.'

I think her spine had been hit: her blond head was heavy and helpless on my arm. Her wide, suddenly innocent, eyes stared up at the moon-washed sky. She muttered something in Swedish and then her memory returned. 'He hit me in the back, with a stick, but I'll be all right in a minute. And then we can go...'

I nodded, holding her hand tightly. Her eyes turned to me. 'I'm sorry for what I did. But he said you were the one who'd get Max into trouble. And he gave me so much money...'

'Don't worry about it,' I said quietly. 'Everything's all right now.'

She had a moment of delirium. I pressed her hand, conscious that every extra second might cause two more deaths. She quietened down and her wide eyes wandered over the luminous sky. I had to lower my head to hear her last words. I was surprised to hear they were in German but I quickly understood.

'It's gettin' dark, Max. An' you know I'm frightened of the dark. Don't leave me,

Max. You know I never meant those things I said to you…'

She was dead a few seconds later. I would greatly have liked to do something for her, but the needs of the living were now more urgent. I went over to Hacht and picked up his automatic from the frosted grass. I searched his pockets, hoping to find a spare clip of ammunition, but they were empty. With one last glance at them, the weak and the wicked, I started back down the road to Kiruna.

CHAPTER 20

A bitter wind was sweeping across the heath, biting through my wet clothes. It was 9.07: I had thirty-eight minutes to reach the station. Not knowing how long it would take me on foot I ran hard down the road, at the same time wondering what use the train would be to me. Even if I could board it undetected Steiner was certain to see me leave it at Torneträsk. And in my present condition I couldn't hope to out-distance him in the woods and reach the cabin first.

I thought of the police. There was evidence for them now – grim evidence. Then I realised there was no time. Before I had found them, been given an interpreter, and was halfway through my story, Steiner would be on his way. I could do nothing but make certain I caught thc train and hope some idea would come to me then.

Running was agony. A vicious pain kept stabbing through my right side and my head throbbed as if a demon astride my shoulders were striking it rhythmically with a hammer. Car headlights came out of the darkness towards me. I stopped and waved frantically. My wild, dishevelled figure must have frightened the driver for he swerved and accelerated by.

Damning him, I ran on. The road sloped uphill all this time, a cluster of houses appearing as I reached the crest. I was forced to pause here for breath. Below me shone the lights of the town. Across the moonlit lake shifting lights round the foot of the mountain showed night work was in progress. The icy wind brought with it the distant, mournful hoot of a shunting diesel. The sound made me start. It was as though the idea had been trapped in my subconscious for some time and the siren had triggered its release. I remembered a Narvik-bound freight train had passed me on my arrival in Kiruna. I had looked at my watch and it had been 7.30. If it was true they ran punctually every hour another one was due in twenty minutes, fifteen minutes before the passenger train was due to leave. If I could reach the track in time and somehow board it I would reach Torneträsk before Steiner. Only by a few minutes, but minutes that could mean a difference of life and death to us.

No longer able to nurse my pain I ran wildly down the dark road. The outskirts of the town couldn't have been more than a mile away, but by the time I reached the first of a row of wooden houses my legs were shaking with weariness. The pavement here was unfinished: I stumbled and sprawled full length over a pile of stones. Picking myself painfully up I ran on, grateful that all the roads ran slightly downhill towards the lake, so keeping it in my vision. I knew that if I kept running towards it through the centre of the town I must eventually come out somewhere along the railway track.

The wooden houses began giving way to blocks of flats, then to neon-lighted shops. There was little night traffic on the roads, no sign of any taxis. Ahead of me a group of miners were clustered around a stall selling polser sausages. They must have thought my wild figure belonged to an escaping fugitive: one stepped out to grab my arm. I ran wide and past him. To my immense relief none of them followed, although they all stood staring after me.

I crossed a road and came to the fringe of a park that dropped steeply towards the lake. Scrambling down a grassy bank I found a path and ran down it, startling a young couple embracing under a tree. At intervals there were flights of stone steps. I fell down one, badly grazing my legs. Pain and dripping sweat blurred my vision. I came out of the park at the intersection of two roads. Below me was a long brick building that I recognised as the station. It was no use to me, particularly with Steiner there. I had to get further down the line where I could jump on the freight train unseen.

A road ran past the station, parallel to the track. I remembered it from our journey to Torneträsk earlier in the day: about half a mile long and lined with sheds and station- ary wagons. To reach it I had to run right past the station and could only hope the few blurred figures standing in the ticket-office entrance did not belong to Steiner or his two men.

The road curved left, then straightened, running straight alongside the track. I ran for fifty yards and then glanced back, into the station. There was an engine alongside the platform, coaches strung out behind it. The 9.45 was already in.

The sight gave me a shock. I glanced at my watch and saw it was just on 9.30. Feeling my sobbing lungs would burst at any moment I ran on. The track along this stretch was multi-lined for shunting purposes and il- luminated by arc-lights suspended on pylons. I knew I would be seen if I tried to board the train here, yet was afraid it might gather too much speed further down the line. I ran on until I found a spot where a high shed threw a dense black shadow across the track. Then I flung myself down and fought to get air into my retching, tortured body.

It was a full minute before I recovered and could take stock of my surroundings. The station was now hidden from me by sheds. Because of the brilliance of the arc-lights the only thing clearly visible was the track. With its tall pylons, its taut cables, and its steel lines all glinting silver, it stood out of the darkness like some fantastic stage set. It held my eyes as I waited for the massive freight train to thunder down it.

It was very quiet. I could hear the throbbing of an engine coming from across the lake: the moan of the night wind in the cables overhead. My sweat-soaked clothes turned icy on my body and I began to fear the freighter had already gone when I heard the drawn-out hoot of a siren. For a few seconds I could hear nothing more and feared it was only an engine shunting at the mine. Then I heard a distant approaching rumble and felt a tremor through the ground.

I rose to my feet, trying to penetrate the darkness beyond the arc-lights. I had no idea how I was going to board the train and yet the penalty of failure was something I dared not consider. In the agony of waiting even my pain was forgotten.

The massive train appeared suddenly in the arc-lights, dragging its sixty loaded wagons behind it. With its metal surfaces glinting dully and its power-packed wheels thrusting at the rails it gave an impression of weight and strength that was almost overpowering. It had not built up any great speed yet but the arc-lights exaggerated its movement, making me feel like an ant about to be crushed by a steam roller. Somehow I positioned my stiff and frightened body alongside the track. Forty yards, thirty, twenty – the gap closed with alarming speed. I crouched low, hoping its crew would not see me. The noise became deafening, the ground shuddered, a wave of hot oily air struck me in the face, and then the enormous thing was past. As the huge wagons rumbled after I searched them frantically for a foothold.

I saw each of them had a metal rail running around its ore-container and a small platform behind it to facilitate coupling. Without daring to think of the consequences of a slip I chose one and leapt at it.

My hands caught the rail cleanly enough but my feet slipped off the metal platform. For a moment I swung helplessly, feet inches from the grinding steel wheels. Drawing them up frantically I scrabbled for a foothold. My toes caught on a steel girder that ran over the wheels. I edge along this until I was standing on the metal platform. There I crouched, fighting off the effects of shock and fright.

When I recovered the lights of Kiruna were well behind. Holding on to the rail I stood erect. This brought my head above the level of the iron ore in the huge container. Ahead of me the rising and falling black wagons looked like a row of whales swimming in a moonlit sea.

At first I was content enough to stand there and rest. But soon I felt a new discomfort. We were travelling at speed now and the rush of icy air cut through my wet clothes like a knife. I was forced to twist sideways and crouch down behind the protection of the container. It was an insecure position: I could only hold on to the rail above me with one hand and in the yawning gap a few inches from my feet the huge wheels sang and sparked on the steel track.

We clattered over a bridge. A torrent of rushing water shone white in the moonlight. On the left mountains were closing in. Twenty minutes later we passed at speed through a small siding. It was in darkness and I could not see its name. A new danger was brought to me. At night most of the sidings would look alike and unless I kept careful watch I might easily miss Torneträsk.

The noise of the freighter took on a sterner note as we climbed more steeply. Mountains were black on either side of us now, laced with threads of silver waterfalls. We swung round a sharp bend and passed through another siding. Ignoring the wind I stood up. A name was suspended over the doorway of the darkened cabin and the moonlight was full on it. Rensjön. I had lost my timetable and struggled without success to remember its distance from Torneträsk.

There was a lake on our right. For a

moment I believed it the eastern end of Torneträsk until it disappeared among the mountains. The cold was agony now, my half-frozen body found more and more difficulty in balancing on the jerking platform and I became afraid of falling through the deadly gap at my feet.

Another tiny siding flashed by. I dragged myself upright. The wind was like ice-water, bringing tears streaming from my eyes. I peered back but the siding had already disappeared among the woods. Moonlit patches of snow streaked the mountains: over on the right a sheet of water glistened silver among the dark trees.

We crossed a gorge. The high white plume of a waterfall showed at its far end. The mountains on the right fell away and I saw the sheen of a large lake. I thought I recognised the view and felt renewed hope. Determined not to miss the next siding I stayed upright, ignoring the bitter wind.

Torneträsk came suddenly out of the tundra. I recognised the peculiar dome-shaped building, black against the luminous sky. My relief was intense but short-lived. The sides of the track here were lined with stones and pebbles. With so much at stake it would be fatal to jump, for although the train was still climbing its speed was considerable.

Yet I dared not wait long. Stiffly I lowered

myself down to the step beneath the platform, my hands clinging to the metal girder over the wheels. The step was only wide enough for my left foot, my right swung over the track. I knew I would only have the strength to cling there for a few seconds and prayed for a return of the bushes.

Tears streamed down my face, my leg trembled with the strain, and in desperation I was about to jump when suddenly the tundra closed in again. First a corridor of stunted trees, then a carpet of dark shrub that almost brushed the sides of the speeding wagons.

I crouched lower and waited. A large bush swept into view, black in the shadow of the racing train. I braced myself, timed its approach as best I could, and jumped.

My feet struck the track a few feet ahead of the bush, pitching me into it as if a giant hand had struck me. There was a wild snapping of branches. A blow in the stomach drove the breath from me, another numbed my arm. For a few seconds I lay coughing for breath, with the bitter taste of leaves in my mouth. I rose gingerly, afraid of finding a limb broken, but I appeared to have escaped with only cuts and bruises. The train was already far away, a long black snake sliding over the silver tundra. I turned back to Torneträsk.

Because of the bushes I could make progress only along the track itself. Running was difficult because of the awkwardly-spaced sleepers, but I stumbled on, knowing every second was whittling down my few minutes' lead on Steiner.

The going became easier when I reached the pebbled stretch. I found a path here, running diagonally behind the station. It led me to the track down which Lars had taken us that afternoon, and a moment later the jet and silver woods closed around me.

In the darkness I ran past the narrow path that branched off to the cabin and had to search back for it. At first I could hear nothing for the agonised gasp of my breathing and the pound of blood in my ears. Then a mournful hoot sounded as the approaching passenger train rounded a mountain bed. Fear gripped me, and I searched for the path like a maddened, hunted animal.

By the time I found it the clatter of the train was loud and clear as it approached the siding. I was delirious with exhaustion now and the path became a tunnel of horror in some diabolical fun-fair. Tree roots took life and clutched my feet, branches threw me gleefully from side to side. When the white shimmering blur of Torneträsk appeared through the trees I thought it another vision. Then, unbelievably, the woods fell away and the cabin stood before me.

CHAPTER 21

The door had been left ajar for me. I threw it back and stumbled inside. Warm air and the smell of cooking met me: it was like entering another world. Three more steps took me into the living room. Carl was lying on his bed just as I had left him, Anna was in a chair at his side. She had turned to greet me, her face glad with welcome. In the yellow light of the paraffin lamp it was like a domestic tableau, warm and secure...

Only to shatter like glass when Anna saw my condition. She gave a gasp of horror, leapt to her feet. 'John! What is it? What has happened?'

I fought for breath. 'Steiner... On his way here. You've got to leave ... at once.'

The shock seemed to freeze Carl to his bed. Anna caught hold of me, voice frantic. 'You! What have they done to you? Are you badly hurt? Tell me!'

I shook my head. 'No. But never mind me... Get your coats. Hurry, for God's sake... They'll be here any minute now.'

Instead of bringing me relief my safe arrival brought me hysteria – a frantic fear that Steiner would catch us yet and make everything in vain. I caught hold of Carl, dragged him brutally from his bed. 'What are you lying there for? Can't you hear what I'm saying?'

It was Anna, resisting me, that brought me back some measure of control. 'But where are they? You must tell us more so we know what to do.'

I threw Carl's coat around him, thrust the remainder of his clothes under his arm. 'They've come on the train. And it got in minutes ago. They'll be halfway to the cabin by this time. We'll have to take the path along the lake.'

Her shocked eyes were on Carl. My brutal news had brought on a reoccurrence of his attack: he was trembling from head to foot. He would not last a mile in the woods, but we had to get out of that death-trap of a cabin. I pushed them through the doorway and followed them outside.

An icy circle of moonlight lay around us, like a spotlight on a stage. Beyond it crouched the woods, black and full of whispering things. We stumbled round the cabin towards the lakeside path. Something tugged at my mind, trying to show me a better way of escape. It stung like a thorn but I was too pain-drugged to recognise it. Then Anna turned to me.

'The boat, John! If we take that they cannot follow us.'

That was it – the boat. I ran to it and tore off the tarpaulin. Its bows were about six feet from the water's edge. I kicked away two pieces of timber supporting it and ran round to the stern. In my weakened state it seemed cruelly heavy. Anna pushed with me and this time it moved a few inches, pebbles scratching along its planks.

Carl added his pitiful strength to our efforts and its bows touched the water. A last desperate heave, a splash, and it was riding gently alongside the bank.

We helped Carl into it. Anna turned back to the cabin. I caught her arm. 'Where are you going?'

She pulled away. 'We must have blankets or we'll freeze to death out there. And we shall need food too.'

I realised she was right but it took all my courage to run back with her. I tore blankets form the bunks, slinging them over my arm while Anna threw tins of food and bread into her grip. I heard a cry outside and my breath locked in my throat until I realised it was Carl urging us to hurry.

'Your gun,' I panted. 'Have you got it?'

In the confusion of the room she could not find it. Remembering Hacht's automatic in my pocket I pushed her out into the moonlight, half-expecting a rush of bodies to overwhelm us.

Carl was muttering feverishly for us to

276

276

hurry. I threw the blankets into the boat, then turned to help Anna. I felt a hundred eyes were watching us from the dark woods, gloating and waiting to pounce the moment we tried to pull away. As Anna jumped aboard a dried twig snapped like a pistol shot in the woods, followed by the startled, high-pitched cry of a ptarmigan. The urgent whir of its wings as it flew over us gave me a surge of intense panic. I shoved hard at the boat, floundering in the icy water as it ran away with me. I waded after it and Anna helped me aboard. I grabbed the oars and dropped them into their locks. The footrest was askew but there was no time to adjust it. I swung the oars out and pulled with all my strength. The boat quivered and then surged out on the silver lake.

The feeling of exposure out there was frightening. I felt like a hunted insect crawling across an illuminated leaf. At any moment I expected a pistol flame, like the tongue of a chameleon, to flash out from the dark shore and destroy us. I heaved on the oars without any thought of direction – every ounce of remaining strength going into the task of widening the gap between us and the shore. When I collapsed over the oars, retching for breath again, we were two hundred yards out and, for the moment at least, safe from Steiner.

A hand tugged at my arm. I raised my aching head, to find Anna had crept forward in the boat towards me. Her eyes were bright and moist in the moonlight, full of a hundred things she wished to say and could not because of Carl.

'You must go and rest. I can row the boat now.'

I was afraid to look at her. Now that the immediate crisis was over reaction was clawing at my defences and I wanted her as much as I wanted life at that moment. Not to love physically but to hold on to: to feel the softness of her hands and to reassure myself there was another side to life but brutality and pain.

Her expression told me she knew my needs. 'What did they do to you?' she asked again, unsteadily. 'Are you badly hurt?'

I shook my head. 'No. But I must rest. We should be safe out here for a while.'

I dragged myself to the stern. Carl made room for me on the seat but I felt too unsteady to sit there, slumping down instead on the bottom of the boat. Carl took off the blankets Anna had given him and tried to wrap them round my wet body. His action brought an odd rush of tears to my eyes, a yardstick by which I could measure my weakness. I accepted one and lay back. It was luxury to lie there and do nothing. I felt the strong pull of the oars and heard the gurgle of water beneath me as Anna pulled us yet further from the shore. I closed my eyes and instantly felt myself slipping into unconsciousness.

Carl's anxious voice dragged me back. 'Do you feel able to tell us a little what happened, John?'

Anna gave a murmur of protest. 'Let him rest, Carl. He can tell us later.'

One of Carl's legs was resting against my shoulder: through it I could feel the incessant trembling that was racking his body.

'I'm sorry, *Liebchen*. But we know nothing yet – not even where we ought to row this boat.'

Somehow I lifted my head. The cabin had merged into the dark shore but the blunt promontory told me its position, a good half-mile to our right. I saw now that the night wind and a strong current were taking us westwards.

My knowledge of the territory was very sketchy, and without a map it was difficult to decide which way to take. I knew Torneträsk was over a hundred kilometres long, lying like a bent finger between Kiruna and Narvik, and that we were approximately halfway between the two towns. I also knew Torneträsk ended well north of Kiruna, making a perilous land journey unavoidable if we went in that direction. But I had no idea how far it extended westwards, and the chance, however slim, that it might extend as far as the Narvik Fjord was more than enough to decide me. I knew that Steiner would probably be able to keep pace with us along the shore, but at the same time the current would not make things easier for him.

'I think we ought to keep going this way,' I muttered. 'It's easier than backing the current and no more dangerous.'

None of us wanted to pass by the cabin again, not even at a distance, and they nodded without argument. As I dropped back Carl laid a pleading hand on my shoulder.

'Do you feel strong enough to tell us what happened, John?'

I was dreading telling them. I played for time, lifted myself up on one elbow. 'Give me a cigarette first.'

He reached down and put one in my mouth. He struck a match for me, but suspense was shaking his hand so much I had to grip his wrist to guide it. Anna stopped rowing, her white face watching me.

I sucked smoke deeply into my lungs. 'It was Inga,' I said. 'Steiner bought her. She let me believe Kleinberg was up here. Instead it was Steiner, waiting for us to enter his web.'

Carl jerked as though he had been stabbed. Anna leaned forward incredulously. 'But how did he get to know her?'

'Because of me,' I said bitterly. 'Like a fool I'd forgotten our hotel in Stockholm was on an island. All he did that day was drop a man at each of the three bridges and watch for us to cross them.'

Carl's face was like a death-mask. 'But that means he traced Kleinberg too. It means Kleinberg is dead.'

I sucked in smoke again, nodded. 'I'm afraid he is.'

Frozen with shock, they stared blindly at one another. In the moonlight, grey-faced, they looked as if they had died themselves. My task was to bring them back to life. I spoke hurriedly.

'It isn't as bad as you think. Kleinberg wouldn't have been any use to you. He was a crook himself – he'd once been one of Steiner's men. The men who called at the house that night and were shot by Steiner weren't his friends – they were special Federal agents going to arrest him. That was why Kleinberg never went to the police after you released him. And that's why he would never have gone as a witness to Germany, no matter what we'd offered him.'

I could see the horror breaking in Anna's eyes as she stared at me. 'You say it is not as bad as we think... *Mein Gott*, do you know what you're saying? All our money gone, our strength, our hopes... And for nothing...'

I had never seen her break down before.

281

Her bowed body suddenly looked small, crumpled over the oars. It was her suffering that brought life back to Carl.

'Don't cry, *Liebchen*. You have always been so brave, have always fought so hard. You mustn't break up now...' Then, as hopelessness returned, his plea became a low, gritted cry of pain. 'Oh, *Liebchen;* what have I dragged you into? Why have I spoiled your life like this?'

His words checked her sobs just as her distress had rallied him. 'You must not say such things... I have been happy. I would change nothing...'

I interrupted them quickly. 'Things aren't as bad as you think. Before I escaped I learned where the two men Steiner killed were buried. Now we know who they were it will be easy for the police to identify them. And when they've done that they will be as keen as we are to have Steiner re-tried.'

They had both started and glanced at one another. Fear was in their glance – fear of being betrayed again by false hope. Carl turned his haggard face to me.

'Does Steiner know you found this out?'

I hesitated. 'Yes. It was he who told me.'

His eyes dulled. 'Then it is no use. Now you have escaped he will realise the danger and have the bodies moved elsewhere.'

The danger existed but I argued against it. 'He won't find that easy to do. He can't do it himself – he and Müller and a third man are somewhere on that shore at the moment. If we could make contact with the German police they could have the bodies exhumed before he could make a move.'

Carl shrugged despairingly. 'If. But how?'

'Through the Swedish police.' My voice was eager. I was thinking of Hacht and Inga, forgetting Carl didn't know they were dead. 'Don't you see how the situation has changed? If we can only reach them we have evidence to make them take action.'

He stared at me, puzzled. 'What evidence? We have nothing to make them hold Steiner. And while they are questioning us, he will have all the time in the world to move the bodies. He can go back himself or send Hacht.'

There was grim satisfaction in giving him this news. 'Not Hacht, Carl. He's the evidence. He shot Inga and I killed him. His body is lying in the front garden of a lonely house in Kiruna.'

They both stared at me, wide eyed and awed. 'You killed Hacht,' Carl muttered. *'Lieber Gott;* what have you done? Steiner will go crazy for blood.' Fear dug its claws deeply into him, swinging him round to stare at the dark shore. 'He'll know he must keep us from talking. And this is his opportunity, while we're miles from anywhere. If he once gets a boat we won't have a chance.'

His words had an immediate effect on me. Until now reactions had made the great shimmering lake seem a haven of refuge, but now that illusion burst like a bubble. Somewhere along its shores there must be other boats, waiting as ours had waited for the occasional visits of the owner, and if Steiner discovered one we were as good as dead. His great strength, aided by his two men, would bring him upon us like a shark on a wounded turtle.

Anna made no protest when I crawled painfully forward and took an oar from her: an indication the sense of peril and urgency had descended on her too. About five miles to the west a long mountain spur jutted out halfway across the lake. If we could round it tonight we might at least be out of Steiner's sight for a while. We pulled together on the oars and the boat moved forward again.

CHAPTER 22

Rowing was agony for me: each time I pulled on the oar pain jabbed like a knife in my side. To some extent I could conceal the pain but not my exhaustion which soon returned. Anna stopped rowing and turned to me.

'If we are to escape we must be sensible. I am the strongest of us all tonight. Leave me to row until I'm tired, and then perhaps you can take an oar again.'

I realised she was right, lay on the bottom of the boat, and was asleep in seconds. The loud thump of an oar and an icy douche of water in my face awaked me. Struggling to my elbows I saw Carl fumbling to replace his oar in its lock. He was seated alongside Anna and from the raggedness of their rowing it was obvious they were both exhausted.

I glanced at my watch and saw it was nearly half-past one. Protesting at having been left to sleep for so long I told them I would take over. Anna, tight-lipped and breathing heavily, shook her head. 'Not both oars,' she panted. 'You can take Carl's place.'

I helped him into the stern and took his

seat alongside Anna. Her face was drawn with pain. I glanced down at her hands and started. As I tried to take one of them she pulled it sharply away.

'Let me look at your hands,' I insisted. For a moment it seemed she was going to refuse. Then she held them sullenly out. The skin on the palms was raw and wrinkled where huge blisters had burst. I pointed to the rear seat. 'You've done enough for one spell. Take a rest now.'

She hesitated, gave an exclamation of impatience, and joined Carl. I glanced around. The shore seemed very close, giving me a shock until I realised we were standing off the end of the long mountain spur. Unless Steiner had followed its long and exhausting coastline we ought to be well out of his sight by this time.

The knowledge heartened me and gave me strength to row for another fifteen minutes. The lake widened again as the promontory fell away. A small island lay ahead, black in the moonlight. Waves of weakness began surging through me and I knew I couldn't go on much longer. Carl was lying back in the seat with closed eyes. The night had taken its toll: his face looked waxen. I caught Anna's anxious eyes and nodded.

'I don't think we can go on much longer without rest and food. I think we'd better make for the island.'

Neither of them made any protest and I turned the bows towards it.

I stopped rowing and steadied my right oar in the water. The boat pivoted on it and slid sidewards under overhanging willows. Twigs scraped its side: we thudded gently against a grass-matted bank. It was dark after the moonlight, like entering a cave. I held on to a branch while Anna jumped out. We secured the boat to a tree and then helped Carl ashore. His shaking body was ice-cold and I found something ominous in his making no protest at our assistance. We found a small clearing behind the willows and helped him down to the rimed grass. Anna tucked blankets around him, and then turned the pale oval of her face up to me.

'He's half-frozen. Can we make a fire for him?'

He heard her and made an immediate protest. 'No, *Liebchen*. Steiner will see it. I will be all right when I've had a short rest.'

Her pleading eyes stayed on me. I nodded and turned away. 'Wait here. I won't be long.'

I pushed my way through a tangle of bushes deeper into the island. Trees rose all around me, black silhouettes against the moon-washed sky. My feet sank into a soft pocket of pine needles. From somewhere nearby I heard the squeak of a startled animal: the scurry of it through the dry leaves.

Then the silence returned, the ear-aching silence of the Arctic. Rocks appeared, grey in the filtered moonlight. Over to my left the ground sloped more steeply. I followed it and came to a craggy ridge, covered in bushes and clinging pines. On the north side it fell away in a series of rock terraces into the lake. Satisfied I returned to Anna.

'There's a ridge at the other side of the island. I think we can light a fire behind it.'

Carl protested again. 'It will still throw up a glow. Don't be a fool, John. I don't need it.'

I helped him to his feet. 'We do, even if you don't. So let's not argue about it.'

Anna followed us, bringing the blankets and the food. We found a wide ledge on the north side that was quilted with pine needles and made Carl comfortable on it. Then Anna and I searched for fuel. It was not difficult: there was plenty of dried wood on the island. Soon we had a brisk fire going.

We found six tins in the grip, three of baked beans, the others a miscellaneous collection of soup, steak, and vegetables. There was also a loaf and a half of bread. We decided to eat the beans and keep the other tins for a future meal. With no utensils to heat them in, the best we could do was open the tins and plant them among the embers at the end of the fire.

The fire was burning well now and infinitely comforting: I longed for nothing more than to lay my aching body down in front of it. But before anything else I had to remove the filth from my clothes. Borrowing a blanket from Carl I went back to the boat where I could keep watch on the stretch of water Steiner had to cross to reach us. Its width was deceptive in the moonlight but I estimated it at about two miles. I searched it carefully but could see nothing suspicious among its dancing waves. I then climbed a hillock to see if the fire were visible. In spite of the moonlight there was a faint glow: I could only hope it was invisible from the mainland. Then I stripped off my outer clothes and washed them as best I could in the icy water. Shivering with cold, with the blanket wrapped around me like a toga, I returned to the fire and laid the wet clothes before it.

The beans were simmering now. Anna gave us a tin each and we ate them as best we could, pouring them out on slices of dry bread. Simple though the meal was, it brought some life back to our exhausted bodies. Its effects were paradoxical, making us more sensitive to the dangers of leaving the two-mile stretch of water unobserved. I saw Anna fastening up her windcheater and I rose quickly to my feet. She turned on me angrily.

'No. It is something I can do as well as either of you, and you are both half-dead for sleep. Stay there by the fire. I shall call you at once if I see anything.'

Carl protested too, but she was as curt with him. She took the blankets we no longer needed and slipped away. I watched her go, then felt Carl's eyes on me. I wondered for a moment how much my expression had given me away.

'Let her go, John,' he said quietly. 'She won't be happy otherwise. We can relieve her later.'

I nodded. 'I'll go as soon as my clothes are dry.' As I lay back his voice came again.

'You still haven't told us the details of what happened in Kiruna, John. Will you tell me now?'

I told him as much as I thought fit. His wincing face made it clear he guessed the rest. When I finished he dragged himself towards me and held out his hand. 'I will not ask why you did this for us, my friend. But I thank you from the bottom of my heart.'

I had grown to respect this man, to admire the ceaseless battle his courage waged against his shattered nerves. But I was wondering what his first sentence meant, and because Europeans believe love is finite and indivisible and I was in love with Anna, guilt made my voice abrupt.

'It was to my advantage to hold out as long as possible. I was certain they'd kill me as soon as they knew. Now get your head down or you won't be fit to travel at dawn. I'll take the next watch.'

His smile was warm and comradely. 'An hour each, John. Don't let me sleep longer.'

We lay silent after that. The red firelight stained the terraces and trees and shone like blood in the water below. Carl, wearied beyond measure by his illness and the events of the night, dropped off almost at once into an exhausted sleep. Pain and the knowledge I must soon relieve Anna kept me awake. As we lay side by side a sense of comradeship for Carl deepened in me. We had much in common, he and I, fearing the same man, loving the same woman, perhaps sharing an equal unhappiness... For he was married to her in name only and I knew she could never be my wife. These thoughts and others made the vague jealousy I sometimes felt for him slough away like a dead and untenable skin.

I waited until my clothes were reasonably dry and slipped them on. The rest had stiffened me and I was in considerable pain, particularly when I breathed. I built up the fire and then went to relieve Anna.

I found her some distance from the boat, on a pine-covered ridge of rock overlooking the southern channel. She was staring across the water, the blankets tucked around her, her thoughts far away. Below her ripples ran like quicksilver into the shadow of the bank. A twig snapped under my foot. She started, then gave a cry of protest.

'Why are you here? You've been badly hurt today; you should be sleeping.'

Painfully I climbed the ridge. Her wide eyes never left me. I reached her side, looked at her. She gave a sudden, helpless sob and threw herself into my arms. Her lips were fierce on my bruised face, as if trying by their very fervour to prove I was still a creature of flesh and blood. Words poured from her in a wild torrent.

'*Lieber Gott,* how I was frightened tonight when you entered the cabin... It was like being taken back many years. I thought you were dying ... if you had died I would have died myself. I wanted to hold you, to dress your wounds, to cry over you... Let me help you now, *Liebchen*. In the boat I noticed you kept holding your side. Show me where the pain is.'

She was like a frantic mother in her anxiety. There was a hollow filled with pine needles a few yards away, in the shadow of the trees. She threw the blankets down there and made me lie on them. Opening my shirt she probed for the injury. She found it and lifted her head.

'It is possible a rib is cracked. It must be

bandaged tightly.'

She used my shirt, ripping it laterally into a single strip. Over it she bound a second strip we managed to tear from one of the blankets. The relief was immediate. She helped me back into my pullover and windcheater, then eased me down on the blankets. I was shivering, the exposure to the night air had chilled me again. She tucked the blankets around me, then took my hand from which Steiner had ripped the nail. She pressed it to her lips: I felt tears fall on it.

'That you should suffer this for us... I have prayed it would not happen.'

I needed her badly. I hadn't recovered yet from the shock of the torture, and the contrast of her solicitous hands to the hellfire of Steiner and his devils was too much. There was a wetness on my face.

'Anna,' I muttered, reaching out to her.

She knelt beside me for a long moment, a lovely jet and ivory statue. Then she pressed my hand to her lips and rose. 'Wait for me here,' she said quietly. 'I shall not be long.'

The night was suddenly empty without her. I lay listening to the wind, sighing like a lost spirit among the pines. Then I heard her footsteps again, driving my loneliness back.

'I have built up the fire,' she told me. 'It will last the night now. Carl is comfortable and is fast asleep.'

She lay alongside me beneath the blankets, her body pressed to mine. For a long time that was enough, to hold her and feel the warmth of her womanhood bringing back my strength. Only when she felt that strength return did she move, taking my hand and pressing it to her heart.

She was grave and gentle in her love that night. It was not for her, it was to win back my confidence in a world that for a while had seemed overwhelmingly harsh and brutal. When it was over her face was peaceful, and I knew it was one time she felt no remorse.

We lay together while the moon floated towards the mountains like a great silver bubble. It vanished behind them and for a while the lake grew dark. Anna kept watch, stroking my head until I fell asleep. When I awoke she was no longer with me. Over the mountains to the east the sky was turning light and the dawn song of the birds was growing on the island. It was cold: I was shivering as I went to the boat. As I was piling the blankets into it, Anna returned.

'I went to see if the fire was all right,' she told me. 'Carl was still sleeping: I think the rest has done him some good. He is awake now, looking after our breakfast.'

Light was coming quickly now, bringing the autumn colours back. The shore opposite took shape and definition. It swept westwards in a series of undulations, dense with woods and backed by snow-capped mountains. There was no sign of habitation or life but we knew Steiner was somewhere among the woods. Anna voiced my thoughts.

'Either he has not managed to find a boat and so could not follow us, or he doesn't know where we are. But he will see us the moment we leave.'

'I'm hoping he hasn't found a boat,' I told her. 'And in that case the sooner we get away the better.'

I stayed to watch while Anna brought me a sandwich of hot steak. After eating it I was going to fetch Carl but she protested. 'I'll see to him: you must conserve your strength. In any case, I think he can manage without help this morning.'

They reached me ten minutes later. Carl, although still pale and unsteady, was walking unaided. His quietness as we prepared to leave told me he was hurt at having been given no part in the night watch.

We put the grip containing the remainder of the food into the boat and were ready to leave. The eastern sky was a great slash of crimson now: I noticed Anna give a shudder as she looked at it. The dread of what the day might bring was in us all, bringing a reluctant slowness to our movements. Rightly or wrongly, hidden from view and with a two-mile moat around us, we felt safe on the island. But out on the lake we would be visible for miles and could be followed with ease.

At the same time, if we were to reach the police before Steiner caught us, and if he were still hunting for a boat, every minute was precious. Carl insisted on taking an oar and to avoid hurting his feelings further neither Anna nor I protested. I dug my oar into the bank and pushed to get way on the boat. An outraged black-throated diver broke cover and fled into a clump of rushes. A minute later we were out exposed in the centre of the lake with the island fifty yards behind us.

CHAPTER 23

A draughty wind was blowing down the lake, making us shiver. Our eyes were on the shore, afraid that at any moment a boat would dart out and make towards us. As the minutes passed and nothing happened our nerves began to relax. It proved a mixed blessing, because without the stimulus of fear we became conscious of our physical condition. Pain caught my breath each time I pulled on the oars, and Carl's rowing was ragged and laboured. The boat swung unevenly but when Anna looked at me anxiously I shook my head. For Carl's morale as well as his feelings I felt we had to let him take some part in our efforts to escape.

The first arc of the sun appeared over the eastern mountains, shining right in our eyes. It brought a final burnish to the autumn colours: the distant mountain slopes became stretches of smouldering fire. To our right a heron spotted a fish and dived with barely a splash beneath the glistening water.

The silence was complete but for the splash of water and the creak of oarlocks. Carl was beginning to pant for breath. I eased my stroke, waited a few more minutes, then ceased rowing and looked at Anna.

'You must be feeling cold. What about a change-over? We shall have to keep this up for a long time, so there's no point in overdoing the first shift.'

I made her wrap handkerchiefs around her blistered hands before she took over the oar. As I was tying them we heard the far-off familiar hoot of a train. We stared at one another, then at the south shore from which the sound came.

'It's one of the freight trains,' I muttered. 'The track must continue along the lake after all.'

We waited, listening. At first there was nothing but the lap of water against the side of the boat. Then we heard the train's clatter, moving from east to west. We could see no sign of it, but the fact that the track was close to the shore gave us all the same thought. Somewhere along its length would be a siding which would have telephone communication with Kiruna and Narvik.

My hope was tempered at once by reality. As far as reaching the railway went we were no better situated than we had been in the cabin the previous night. By this time Steiner would have seen us and certainly realised the necessity of keeping between us and our one lifeline to escape. And our slow progress would make this task easier for him.

Yet the knowledge that the track was there heartened me until I had another disturbing thought. If similar sidings to Torneträsk were spaced along it, was it not possible that one of their resident staff might be an amateur fisherman like Engestrom and have a boat moored alongside the lake?

I said nothing, but the thought put an extra urgency into my rowing. With Ann pulling alongside me we made better time. Miles ahead another promontory reached out into the lake. We kept scanning the shore in the forlorn hope of seeing a village or hamlet near enough for us to risk a landing, but it remained wild and uninhabited. The sun was well up now. I was sweating freely and the pain in my side was severe, forcing me to let Carl relieve me for a while.

We made two more changes at the oars and heard the distant clatter of another freight train before we reached the promontory, passing no more than a hundred yards from its northerly shore. It was shallow, covered in bushes and dwarf trees, and was a blaze of hot colour. I thought I saw one or two paths running among the trees but there was no sign of life.

The promontory was wide and it took us twenty minutes to round it. It was mid-morning now and we were all nearly spent. I could breathe only with difficulty; Anna, although as tight-lipped and resolute as ever, was obviously suffering greatly from her blistered hands; and Carl was in no state to relieve either of us. Feeling the promontory might hide us for a while from Steiner's view I motioned to Anna to stop rowing.

The boat drifted gently on the slight westerly current. Anna and I leaned over the oars, regaining our breath. The lake was very wide at this point. South-westwards a wide and lush valley lay between a break in the mountain range. My attention, however, was drawn to Carl. He was staring westwards, over our heads. I turned and stiffened. In the far distance, six or more miles away, the mountains suddenly swept inwards and appeared to enclose the lake. Anna followed our gaze and her face turned pale.

'It might only be the mountain spurs interlocking,' I muttered. 'The lake looked much the same last night before we rounded the first promontory. We'll probably find a way through when we get there.'

Yet the thought that we might have come all this way only to be trapped made our hearts sink. Our weariness suddenly became a heavy burden, and we sat in silence as the boat drifted slowly westwards. At last I roused myself, found I had a few cigarettes left and handed them round. I was reaching forward to give Carl a light when Anna gave an exclamation. 'What is that? Over there in the valley!'

I stared round, and over to the south-west saw a building of considerable size standing alone in the valley. It had been hidden from us previously by a low hill, but now our drift had brought it into view. Although as yet a considerable distance from us, it gave the appearance of being some kind of hostel. (I learned later our guess was right. The valley was the Abisko nature reserve, and the building a hostel for mountaineers and nature-lovers.) One thing was certain from its size – it would be in telephone communication with Kiruna. I grabbed my oar and turned to Anna. 'Come on. This is our chance.'

She swung back her oar, then paused. 'What about Steiner?'

'He may not have reached it yet… But in any case it's not much more than three hundred yards from the shore. You and Carl must stay in the boat while I make a run for it.'

Two, perhaps three miles to go, then rest, food, safety… I forgot even my pain as we pulled on a diagonal course for the shore. We rowed for perhaps five minutes before Carl reached forward and checked us. We followed his eyes to a point on the shore east of the hostel. A curiously-shaped rowing boat, pointed at both ends, had suddenly darted out from a hidden cove. It was cutting diagonally across the lake on a course that must intercept us well before we reached the hostel. As yet it was too distant for its occupants to be identified but the same fear was on all our faces. Carl gave voice to it.

'It is Steiner. He has got the boat from the hostel.'

Anna looked at me. I hesitated. 'We can't be sure. It might be anyone, visitors or fishermen...'

Carl shook his head, voice dull with despair. 'No. Look at the way he has changed course now you have stopped rowing.'

I saw he was right. The boat had turned and was now heading straight at us, a dancing black speck on the sunlit water. To the right of it the distant hostel stood alone among the red-gold trees, a haven we could no longer reach.

The temptation to turn round and flee across the lake was almost irresistible, but I knew we had to fight it at all costs. The northern bank was utterly desolate, and once there we would be entirely at Steiner's mercy. Nor was the shallow promontory we had passed any use to us. Even if we were not intercepted on our way back to it, Steiner could land further south and cut us off from the mainland. Our only hope was to head westwards. If we could avoid interception and strike the coast where it began its northern encircling sweep we might be able to double back on foot to the hostel.

At first we rowed frantically, fear finding a

welcome outlet in every wild heave of the oars. I found the bows were swinging too far towards the centre of the lake as my extra strength made itself felt. I steadied myself, lowered my rate of stroke. If we were going to reach the shore we had to conserve our energy.

'Slower,' I panted to Anna. 'We've a long way to go yet.'

Realising our intention the other boat had changed direction again, trying to drive us out across the lake. It was agonisingly difficult to decide on the right course to take. If we struck the coast too far north Carl would never make the journey to the hostel. On the other hand, if we cut the angle too fine, Steiner would either catch up with us on the lake or be upon us before we had fled a hundred yards into the woods. We could only watch his boat coming on our port quarter and change course accordingly.

Although still distant it was approaching rapidly. Its three occupants could be seen now, two of them rowing. On the distant shore the hostel slowly came opposite us, peaceful among the trees. For a moment I had the wild idea of jumping up and waving for help. I crushed the impulse back. In the unlikely event of being noticed – we would be little more than a speck among the waves to a casual observer – there was no chance of help reaching us before Steiner. And every stroke of the oars was precious: the vectors were shortening remorselessly, driving us further and further north. Beside me I could hear Anna's harsh breathing. She was tugging the life from herself and Carl's agonised eyes turned pleadingly from her to me. Abruptly I stopped rowing and nodded to him.

'All right, come on. Quickly.'

Anna was half-delirious with exhaustion and struggled to continue rowing. I caught hold of her, held her tightly. 'A short rest,' I gasped. 'Go on. You'll be all the stronger for it.'

Her eyes stared wildly at me as I pushed her past Carl. The boat lurched unsteadily. She could not reach the seat, dropping down on the bottom of the boat. Her face was pale and her breasts heaved as she fought for breath. I could do nothing to help her: the pain in my side was exquisite. If I had been alone in the boat I could never have driven myself on. As it was I somehow got the oar swinging again, closing my eyes to the agony of it. Time became meaningless, and we rowed as the galley slaves of the Pharoahs must have rowed when the overseer's scourge was tearing the skin from their backs. Anna took over from me when I was exhausted, then I from Carl. By this time the gap between the boats had shrunken terrifyingly. I could recognise each figure clearly now: Müller and the stocky man at the oars, Steiner crouched forward in his seat, urging them on. As I watched he threw off his jacket and motioned them both astern. The long-prowed boat seemed to leap forward as he bent his enormous strength to the oars.

But the shore was close now, no more than two hundred yards away. A pebbly beach sloped back to a shallow bank. A hillside rose behind it, densely carpeted in trees. Beyond it were the mountains, barren and snow-capped. We were well past the valley now and the hostel was hidden by a mountain spur.

Steiner was between three and four hundred yards away, his shirt gleaming white in the sun as he rowed. As I watched he turned the sharp prow of his boat a good twenty-five degrees south. Realising he could not catch us on the lake he was going to make certain of cutting off our route to the hostel.

Anna's oar struck bottom. The boat heeled, then steadied. We shipped oars and slid forward, keel grating over the pebbles. I leapt out into the icy water and dragged the boat forward. Leaving everything in the boat we stumbled across the beach and up the shallow bank. Steiner's boat was approaching the shore well south of us, making it obvious we could never get past him that way. Our only hope left was the railway, yet we had no way of knowing whether it followed the northern sweep of the shore: there was no sign of it among the trees ahead. I don't think any of us had much hope of escape left by this time. It was a matter of running from terror as long as one could run and then fighting in the hope of dying quickly.

The hot red and gold trees closed around us. We found a narrow animal path and stumbled along it. Carl, refusing aid, kept up with us gallantly although his tortured face told what it was costing him. A rivulet crossed the path. We waded through it, helping one another up the muddy bank opposite. We were well up in the hillside now and had a view of the lake over the trees. There was no sign of Steiner's boat and we knew he had landed.

A narrow path ran off to our right. I hesitated, then motioned to it. 'If we keep on going inland he'll be able to cut us off,' I panted. 'We'll have to head away from him and work our way inland gradually.'

Working our way along the hill instead of over it made the going a little easier. After a few minutes the trees around us thickened, closing in our visibility. They brought deception with them. We knew that Steiner and his men were coming after us like wolves after a crippled reindeer, and yet the red-gold trees, the hot sunlight, and the silence made the imminence of cruelty and death seem an absurd delusion.

A startled ptarmigan rose from a nearby tree and flew away, the white patches under its shoulders bright against the blue sky. It took with it much of my hope that we might remain hidden in this wilderness while we searched for the railway. Carl stumbled and fell over a tree root. Anna ran forward to help him. His breathing was rapid and shallow and his face grey with exhaustion. He whispered something hoarsely to her: she shook her head angrily. As I came alongside them he turned to me. 'He mustn't catch her, John... Take her and get away. Please.'

Her resolution was such that she did not even waste words in argument. She motioned me to take his other arm. He checked me.

'Please go... I beg you. Get her away while you have a chance...'

She read my thoughts from my expression. Her eyes flashed angrily as she reached down for him. 'Don't be a fool, Carl. Take hold of my arm.'

We helped him to his feet. He leaned against me for a moment and I felt the violent shuddering of his body. Then he pushed me away and lurched on again.

The path rounded a bend, then dipped downhill. Carl halted abruptly. We came up to him and Anna gave a gasp of dismay. Below us, shining in the sunlight, was a flat expanse of swamps and reeds, an extension of the lake whose western limit we had now reached. There was no hope of crossing it: we had to turn inland again and make for the higher ground on our left.

We had to retreat a hundred yards before finding a path, the hardest thing we had yet been called on to do. The path we found was narrow and steep, forcing us into single file. We let Carl go first so he could set his own pace. We had covered no more than fifty yards when he stumbled again, falling heavily this time. As we helped him to his feet a distant rumble made me pause. It faded almost at once, to return a few seconds later. I swung round towards them.

'The railway! It can't be far away. Listen.'

The train was coming from the west, probably an empty freighter from Narvik. The noise of its approach kept dying away, puzzling me. On our left the ground rose steeply: I ran up it to gain a better view. Ahead of me the woods swept like an enormous wave against an almost perpendicular rock face. I heard the clatter of the train, coming from the western end of the rock face, and ran higher to try to catch a glimpse of it. A siren hooted and then the noise disappeared again.

Half a minute passed and my uneasiness grew. Then the clatter returned, appreciably nearer now. A moving shape flickered behind the trees and grew longer as I watched. I understood now. The train, skirting the mountains, ran through a series of tunnels on this part of the track.

I scrambled down the path. 'Straight ahead,' I panted. 'About a quarter of a mile.'

Hope never dies in man. I had learned that truth during the war and was reminded of it now. We had no idea when the next west-bound freight train was due: the last one must have passed when we were nearing exhaustion on the lake and none of us had heard it. And, even if it reached us before Steiner, we had no idea how we could make our peril known and halt it. Yet even Carl found the strength to stumble up that last killing stretch of hillside. Halfway to the rock face the path branched away. Gasping, scratched, soaked in sweat, we fought on through the dense bushes.

Then the track, our one lifeline to civilis-ation and safety, lay at our feet. It was a fragile thing – a single line bedded on black-ened pebbles, with the wilderness encroach-ing on both sides. Eastwards it curved and vanished into the woods. Westwards it ran along the foot of the rock face and then vanished into a mountain spur.

For Carl's sake we were forced to pause. Below us the woods swept like a great multi-hued carpet to the lake. Eastwards where the track disappeared among the trees, a hawk rose sharply, hovered, and then flew in our direction. I fought back my panic. 'We shall have to get moving again,' I muttered.

Anna was in torment, longing to give Carl a rest, knowing Steiner was closing in. She helped him upright and put one of his arms around her shoulders. He tried to pull away but was too weak. I took his other arm and in that fashion we started down the track.

After the shelter of the woods we felt exposed and I soon realised that unless we could board a train soon or reach a siding that could offer us protection we were playing right into Steiner's hands. The dense bushes on both sides of the track forced us between the sleepers and their awkward spacing made us slip and stumble like drunken men.

We reached the tunnel and paused. Over the last hundred yards the hillside on our right had fallen away more steeply, making a detour around the mountain spur impossible. Anna gazed apprehensively at the tunnel.

'It seems very narrow. Will we be safe if a train comes?'

'There are sure to be man holes inside,' I muttered. 'And if he hasn't spotted us already it'll help to hide us from Steiner.'

It closed around us, shutting out the sunlight. The gloom deepened rapidly, became darkness. Water dripped from the rock sides. Above us we could feel the mountain, pressing downwards with its massive weight

of rock. The darkness became unlike anything I had ever known before, the solid
darkness of the grave. At first I could see
nothing of the exit ahead of us. Then it
appeared, a pinhead of light that stung my
eyes.

Without a torch we kept stumbling into the
jagged rocks alongside the track. It drove us
into feeling our way, making us waste the
precious seconds. The silence made my ears
ache. Twice I stopped, mistaking the rush of
blood in my ears for the sound of an oncoming train. The cold grew, chilling our
sweat-soaked bodies.

The tunnel seemed of interminable length
and I remembered the time the freight train
had taken to pass through it. Yet our slow
progress had one thing in its favour: it gave
us, and particularly Carl, a chance to recover.
The light began returning and we could see
the rocky walls again, grey and dripping. Carl
stumbled over a sleeper and as he was
recovering I glanced back. For a moment I
could see only darkness. Then a tiny circlet of
light appeared. For a second it shone steadily
like a tiny eye. Then it half-closed, to open
again a moment later. Anna saw me start and
looked back herself. She saw the unsteady,
blinking light and knew what it signified.
Supporting Carl as best we could, we
stumbled madly down the remainder of the
tunnel and out into the pitiless sunlight.

CHAPTER 24

Beyond the tunnel the mountainside dropped steeply away to the wide marshes alongside the lake. On our left the unscalable rockface stretched as far as we could see, curving away as it followed the westward sweep of the mountains. We had wanted the railway, our hopes had risen when we found it, and now it looked as if it would be our death trap. Panic-stricken, we could only run along the track, knowing it was only a matter of minutes before Steiner and his men caught us.

Our feet sank into the soft pebbles, tripped over the sleepers. For a moment Carl was able to manage alone. Then he fell heavily, striking his shoulder against one of the fish-plates. I turned back for him, throwing a glance at the tunnel two hundred yards back. Its exit was still empty. I bent down to help Carl up and he pushed me away with a thin, protesting hand.

'No. Leave me... Please.'

Anna ran up. He lifted his agonised, unshaven face to her. 'Leave me, *Liebchen*. I beg it of you. He mustn't catch you alive. Go with John...'

312

Her lips tightened. 'Never. We stay to-gether, you and I. Always. Now get up. Please get up.'

His thin chest was arising and falling agonisingly. 'I cannot, *Liebchen*. I have done my best but I can go no further. Please go. It is my wish.'

Her eyes were wet but her voice fierce. 'Never. If you can't get up I shall stay here with you.'

'But we have no chance, *Liebchen*. And there is John. We must think of him too.'

She went rigid at his words, then lifted her eyes to me. A wild pleading to escape was in them: an equally fierce challenge for me to stay. Fear and courage, love and loyalty, de-spair and the wild ecstasy of sacrifice: every emotion that has ever harrowed mankind was in those two blue-grey eyes.

'Of course... You must go. Please go. Only leave us the gun.'

It would be a lie if I said I felt no tempt-ation. Reason, self-preservation, all the protective devices nature has given to man screamed that I'd done all a man could do and that it was madness to stay and die with them. And I was terrified of Steiner as I was terrified of no other man. The thought that stopped me was how I was going to face all those days I saved, morning after morn-ing... That and the look in Anna's eyes.

I grabbed Carl around the shoulders.

313

'Come on,' I muttered. 'You aren't finished yet. Let's first go and see what's round that corner.'

We got him on his feet, slung his arms over our shoulders and stumbled on. For fifty yards the track curved westwards around the mountain talus, hiding the hollow eye-socket of the tunnel from us. Then it straightened again and Carl gave a sob of despair. There was nothing ahead of us but the narrow shelf of rock and another mountain spur covered in spruce and pine. The rock face on the left and the precipitous drop on the right made concealment impossible.

'The tunnel ahead,' I gasped. 'It's our only chance.'

Carl was almost a dead weight now. The pain in my side was turning me delirious. The endless sleepers became a devil's treadmill, the sun an enormous lamp spotlighting our misery. Behind us we heard voices, harsh voices that grew louder and more exultant as the treadmill lurched round and our lungs raved for air.

Then the arc-light above us dimmed and went out as we stumbled into the tunnel. Carl collapsed on the track, Anna alongside him, utterly spent. I clung to the rough-hewn walls, pulled myself round. For a moment the sunlit track swam dizzily before my eyes. Then I saw them, not more than eighty yards away. Steiner, bald head glisten-

314

ing in the sunlight, was running ahead of the others, his huge body looking as massive and irresistible as a locomotive.

I dragged Hacht's automatic from my pocket. It had nine rounds in its clip, each one infinitely precious. I tried to steady my shaking hand on the side of the tunnel. For a moment I had the wild and absurd hope Steiner had not seen us stop and was going to run into range. It died a second later as he checked his stride. His voice reached me, exultant and mocking.

'This is it, Drayton. The game's over. Throw your gun away.'

I couldn't trust my voice to answer him. He was perhaps fifty yards away. I knew I shouldn't waste the shot but the temptation was too great.

The explosion sounded loud in the tunnel, making my ears sing. Müller and the stocky man jumped back. Steiner did not move. His laugh mocked me.

'Your nerves have gone, Drayton. Better give up.'

Behind him Müller was assembling something. Steiner turned and motioned him forward. I saw now he was holding a long-barrelled Mauser pistol complete with butt: a weapon that could probe into the tunnel while they stood out of range of my automatic. Somehow we had to nullify the advantage it gave them. From the corner of my eye I saw Anna crouched on the ground alongside Carl, her white face staring at Steiner. I nudged her with my foot. 'Get Carl to the other end of the tunnel,' I whispered. 'Hurry, for God's sake.'

I drew further back into the shadows myself as Müller lifted the Mauser. Steiner held out a hand, restraining him. He was enjoying the cat-and-mouse game.

'Well, Drayton. Will you throw your gun away now?'

Carl and Anna had vanished into the darkness. I found a protruding rock, squeezed myself behind it. Desperately I played for time.

'What's the use if I do? You'll kill me just the same.'

'I've no interest in you, Drayton. I never had.'

'How do I know that? What guarantee will you give me?'

He was having difficulty in keeping the mockery from his face. 'We'll let you go. I'll give you my word.'

The scrabble of Ann and Carl's feet was well up the tunnel now. 'You're lying,' I said. 'You'll be too afraid I'll go and tell the police what has happened.'

Steiner glanced at Müller. 'We're crediting you with more sense, Drayton. We think this might have taught you a lesson.' He was moving forward as he spoke, eyes probing

316

the tunnel. His voice suddenly hardened. 'All right, Drayton. You've played for time long enough.' With that he stood aside and made an abrupt motion to Müller.

I squeezed back against the tunnel side. The flash of the Mauser was barely visible in the bright sunlight but the bullet was real enough. It struck the protruding rock and ricochetted with a scream into the tunnel. Before I could change position Müller fired again, this time striking the wall a few inches above my head. To unsettle his aim I was forced to fire back. As I hoped, he retreated a few paces. Steiner leapt forward and seized the Mauser from him. I grasped the opportunity and ran back into the tunnel.

Bullet after bullet followed me, screaming like devils as they ricochetted from one rock wall to the other. The darkness became intense but I ran on, heedless of injury. I could see no circle of light ahead of me and realised the tunnel curved under the mountain. The entrance behind me disappeared, the gunfire ceased, and for a moment the blackness and silence seemed almost solid. Then the exit appeared, with the black struggling figures of Carl and Anna outlined against it. Knowing we were going to be silhouetted targets for Steiner unless we cleared the exit in the next thirty seconds I ran madly after them.

There was no time for words even if we could have spoken them. I slung Carl's arms over my shoulders and carried him bodily down the track. Through the widening tunnel I could see down the sunlit rails ahead. There was no siding: as narrow and fragile as a thread it stretched on endlessly into the wilderness. A sense of futility almost overwhelmed me. All this enormous effort, this torment, and only to give us a few extra minutes of agonised life. There was no pity in this wilderness. We were doomed and only man's incomprehensible will to live drove us on.

The grey wet walls around us reappeared. They hugged the track very closely: since the tunnel had been built there had been a rockfall and the last seventy yards had been cleared as economically as possible. I saw my first bay, a niche between two rocks barely deep enough to take a single man. It reminded me of something I had completely forgotten by this time – the hourly freight train – and brought me a last faint glimmer of hope.

We reached the exit just in time, the first shot coughing like a savage animal behind us. The bright sunlight half-blinded me as I searched for a place to make our last stand. Twenty yards down the track a boulder-strewn shelf overhung the steep slope to the marshes. We stumbled to it and dropped exhausted behind the larges rocks.

It is strange how acute one's aesthetic senses become when death is near. I remember looking around and thinking how beautiful everything was. The bottle-green pines clinging to the mountain talus around us; the smouldering red-gold woods below. The marshes, cloud-shadowed and mysterious. The great Torneträsk, majestic among its snow-crested mountains. A hawk soaring high above us, wondrously free. The sun, the pine-scented air, the good earth.

And Anna. Anna of the brave heart. Bleeding, weary, unconquerable. Lying with her arms around Carl, waiting to die with him. Beautiful beyond words to me. It was a long time since I had prayed, but I prayed then. Don't let them die, God. Not after all this effort and loyalty... Don't let them die now.

Carl, unshaven, shirt half-torn off his back, thin arms scratched, looked like a scarecrow that had been cast to the ground. He turned his agonised face to me, moved his lips. I had to edge closer to hear him.

'In the name of God get her away, John. That devil mustn't get his hands on her...'

I had a sudden hellish picture of it and felt sick with fear. Below us the mountain talus was steep, but an active person could descend it by clinging to the base of the pines and the bushes. I turned to her fran-

319

tically. 'Climb down there and make your way back to the hostel. Hurry – before they see you go and send a man to cut you off.'

Her arms tightened around Carl. 'No. I'm staying here.'

In the few seconds left I tried to be cunning. 'You might save us by going. We might be able to hold them off in the tunnel – in time for help to arrive.'

Carl lifted his head, nodded eagerly. 'He is right, *Liebchen*. It would be better that way – it would give us hope.'

Again she shook her head. 'You both know I could never reach the hostel in time. I'm staying here with you.'

Panic exploded in me. I grabbed her by the shoulders, sank my fingers cruelly into her flesh. 'Get down there, damn you. Can't you see you're making things a hundred times worse. Get down there before they see us…'

Then it was too late. I saw a movement in the tunnel entrance, flung her down and dropped flat myself. They had seen us: they emerged from the darkness cautiously. I took aim, waited. Steiner saw the danger and drew them back.

From my elbow I heard Carl's hoarse whisper. 'How many rounds have you?'

'Seven,' I muttered.

He was watching the tunnel. He knew their next move and so did I. In spite of its obvious advantages our position had one thing against it. A man could stand far enough back in the tunnel to be hidden in the darkness and yet see us clearly. That meant he could pin us down with cowering fire from the Mauser while the other two attempted a rush.

I pushed the automatic along the ground to Carl. 'Would you like it? Perhaps you can do better than me.'

He grimaced, shook his head. 'Only if you agree to go.' He turned to Anna again. 'Please, *Liebchen*. They must not capture you. I would die in hell if that happened. Go … for my sake.'

There is no reason in love and loyalty. She only tightened her grip on him. He groaned and writhed on the hard ground like a man on the rack. A movement in the tunnel tore my eyes from him. Urging both of them frantically to keep down out of sight I wriggled sideways, found a niche between two rocks on which to rest my automatic. I knew the attack would be concentrated on me, and with the need to return their fire I could not keep wholly out of sight. Skin cringing I awaited the first shot.

It smacked brutally into the left-hand boulder, the crash of it rolling out of the tunnel. Gritting my teeth I burrowed lower, waiting. I knew I had to stop them early if I was to stop them at all. The second shot screamed off a rock past my face, making me drop flat for a moment. Then I heard the clink of pebbles and the scuffle of running feet. Lifting my head I saw Steiner and the stocky man just clearing the tunnel entrance.

I tried to steady myself and line up on Steiner. But Müller's covering fire was too accurate. A bullet smacked the left-hand rock again, splinters flew from it like shrapnel and struck my head. A sudden red haze came before my eyes. Through it two indistinct figures appeared. I fired at the first one, missed and fired frantically again. I saw him stumble, heard a gasp of pain. The mist cleared and I saw Steiner, savage-faced, dragging the stocky man back into the shelter of the tunnel. I took a rash shot at him and missed as Müller's counter fire made me flinch.

I lay trembling with shock. My head was throbbing with pain and blood soaked through my hair. Anna tried to reach me. I motioned her back frantically as Müller fired again. I turned to Carl, who was also trembling violently from reaction.

'The stocky man,' I panted. 'How badly was he hit?'

'In the leg, I think. He was stumbling badly.'

I tried to work out what they would do next. Give the wounded man the Mauser, I was certain of that. And Steiner and Müller would either try another rush or go back along the tunnel to outflank us while the Mauser pinned us down. I squirmed half-round in an effort to assess our chances of getting down the talus without being hit. A puff of dust from the dry earth alongside my feet told me they were nil.

As the crash of the Mauser died away I saw Anna turned her head sharply. I listened with her and for the moment could hear nothing for the ringing in my head. Then I heard it too – the clatter of an approaching train. It sounded quite close – the outward sweep of the mountains and the gunfire had deadened the noise of it until now.

Anna's widened eyes were on me, trying to see what hope I drew from the sound. For a moment I could find none. It was clear we had no chance of stopping the train – before its crew could accustom their eyes to the bright sunlight again they would be a hundred yards past us. And it was certain death for us to go out on the track to be seen. And yet something was hammering at my mind, driving a stake of hope among the stones of its despair. I recognised it and gave a violent start.

'The tunnel,' I muttered. 'The last seventy yards are very narrow. If Steiner doesn't know these freight trains run every hour and is caught at this end...'

There was conflict in Anna's eyes, fear of

this new hope that might only betray and weaken her resignation of death. I felt it myself as I turned back to watch the tunnel. Everything depended where Steiner was at this moment. If his intention had been to outflank us and he had started back along the tunnel but had not yet reached its bend he wouldn't be able to see the approaching train. And the gun fire, deafening in the tunnel, would keep the sound of it from him. Alternatively, if he was still in the entrance he would be able to escape on to the open track. It would then be the three of them without the advantage of hidden covering fire against me with only four rounds left. A slim chance, but I would get Steiner. That I promised myself.

But the hope I was clutching was that they had already started back along the tunnel. In my anxiety to keep the Mauser firing I nearly had my head taken off by a bullet that richochetted viciously off the boulder in front of me. Lying flat I reached out with my right foot and pushed a small rock sideways. The roar of the Mauser came again. The train was close now, the clatter of its approach echoing among the mountains. The noise died away into a low rumble: it had entered the other tunnel. Remembering the tunnel was a long one I drew the Mauser's fire again, trying to guess how long it would take their ears to recover from the explosion.

The clatter returned, loud and moving at speed. A few seconds later a siren hooted and again the noise died into a dull rumble. This time it seemed to come from the ground beneath us, shuddering the track. Muscles aching from tension, forgetting the danger, I lifted my head and watched the tunnel entrance.

The rumble grew louder, became deafening. A figure dragged itself frantically from the tunnel entrance. Before I could fire at it the train, massive and overwhelming, burst out and thundered between us. Behind it rumbled the huge, ore-filled wagons. I turned exultantly to Carl and Anna. 'Only one,' I shouted. 'The others must have been caught inside.'

They both looked stunned at this dramatic change in our fortunes. Between the speeding wheels of the wagons I watched the wounded man. He was dragging himself painfully along the rockface, searching for cover. There were a few clumps of willow herb about seven yards from the tunnel: in desperation he lay behind one of them, his Mauser ready. I rested my automatic on the boulders in front of me. He tried one shot but it must have struck one of the steel wheels because it never reached me. Then we both waited.

It seemed an interminable time before the last wagon cleared the tunnel. I fired the instant it passed me. I saw him jerk but from his return fire, as vicious as a cobra's tongue, knew he wasn't badly hurt. I missed him with my second shot: he was that extra yard too far for accurate shooting with an automatic. I gritted my teeth, aimed in the dead centre of the bush, and squeezed the trigger carefully. He leapt up and rolled over sideways. There was no mercy in me; I fired my last shot into him. His kicking feet brought dust up from the dry ground. Then he lay still.

I fell back sick from reaction. I head Carl's hoarse whisper. 'The gun, John! We must get it ... in case either of the others has escaped.'

I knew he was right but Anna was too quick for me. While I was staggering to my feet she was already running down the track towards the tunnel. She was no more than four yards from the dead man when she stopped as if a bullet had struck her. I followed her eyes and froze. In the tunnel entrance, shirt wet and lichen-stained, blood welling thickly from a gash in his head, stood Steiner.

It was a moment I shall never forget. In the shadows he looked as huge and evil as Mephistopheles. Too late I remembered the manhole in the tunnel. It had been he or Müller, and Müller had been sacrificed...

Then the frozen tableau sprang into life. Anna darted for the Mauser, tried to seize it. Steiner moved with fantastic speed, leaping forward and striking her with one of his huge hands. She was flung backwards like a child, striking her head against one of the steel rails. Steiner snatched up the Mauser and spun around.

Neither Carl nor I had moved. Carl, a ten-year-old nightmare suddenly alive before his eyes, was helpless with shock while all that kept me from collapse was the sight of Anna lying motionless on the track, a trickle of blood running down her chalk-white face. Seeing we were unarmed Steiner came across the track towards us. Slowly, like doom itself... His gun was covering us both but his eyes were on Carl. The ferocity in them was inhuman.

'So, Carl. The moment I've been waiting ten years for... No; I'm not going to shoot you yet. A little pain must come before the bullet. And it must not kill at once. It must let you lie helpless and watch your pretty Anna play with me...'

His eyes moved to me and I saw he was mad. There was foam at the corners of his mouth. 'And you, Drayton. We have a score to settle... And you wouldn't want to be treated differently to your friend, would you – not after having shared so much with him already. So you shall be first...'

Without warning he slashed down with the Mauser. I managed to save my face but the sharp sight ripped agonisingly down my shoulder. He slashed again, this time driving me to my knees. He could have killed me with a single blow but that was not his intention. He wanted to mutilate first, to prolong consciousness as long as possible.

It was this sadism in him that saved me. As he struck again I lurched forward in desperation and grabbed his legs. He tried to kick me, overbalanced, and fell heavily forward. The shock jarred the Mauser from his hand; it skidded away and toppled over the edge of the track. As I staggered to my feet I saw Carl had not moved – fear of Steiner was holding him paralysed as I had always believed it would. I was sweating with terror myself when Steiner snarled and leapt at me. I lashed out with my fists, trying to keep him off. One blow with all my remaining strength behind it landed full in his face. I might as well have hit him with a rubber hammer. He came straight through the blow and grabbed me.

It was like being seized by a mad gorilla. He threw me to the ground and dropped his full weight on me. I threshed madly but could not move. Saliva ran from his mouth, splashed on my face.

'Scald not thy lips, Drayton... Remember?'

His great hands tightened on my throat. My breath choked off, my lungs fought madly for air. Through a red mist his devil's eyes stared down at me, enjoying my agony. 'I always mean what I say, Drayton. You should have believed me.'

My head felt as if it would burst at any moment. A great drum beat frantically in my ears. I threw my remaining strength in a last frenzied effort to escape. Pain and terror overwhelmed me as his grip only tightened.

Then I saw Carl, and at first believed it was only a vision before death. He was standing like a grey scarecrow behind Steiner, gripping the empty automatic in one hand. He lifted his arm, grimacing with pain as he tried to find the strength for the blow. Not daring to watch I closed my eyes.

I heard a thud, felt Steiner's hands momentarily relax. Frantically I tore away and dragged myself clear. Steiner was crouched low, staring up at the helpless Carl. 'You!' he said thickly. 'Frandl...'

I believe he forgot my existence at that moment. Like myself he had believed Carl broken, a terrified man waiting for death. To learn there was still defiance left, to be struck by him in this way drove the last remnant of sanity from him. The cry that broke from his throat was inhuman as he sprang at Carl.

I knew Carl and I together had no chance

against such maniacal strength. Sobbing with haste and fear I ran to the edge of the track. The Mauser was about fifteen feet down the slope, wedged in a bush. I leapt down, tearing unheedingly through bushes and scrub. Seizing the Mauser I fought my way back to the track. Above me I could hear the vicious thud of blows. As I scrambled over the edge I saw Steiner, his back to me, crouched like a predatory animal over the helpless body of Carl. Over by the tunnel Anna had recovered consciousness and was running towards them, a look of horror on her face.

Frantically I waved her back. Steiner's huge body lurched unsteadily in the Mauser sights. Fighting to control my gasping, shaking body I moved a few paces nearer. Then I fired.

He stiffened, gave an inhuman grunt as he spun round, and came at me like a great ape, body crouched low. I ran a few yards towards the tunnel, then turned again. I had no idea how many rounds were left in the Mauser and sweat and terror blurred my vision. I fired again and a red spot appeared on his shirt, just below his ribs. He grunted again but kept coming on, his face a devil's mask of hate. I fired again, almost at point-blank range. He lurched forward, missed me and fell. I pulled the trigger again and heard only a metallic click.

His vitality and determination to kill were terrifying. Blood was running from his mouth but somehow he rose again and lunged forward, huge hands outstretched to crush me. I could retreat no further, my back was pressed against the bank alongside the tunnel. He was almost on me when he fell again, right at my feet.

Even then he was not finished. One hand crawled along the ground like a great spider and seized my ankle. For a moment its grip was crushing and then I felt the evil life run out of it. He jerked spasmodically and lay still.

There was a sound like rushing wind in my ears. I tore my leg away and stepped over his body, trying to reach Anna. Then the sky went black and fell down on me.

When I regained consciousness Anna was bending over Carl, her body racked with grief. The greyness of death was on his face, but as I approached he tried to smile at me. I had to bend low to hear his hoarse whisper. 'It is over at last, John… Well done.'

Then his eyes winced in distress as they moved to Anna. 'Don't cry, *Liebchen*. You must not cry.'

'We shall get a doctor from the hostel for you.' Her voice was fierce, willing him to live. 'You must not give up. Not now.'

His smile was gentle but infinitely weary.

'No, *Liebchen*. This is better… The pain has gone at last.'

I saw now that his grey, sweat-stained face was more relaxed than I had ever seen it. As she sobbed again his voice saddened. 'So many years of your life, wasted, *Liebchen*. I am sorry… Make up for them now, you and John.'

She stared at me with eyes that were wide and shocked. Then she gave a wild cry and buried her face in his shoulder. 'Carl, forgive me. Say that you forgive me…'

He lifted a thin, distressed hand and tried to stroke her head. 'There is nothing to forgive, *Liebchen*. It was not your fault I could not give you love.'

Her words were fierce and urgent, driving themselves into his soul before it slipped away. 'You did give me love. All the love any woman could want. The flesh is not love … sometimes it comes between love. If I had to choose again … if I had to choose a hundred times more … always it would be you. Do you hear me, Carl? *Do you hear me?*'

He nodded and tried to smile at her. I turned and stumbled away. Time was running out fast and their last hurried whispers belonged only to themselves. A grey wagtail landed on the stem of a rose bay near me. It cocked its head sideways, one bright eye watching Carl and Anna. I looked up and saw the hawk had disappeared. Beyond the dipping red-gold woods Torneträsk lay silver and peaceful in the sunlight. The silence was intense. It was broken by a single jagged cry from Anna. The wagtail threw open its wings and climbed swiftly away. I knew Carl was dead.

At first her bitterness was intense, shunning all my efforts to comfort her. 'All his life he has suffered. The war, his injuries, his unhappiness... His fight to make a life for us... His fight to live at all. And now, just as the battle is won, he has to die. *Lieber Gott,* where is the justice of it? Why are some given all and others nothing? Why...?'

I had no answer to her bitterness, because I was alive and he was dead. Unable to look at her I could only stumble about the side of the track, covering his body with twigs and stones until it could receive decent burial. In the end it was the tundra that came to her aid, the tundra I had thought cruel. Its vast silence calmed her, its red-gold beauty drew her eyes mercifully from the track. After gazing over it for long silent minutes she turned and came across to me.

'I have been selfish, John. You are badly hurt – we must get to the hostel and find a doctor for you. Put your arm around my shoulders...'

Only sadness remained in her now, because she was very gentle with me. And so it was we stumbled through the long tunnel that was so

black and cold and full of terror, and came
out at last into the bright sunlight that lay
beyond it.

This Large Print Book, for people
who cannot read normal print,
is published under the auspices of

THE ULVERSCROFT FOUNDATION